Praise for *Cover Me*:

"Relentless suspense, heroes to fall in love with right from page one—this must be another military romance by the fabulous Catherine Mann!"

—Suzanne Brockmann, *New York Times* bestselling author of *Tall, Dark and Deadly*

"Catherine Mann delivers a powerful, passionate read, not to be missed!"

—Lori Foster, *New York Times* bestselling author of *Bewitched*

"From page one, Catherine Mann's dangerous Dark Ops warriors explode onto the page to command your attention and hold your heart, refusing to let go until that last satisfying page when you finally get your breath back."

—Dianna Love, *New York Times* bestselling author with Sherrilyn Kenyon of *Blood Trinity*

More praise for Catherine Mann's hot military romantic suspense:

"As we say in the Air Force, get ready to roll in hot! From page one, Catherine Mann's military romances launch you into a world chock-full of simmering passion and heart-pounding action. Don't miss 'em!"

—Merline Lovelace, *USA Today* bestselling author of *Full Throttle*

HOT ZONE

CATHERINE MANN

sourcebooks
casablanca

Published by Sourcebooks Casablanca, an imprint of Sourcebooks, Inc.
P.O. Box 4410, Naperville, Illinois 60567-4410
(630) 961-3900
FAX: (630) 961-2168
www.sourcebooks.com

Printed and bound in the United States of America
QW 10 9 8 7 6 5 4 3 2 1

*In memory of PFC Zachary Salmon
(United States Army)*

1989–2011

*A father, a son. A friend, a patriot.
Thank you for touching the lives of
my loved ones so profoundly.*

Chapter 1

THE WORLD HAD CAVED IN ON AMELIA BAILEY.

Literally.

Aftershocks from the earthquake still rumbled the gritty earth under her cheek, jarring her out of her hazy micronap. Dust and rocks showered around her. Her skin, her eyes, everything itched and ached after hours—she'd lost track of how many—beneath the rubble.

The quake had to have hit at least seven on the Richter scale. Although when you ended up with a building on top of you, somehow a Richter scale didn't seem all that pertinent.

She squeezed her eyelids closed. Inhaling. Exhaling. Inhaling, she drew in slow, even breaths of the dank air filled with dirt. Was this what it was like to be buried alive? She pushed back the panic as forcefully as she'd clawed out a tiny cavern for herself.

This wasn't how she'd envisioned her trip to the Bahamas when she'd offered to help her brother and sister-in-law with the legalities of international adoption.

Muffled sounds penetrated, of jackhammers and tractors. Life scurried above her, not that anybody seemed to have heard her shouts. She'd screamed her throat raw until she could only manage a hoarse croak now.

Time fused in her pitch-black cubby, the air thick with sand. Or disintegrated concrete. She didn't want to think what else. She remembered the first tremor, the dawning realization that her third-floor hotel room in the seaside Bahamas resort was slowly giving way beneath her feet. But after that?

Her mind blanked.

How long had she been entombed? Forever, it seemed, but probably more along the lines of half a day while she drifted in and out of consciousness. She wriggled her fingers and toes to keep the circulation moving after being so long immobile. Every inch of her body screamed in agony from scrapes and bruises and probably worse, but she couldn't move enough to check. Still, she welcomed the pain that reassured her she was alive.

Her body was intact.

Forget trying to sit up. Her head throbbed from having tried that. The ceiling was maybe six inches above where she lay flat on her belly. Again, she willed back hysteria. The fog of claustrophobia hovered, waiting to swallow her whole.

More dust sifted around her. The sound of the jack-hammers rattled her teeth. They seemed closer, louder, with even a hint of a voice. Was that a dog barking?

Hope hurt after so many disappointments. Even if her ears heard right, there had to be so many people in need of rescuing after the earthquake. All those efforts could easily be for someone else a few feet away. They might not find her for hours. Days.

Ever.

But she couldn't give up. She had to keep fighting. If not for herself, then for the little life beside her, her precious new nephew. She threaded her arm through the tiny hole between them to rub his back, even though he'd long ago given up crying, sinking into a frighteningly long nap. His shoulders rose and fell evenly, thank God, but for how much longer?

Her fingers wrapped tighter around a rock and she banged steadily against the oppressive wall overhead. Again and again. If only she knew Morse code. Her arm numbed. Needle-like pain prickled down her skin. She gritted her teeth and continued. Didn't the people up there have special listening gear?

Dim shouts echoed, like a celebration. Someone had been found. Someone else. Her eyes burned with tears that she was too dehydrated to form. Desperation clawed up her throat. What if the rescue party moved on now? Far from her deeply buried spot?

Time ticked away. Precious seconds. Her left hand gripped the rock tighter, her right hand around the tiny wrist of the child beside her. Joshua's pulse fluttered weakly against her thumb.

Desperation thundered in her ears. She pounded the rock harder overhead. God, she didn't want to die. There'd been times after her divorce when the betrayal hurt so much she'd thought her chance at finally having a family was over, but she'd never thrown in the towel. Damn him. She wasn't a quitter.

Except why wasn't her hand cooperating anymore? The opaque air grew thicker with despair. Her arm grew leaden. Her shoulder shrieked in agony, pushing a gasping moan from between her cracked lips. Pounding became taps… She frowned. Realizing…

Her hand wasn't moving anymore. It slid uselessly back onto the rubble-strewn floor. Even if her will to live was kicking ass, her body waved the white flag of surrender.

———

Master Sergeant Hugh Franco had given up caring if he lived or died five years ago. These days, the air force pararescueman motto was the only thing that kept his soul planted on this side of mortality.

That others may live.

Since he didn't have anything to live for here on earth, he volunteered for the assignments no sane person would touch. And even if they would, his buds had people who would miss them. Why cause them pain?

Which was what brought him to his current snowball's-chance-in-hell mission.

Hugh commando-crawled through the narrow tunnel in the earthquake rubble. His helmet lamp sliced a thin blade through the dusty dark. His headset echoed with chatter from above—familiar voices looking after him and unfamiliar personnel working other missions scattered throughout the chaos. One of the search and rescue dogs aboveground had barked his head off the second he'd sniffed this fissure in the jumbled jigsaw of broken concrete.

Now, Hugh burrowed deeper on the say-so of a German shepherd named Zorro. Ground crew attempts at drilling a hole for a search camera had come up with zip. But that Zorro was one mighty insistent pup, so Hugh was all in.

He half listened to the talking in one ear, with the other tuned in for signs of life in the devastation. Years of training honed an internal filter that blocked out communication not meant for him.

"You okay down there, Franco?"

He tapped the talk button on his safety harness and replied, "Still moving. Seems stable enough."

"So says the guy who parachuted into a minefield on an Afghani mountainside."

"Yeah, yeah, whatever." Somebody had needed to go in and rescue that Green Beret who'd gotten his legs blown off. "I'm good for now and I'm sure I heard some tapping ahead of me. Tough to tell, but maybe another twenty feet or so."

He felt a slight tug, then a loosening, to the line attached to his safety harness as his team leader played out more cord.

"Roger that, Franco. Slow and steady man, slow and steady."

Just then he heard the tapping again. "Wait one, Major."

Hugh stopped and cocked his free ear. Tapping, for sure. He swept his light forward, pushing around a corner, and saw a widening cavern that held promise inside the whole hellish pancake collapse. He inched ahead, aiming the light on his helmet into the void.

The slim beam swept a trapped individual. Belly to the ground, the person sprawled with only a few inches free above. The lower half of the body was blocked. But the torso was visible, covered in so much dust and grime he couldn't tell at first if he saw a male or female. Wide eyes stared back at him with disbelief, followed by wary hope. Then the person dropped a rock and pointed toward him.

Definitely a woman's hand.

Trembling, she reached, her French manicure chipped, nails torn back and bloody. A gold band on her thumb had bent into an oval. He clasped her hand quickly to check the thumb for warmth and a pulse.

And found it. Circulation still intact.

Then he checked her wrist—heart rate elevated but strong.

She gripped his hand with surprising strength. "If I'm hallucinating," she said, her raspy voice barely more than a whisper, "please don't tell me."

"Ma'am, you're not imagining anything. I'm here to help you."

He let her keep holding on as it seemed to bring her comfort—and calm—while he swept the light over what he could see of her to assess medically. Tangled hair. A streak of blood across her head. But no gaping wounds.

He thumbed his mic. "Have found a live female. Trapped, but lucid. More data after I evaluate."

"Roger that," Major McCabe's voice crackled through.

Hugh inched closer, wedging the light into the crevice in hopes of seeing more of his patient. "Ma'am, crews are working hard to get you out of here, but they need to stabilize the structure before removing more debris. Do you understand me?"

"I hear you." She nodded, then winced as her cheek slid along the gritty ground. "My name is Amelia Bailey. I'm not alone."

More souls in danger. "How many?"

"One more. A baby."

His gut gripped. He forced words past his throat, clogging from more than particulates in the air. "McCabe, add a second soul to that. A baby with the female, Amelia Bailey. Am switching to hot mic so you can listen in."

He flipped the mic to constant feed, which would use more battery, but time was of the essence now. He didn't want to waste valuable seconds repeating info. "Ma'am, how old is the baby?"

"Thirteen months. A boy." She spoke faster and faster, her voice coming out in scratchy croaks. "I can't see him because it's so dark, but I can feel his pulse. He's still alive, but oh God, please get us out of here."

"Yes, ma'am. Now, I'm going to slip my hand over your back to see if I can reach him."

He had his doubts. There wasn't a sound from the child, no whimpering, none of those huffing little breaths children make when they sleep or have cried themselves out. Still, he had to go through the motions. Inching closer until he stretched alongside her, he tunneled his arm over her shoulders. Her back rose and fell shallowly, as if she tried to give him more space when millimeters counted. His fingers snagged on her torn shirt, something silky and too insubstantial a barrier between her and tons of concrete.

Pushing farther, he met resistance, stopped short. Damn it. He grappled past the jutting stone, lower down her back until he brushed the top of her—

She gasped.

He looked up fast, nearly nose to nose now. His hand stilled on her buttock. She stared back, the light from his helmet sweeping over her sooty face. Her eyes stared back, a splash of color in the middle of murky desperation.

Blue. Her eyes glistened pure blue, and what a strange thought to have in the middle of hell. But he couldn't help but notice they were the same color as cornflowers he'd seen carpeting a field once during a mission in the UK.

Hell, cornflowers were just weeds. He stretched deeper, along the curve of her butt, bringing his face nearer to hers. She bit her lip.

"Sorry," he clipped out.

Wincing, she shrugged. "It was a reflex. Modesty's pretty silly right now. Keep going."

Wriggling, he shifted for a better path beyond the maze of jagged edges, protruding glass, spikes...

"Damn it." He rolled away, stifling the urge to say a helluva lot worse. "I can't reach past you."

Her fingers crawled to grip his sleeve. "I'm just so glad you're here, that everyone knows we are here. Joshua's heart is still beating. He's with us, and we haven't been down here long enough for him to get dehydrated, less than a day. There's hope, right?"

Less than a day? Nearly forty-eight hours had passed since the earthquake occurred, and while he'd participated in against-all-odds rescues before, he had a sick sense that the child was already dead. But alerting the woman to her own confusion over the time wouldn't help and could actually freak her out.

"Sure, Amelia. There's always hope."

Or so the platitude went.

"I'm going to hang out here with you while they do their work upstairs." He unstrapped the pack around his waist and pointed his headlight toward the supplies. "Now I'm gonna pull out some tricks to make you more comfortable while we wait."

"Happen to have an ice-cold Diet Coke? Although I'll settle for water, no lemon necessary."

He laughed softly. Not many would be able to joke right now, much less stay calm. "I'm sorry, but until I know more about your physical status, I can't risk letting you eat or drink." He tugged out a bag of saline, the needle, antiseptic swabs, grunting as a rock bit into his side. "But I am going to start an IV, just some fluids to hydrate you."

"You said you're here to help me," she said, wincing at a fresh burst of noise from the jackhammers, "but who are you?"

"I'm with the U.S. Air Force." Dust and pebbles showered down. "I'm a pararescueman—you may have heard it called parajumper or PJ—but regardless, it includes a crap ton of medic training. I need to ask some questions so I know what else to put in your IV. Where exactly did the debris land on you?"

She puffed dust from her mouth, blinking fast. "There's a frickin' building on top of me."

"Let me be more specific. Are your legs pinned?" He tore the corner of a sealed alcohol pad with his teeth, spitting the foil edge free. "I couldn't reach that far to assess."

Her eyes narrowed. "I thought you were checking on Joshua."

"I'm a good multitasker."

"My foot is wedged, but I can still wriggle my toes."

He looked up sharply. If she was hemorrhaging internally, fluids could make her bleed out faster, but without hydration...

The balancing act often came down to going with his gut. "Just your foot?"

"Yes. Why? Do you think I'm delusional?" Her breath hitched with early signs of hysteria. "I'm not having phantom sensations. I can feel grit against my ankle.

There's some blood in my shoe, not a lot. It's sticky, but not fresh. I'm feeling things."

"I hear you. I believe you." Without question, her mind would do whatever was needed to survive. But he'd felt enough of her body to know she was blocked, rather than pressed into the space. "I'm going to put an IV in now."

"Why was it so important about my foot?"

He scrubbed the top of her hand with alcohol pads, sanitizing as best he could. "When parts of the body are crushed, we need to be... uh... *careful* in freeing you."

"Crush syndrome." Her throat moved with a long slow swallow. "I've heard of that. People die from it after they get free. I saw it on a rerun of that TV show about a crabby drug-addict doctor."

"We just need to be careful." In a crush situation, tissue died, breaking down, and when the pressure was released, toxins flooded the body, overloading the kidneys. And for just that remote possibility, he hadn't included potassium in her IV.

Panic flooded her glittering blue eyes. "Are you planning to cut off my foot?" Her arm twitched harder, faster, until she flailed. "Are you going to put something else in that IV? Something to knock me out?"

He covered her fingers with his before she dislodged the port in her hand. "There's nothing in there but fluid. I'm being honest with you now, but if you panic, I'm going to have to start feeding you a line of bullshit to calm you down. Now, you said you wanted the unvarnished truth—"

"I do. Okay. I'm breathing. Calming down. Give me the IV."

He patted her wrist a final time. "I already did."

Blinking fast, she looked at the tape along her hand. A smile pushed through the grime on her face. "You're good. I was so busy trying not to freak out I didn't even notice."

"Not bad for my first time."

"Your first time?"

"I'm kidding." And working to distract her again from the rattle overhead, the fear that at any second the whole damn place could collapse onto them.

She laughed weakly, then stronger. "Thank you."

"It's just an IV."

"For the laugh. I was afraid I would never get to do that again." Her fingers relaxed slowly, tension seeping from them as surely as fluid dripped out of the bag. "The second they uncover us, you'll make Joshua top priority. Forget about me until he's taken care of."

"We're going to get you both out of here. I swear it."

"Easy for you to claim that. If I die, it's not like I can call you a liar."

A dead woman and child. He resisted the urge to tear through the rocks with his bare hands and to hell with waiting on the crews above. He stowed his gear, twisting to avoid that damn stone stabbing his side.

"Hey," Amelia whispered. "That was supposed to be a joke from me this time."

"Right, got it." Admiration for her grit kicked through his own personal fog threatening to swallow him whole. "You're a tough one. I think you're going to be fine."

"I'm a county prosecutor. I chew up criminals for a living."

"'Atta girl." He settled onto his back, watching the

hypnotic drip, drip. His fingers rested on her wrist to monitor her pulse.

"Girl?" She sniffed. "I prefer to be called a woman or a lady, thank you very much."

"Where I come from, it's wise not to be nitpicky with the person who's saving your ass."

"Score one for you." She scraped a torn fingernail through the dust on the ground. Her sigh stirred the dust around that shaky line. "I'm good now. So you should go before this building collapses on top of you and keeps you from doing your job for other people."

"I don't have anywhere else to be." He ignored a call from McCabe through his headset that pretty much echoed the woman's words. "The second they give the go-ahead, I'm hauling you out of here, Amelia Bailey."

"And Joshua. I want you to promise you'll take care of him first."

"I will do what I can for him," he answered evasively.

Her wide eyes studied him for seven drips of the IV before she cleared her throat. "You don't think he's alive, do you? I can feel his pulse."

"Yes, ma'am."

"I'm not imagining it, damn it." Her hand flipped and she grabbed his arm, her ragged nails digging deep with urgency. "I can feel his pulse in his wrist. He's a little chilly, but he's not cold. Just because he's not screaming his head off doesn't mean he's dead. And sometimes, he moves. Only a little, but I feel it." Her words tumbled over each other faster and faster until she dissolved into a coughing fit.

Ah, to hell with it. He unhooked his canteen. "Wet

your mouth. Just don't gulp, okay? Or they'll kick my butt up there."

He brought the jug to her lips and she sipped, her restraint Herculean when she must want to drain it dry. Sighing, she sagged again, her eyes closing as she *hmmm*ed, her breathing evening out. He freaked. She needed to stay awake, alert.

Alive.

"Tell me about your son Joshua." He recapped the canteen without wasting a swallow on himself.

Her lashes fluttered open again. "Joshua's my nephew. I came with my brother and his wife to help them with the paperwork for their adoption. They don't want any legal loopholes. What happens to Joshua if they're…?"

She bit her lip.

His brain raced as he swept the light along the rubble, searching for some signs of others—although there hadn't been a helluva lot of survivors in the vicinity. All the same, he made sure they heard upstairs, by speaking straight into his mic as he asked her, "Where were your brother and sister-in-law when the earthquake hit?"

"They were in the street, outside the hotel. They left to buy lunch. They waited until Joshua was asleep so he wouldn't miss them." Her voice hitched. "I promised I would take care of him."

"And you have." He pinned her with his eyes, with his determination, the swath of light staying steady on her face. "Keep the faith. Hold steady and picture your family in one of the camps for survivors right now going nuts trying to find you."

"I've read stories about how babies do better because

they have more fat stores and they don't tense up or get claustrophobic." Her eyes pleaded with him. "He's just napping, you know."

The force of her need pummeled him harder than the spray of rocks from the jackhammered ceiling. The world closed in to just this woman and a kid he couldn't see. Too clearly he could envision his wife and his daughter trapped in the wreckage of a crashed plane. Marissa would have held out hope for Tilly right to the end too, fighting for her until her nails and spirit were ragged.

Shit.

The vise on his brain clamped harder, the roar in his ears louder, threatening his focus. "I'm changing your IV bag now, so don't wig out if you feel a little tug."

She clenched her fist. "You must get pretty jaded in this line of work."

"I've got a good success rate." He didn't walk away from tough odds. Every mission was do-or-die for him.

"About my foot..." she started hesitantly. "Am I imagining that it's okay? Be honest. I won't panic. I need to be prepared."

"The mind does what it needs to in order to survive. That's what you need to focus on. Surviving."

Not that any amount of determination had mattered in the end for Marissa or Tilly. They'd died in that plane crash, their broken bodies returned to him to bury along with his will to live. A trembling started deep inside him. His teeth chattered. He dug his fingers into the ground to anchor himself into the present. Amelia Bailey would not die on his watch, damn it.

But the trembling increased inside him. Harder. Deeper. Until he realized… The shaking wasn't inside, but outside.

The ground shuddered with another earthquake.

Chapter 2

MAJOR LIAM MCCABE LURCHED AS THE GROUND SHOOK under his feet. He grabbed the tractor beside him for support. Debris shifted below his feet, rattling all the way to his teeth. Rescue workers scrambled down the piles, carrying the male victim he'd just stabilized and extricated—a businessman who'd been trapped in his office chair.

Frantic wails filled the air from family members who'd been digging with shovels, even hands, in search of loved ones. A German shepherd jockeyed for balance on top of a shifting concrete slab.

He had to get off this oscillating pyramid of debris. Now.

His pulse ramped with adrenaline. Splaying his arms for balance, Liam tested for firmer ground. The structural triage report on this site had sucked, but Hugh Franco had been ready to tunnel in once Zorro barked a live find.

Liam looked left fast to check on team member Wade Rocha. Combat boots planted, Rocha balanced with the feed line tight in his grip... the other end attached to Hugh Franco somewhere underneath the trembling hell.

Shit. Franco. Stuck below with his victim.

And just that fast, the earth steadied.

The demolished wasteland around him went eerily quiet. Sweat and filth plastered his uniform to his body, his heart hammering in his ears. Relief workers stood stock-still as if the world had stopped. But spirals of smoke affirmed the world hadn't ended, just paused to catch a breath.

He exhaled hard. Adrenaline stung his veins. The tremor hadn't been an earthquake, just another aftershock. Four so far today. Nerves were ragged, especially with the locals.

His headset blazed to life again with a frenzy of orders, questions, and curses from command center, along with check-ins from others on his team—Brick, Fang, Cuervo, Data, Bubbles—spread out at other potential rescues in the sector. But the most important voice was conspicuously missing.

Hugh Franco.

Dread knotted his gut. Liam had lived through hell on earth before, but it was always worse when his men's lives were on the line. They were his family, no question. As his three ex-wives would attest, he was married to the job.

"Franco? Franco?" Liam shouted into the mic. "Report in, damn it."

His headset continued to sputter, some voices coming through piecemeal. None of them Franco.

Crappy headset… Liam's hands fisted.

"Shit." He punched the tractor. Knuckles throbbing, he resisted the urge to pitch the mic to the ground.

Wade "Brick" Rocha edged around the tractor. "I'm going in after him, boss. I'll follow the cable, dig through, and—"

Reason filtered through the rage. He needed to level out, stay in command.

"Hold steady. Not yet. I don't need two of the team

missing." He refused to believe Franco was dead. Only his voice was gone. Just the radio connection fading. "Let's check in with the cleanup crew, maybe nab one of the search dogs again to confirm the exact location, since things have shifted."

Scrubbing along his jaw, he scanned the crews returning to business as if nothing had happened. Training kicked into overdrive at times like these. The cold-sweat stage would set in later, once there wasn't anything to do but sit and think about how very wrong the day could have gone.

How badly it could still go, as they all hung out together in an active seismic zone.

Guards formed a circle around the perimeter. American soldiers armed with M4 carbines stood alongside multinational troops carrying Uzis, all on the watch for looters targeting more than just store goods. Food and clean water were at a premium, which made them a target, since they had both, thanks to the air force's RED HORSE unit: Rapid Engineer Deployable Heavy Operational Repair Squadron Engineers. Whether in a war zone or natural disaster, they responded within twenty-four hours with food and water-purification units filling up water trailers called water buffalos.

Liam scanned the outskirts. Everyone from starving survivors to rapists trolling for a defenseless victim.

His M9 pistol stayed strapped to his hip, loaded. Ready.

For now, he had to find Hugh. He steadied his voice and tried again. "Franco, check in."

"Roger... here..." the familiar voice cut through the chatter, sporadic, but alive.

Thank God.

"Am okay..." Franco continued, the connection crummy with broken interference. "We're shaken... No exit. Would appreciate... dig us... soon."

"We're on it. Not leaving until you're clear," Liam promised without hesitation.

Franco was alive, and if anybody could scrap his way through, he could. The guy was the most fearless, the most tenacious on the team.

All the same, Liam intended to bring as much help to the table as he could wrangle out of the already-overtasked people scurrying around the buckled piles of concrete and rebar. He scanned the construction crews—a mix from around the world—for a spare soul to help out.

And came up empty.

He scrubbed a gloved hand over his face. God, his people were maxed already, working alongside a rescue task force from Virginia for the past eighteen hours without sleep. He was running on the fumes left over from his catnap during the cargo plane ride over.

More C-17s dotted the sky, a trio landing one after the other in the distance with more supplies and personnel. Much-needed help. Except it would be hours before they were in place here.

But the helicopter hovering closer? The supplies and personnel that chopper contained would be available in minutes. His headset buzzed with news of a relief dog handler being sent from the Virginia USAR—Urban Search and Rescue—team.

He zeroed in on the cable lowering from the craft. A wiry figure dangled from the end—appeared to be a female in rescue gear with a dog strapped to her chest.

The helicopter was sending in a fresh search pair. A gold mine for a depleted team stretched to the max after over eighteen hours without sleep. These two were also closer than whatever troops or supplies might be loaded in the C-17 still circling in the sky.

He clapped Rocha on the shoulder. "I'll be right back. Keep talking to Franco."

Sure-footed, he jogged across the jagged debris toward the chopper, eyes homed in on the duo spinning on the end of the descending cable.

He was a scavenger from way back, and intended to be first in line to claim her.

Holding her breath, Amelia squeezed her eyes closed and lips shut tight as the dust settled from the aftershock. Dots sparked on the back of her eyelids. She grew lightheaded from lack of oxygen. But if she gasped too soon, she would choke on pure grit.

She cupped the back of Joshua's head for protection. Precious little to offer, but the best she could offer. The top of her hand stung from something. Better her hand than his vulnerable skull. She was certain she felt him move, heard his tiny whimpers. Helplessness threatened to overwhelm her. How much more of this could she bear?

Consciousness faded. Her lungs screamed for air. Peeking carefully, she exhaled hard. Dust puffed ahead of her.

The thin light lancing through the dark reminded her she didn't have to endure this alone. She had help.

Or did she?

Panic pierced her. "Are you here? Are you okay?" God, she didn't even know his name. "Answer me, please. Let me know you're alive."

The slim glow didn't move. Her savior stared back at her with piercing green intensity. A death stare? She stifled a scream.

He blinked.

She whimpered with relief.

"Hang tough," he said slowly, shifting to pull a rock from under his side. "The worst is past. You okay?"

He was alive. They were all still alive. But for how long? She'd assumed because help had made it through, rescue had arrived. She hadn't prepared herself for another earthquake. Hours of more waiting. The possibility they wouldn't get out at all.

Concentrating on the positive seemed tougher and tougher. Hysteria frothed inside her all over again. She fought the urge to laugh like a lunatic. To sing a flipping chorus of "Tomorrow," like Little Orphan Annie.

She gritted her teeth. *Do not freak out.* She wasn't alone. The people above knew she was here alive.

"Hey," her rescuer said, louder this time. "Are you okay? Need you to answer me."

"I'm all right. Just a little dustier." She pushed the words up and out, even though each one felt like broken glass scraping up her raw throat. She studied the hulking figure behind the light. She clung to the only visible sign of life, of hope, in this hellish tomb. "Did you hear Joshua cry during the aftershock? He's okay, and now you have to know."

He pressed two fingers to her wrist. Taking her pulse, no doubt.

"Amelia," he said with unbelievable calm, his fingers warm and steady against her skin, "we're going to get you both out of here."

She noticed he didn't agree to having heard her nephew. Her lawyerly ear that helped her ferret out nuances in witness testimony was a curse right now. "How much longer do you have on that battery?"

"Long enough. Keep the faith. My guys are close."

"How can you be sure?" She hated the hysteria creeping into her voice.

"I know," he answered simply. "It's what we do. I understand how we think."

She laughed hoarsely. "So they're all as crazy as you are…? I don't even know what to call you."

"My name is Hugh." His large competent hands slid from her wrist to her IV, jiggling the needle, applying a new strip of tape.

The enormity of what he was doing for her and for Joshua flooded through her.

"Hugh…" She tested the lone syllable and accustomed herself to putting a name with the fuzzy blur who was risking his life to save hers. "Hugh, what makes you do something like this for a living? I can't imagine anybody willingly coming down here."

"What can I say?" He settled onto his side, stowing his gear. "I was the kid who climbed trees to rescue stranded cats."

"No kidding?" She grasped at the piece of normalcy.

"When I was seven, the neighbor's Siamese got stuck in a big old oak. The family called the fire department, but it was going to take a while for them to get there because of a three-alarm blaze on the other side of town."

His smooth-as-bourbon bass voice filled the cave with an intoxicating calm. "The neighbor girl was bawling her eyes out. So I figured, why wait? I'd climbed that tree a hundred times."

His story wrapped around her, sinking into her pores and transporting her to the world beyond this murky gray hell, a world with leafy green trees and fuzzy kittens.

"I'll bet the neighbor girl was glad to have her pet back."

"Oh, I didn't save her Siamese. The cat climbed down on its own." He chuckled softly. "I got stuck when my jacket snagged a branch and the fire department had to rescue me."

She laughed with him—how could she not?—until her eyes stung with tears and she choked on the thick air. "You're making that up to distract me."

"Not a chance. I was scared to death up there. Cried like a baby, when I got to solid ground again." A half smile dug a crease into the dirt on his rugged face. "The little kid had her cat back and looked at the firefighter like he was a god."

"Ahhh," she smiled, realizing. "You had a crush on the neighbor girl."

He didn't answer right away, the dull throb of distant engines filled the void.

"Yeah." His voice went flat, the smooth bourbon tones turning gravelly.

The leafy world in her mind faded, landing her back in the drab fissure. She rubbed circles over Joshua's head to soothe the child and keep the circulation going in her increasingly numbing hand. Closing her eyes, she struggled to will herself back to the brief escape from this place.

The sound of jackhammers intensified along with the growl of trucks and maybe even the occasional voice. But her mind could be playing tricks on her. The only thing she knew for sure, her only reality, was this man in front of her. "I hate feeling helpless, *dependent*."

"Hey... Hey," he repeated forcefully. "You're anything but helpless, and there's nothing wrong with needing me. It's my job. You've stayed calm. Believe me, from where I'm sitting, that's huge. A whacked-out victim is a danger to herself, to me, and to everyone around us. You're doing good, Amelia."

She forced dank air in through her nose, out through her mouth, rubbing Joshua's back in time with each breath. "What's your last name? You never told me."

"Franco. My name's Hugh Franco."

"And you're a PJ..." She traced the insignia on his uniform sleeve.

"Master sergeant."

Yeah, she could sink into the comfort of questioning him, like a lawyer finding out as much as possible about the man sent down here to rescue her. The more she knew, the more she controlled her world. Or so she hoped. "Where are you from, Hugh Franco?"

"I'm stationed in Florida." He shifted beside her, extending a leg. To get more comfortable?

"I'm from Alabama. I was looking forward to helping my brother, Aiden, then hanging out at the beach here with his wife and their son."

Debris showered on her head. She stifled a scream.

She bit her lip until she tasted blood. Once the dust settled, she scrunched her nose. "Sorry. I should be used to it by now, huh? People call me a bulldog in the courtroom, but inside, I'm a total wimp. I can't stand mice or snakes. I cover my eyes during scary movies or gory scenes. I don't feel brave at all."

Especially not in comparison to him. She studied his big muscled body, the way he seemed so relaxed and prepped for action all at once. He listened to her, checked her pulse, all while periodically pressing a couple of fingers to his helmet in a way she'd realized meant he was listening in on his headset. He managed a million tasks at once while she wrestled with just lying around waiting to be rescued.

She swallowed hard, scared as hell and unable to stop herself from asking for even more from this seemingly invulnerable man. "Do you think you could hold my hand?"

"Yes, ma'am, I sure can." His broad palm slid against her, callused fingers wrapping around her.

His work glove lay on the ground beside him and she realized how he'd been forced to take off that bit of protective gear to tend her. She'd been selfish, asking for him to stay even a second longer.

She squeezed hard then let go. "Okay, I'm good. I want you to leave now."

"Not a chance." He rolled to his back as if settling in for a nap. "I lose my Superman status if I check out on you."

Right now, he sure looked as ripped and invincible as a superhero. Was he as tall as he appeared? Or was the confined space distorting her perception? Not that it mattered. What he was doing for her now… Superman material, no doubt.

Still, why would he risk staying here with her when

he really couldn't do anything more for her? Her brain raced to the only logical conclusion. "The exit closed off during the aftershock, didn't it?"

He stuffed his pack under his head. "Can't get anything past you, can I? Yeah, you're stuck with me for the duration."

She was too perceptive, and Hugh needed to keep her from rooting around in his brain for answers. While he *could* still leave here, he wasn't one hundred percent sure she was as uninjured as she claimed.

And the kid on the other side of her? Once she realized that baby was dead, she would lose her shit and possibly injure herself. Give up. Die.

Not a fucking chance. Not as long as he was still breathing.

Logic said he should get his ass out of here, but with thoughts of Marissa still clanking around inside his thick skull, he wasn't thinking so straight. What the hell had led him to spill his guts about the cat story, the one about when he'd first met his wife?

Had to be something to do with Amelia's job training. Lawyers. Always digging around in people's lives. "So why did you become a prosecutor? Why not some hotshot corporate attorney making the big bucks?"

"You sound like my ex."

"Damn." He laughed softly. "That's harsh for the guy risking his ass for you here."

She paused. "Maybe my ex was a great guy."

Not if the tone of her voice was anything to go by. "Don't think so. Rotten breakup?"

"Train wreck as bad as anything on a reality show." She rubbed her thumb over her ring finger absently. "Still, for all you know it could have been my fault."

Could be. But his purpose here was to distract her with happy thoughts. "If he lost you, he must be flawed."

She rewarded him with a smile. "Ah, where were you when I was drowning my sorrows in pints of Ben and Jerry's?"

"Chunky Monkey?

"Cherry Garcia." She groaned.

He tensed. "What's wrong?"

"I so didn't need to think of Ben and Jerry's ice cream at the moment."

His muscles melted back onto the concrete slab. "So your smarmy ex didn't like your job choice."

Ex-boyfriend or ex-husband?

"He put me through law school and expected we would lead a more comfortable life once I graduated. When he found out otherwise, we got one of those 'irreconcilable differences' divorces. No kids. Little money. It was quick and far from painless."

"Sounds like he was a jackass." What kind of dumb shit threw away a family?

"Jackass… jerk… cheating scumbag. But he knows what he wants. He's happily married to one of my law-school classmates. Apparently he'd been sleeping with her for months before we split, something he felt compelled to confess—after he'd gotten his fifty-fifty, irreconcilable-differences divorce. From what I hear, they never see each other but they have a crap ton of money to spend on themselves and their two-point-two children. Not that I'm bitter or anything."

"Regrets bite."

"You said it." She finger-doodled small circles in the dirt. "I should probably forgive him in case I don't make it. But then that would be kinda hypocritical, since if I knew for sure I was going to make it, I would kick the rat bastard in the gonads."

A laugh burst out of him. "Lady, if we could harness your spirit, we could lift this building right off you in a heartbeat."

"Yeah, he said I was emasculating."

Hugh was thinking maybe he might like to look this guy up, use him for a refresher course on martial arts skills. After missions like this one, he needed to blow off steam.

She sighed. "The rat bastard was good in bed though. I do miss that."

What the —?

Shock zipped through him, along with an adrenaline surge and a passel of distracting images of this take-no-prisoners woman putting her everything into all-night, sweaty sex.

Not professional thoughts.

He cleared his throat. "You know you're going to live, right? And you're going to be sorry you told me so much."

She stayed quiet so long, he thought for a minute she wouldn't answer. "Maybe. Maybe not. But I'll never see you again, so it doesn't matter. Although I'm sorry if I embarrassed you."

"Surprised, maybe."

For a few seconds there, he'd even managed to stop thinking about Marissa stuck in the wreckage of a plane, stop wondering how long she'd lived, knowing that their child had died instantly. Had anyone else on the craft been alive in her final seconds to offer a distraction from the fear, to give her comfort?

Although one thing was damn certain. Marissa wouldn't have been talking like this. She'd been shy and fragile, and it killed him five times over every single day that he couldn't have been on that airplane instead of her and their daughter.

Amelia kept drawing circles in the sand with a ragged nail, her swirls growing like one of Tilly's scribble-art pieces he still kept on his refrigerator even though the paper had long ago yellowed with age.

"Hugh, it's tough not to think about regrets right now. Especially the huge one. Like thinking about never seeing Alaska or having sex again… Never becoming a mother."

He looked from the ground to her face sharply. "You want kids?"

"Joshua just wriggled his fingers." She smiled softly. "He's really alive."

He didn't want her thinking about the child.

Hell, he didn't want to think about the toddler a few feet away who was likely dead, and if the kid lived in some kind of coma state, not being able to do a damn thing for him… Yeah, that dropped Dante's inferno to a new rock-bottom level.

Time to discuss something else. "I've lived in Alaska. It's incredible. You should take a cruise up there when you get out of here, give yourself a chance to decompress."

She laughed hoarsely. "Maybe you could join me,

and we'll have lots of great sex in our stateroom so I can erase both of my regrets at once."

Again, he chuckled along with her and even wondered what it would be like to "decompress" with her. He hadn't lived like a monk since his wife died. The thought of getting married again made him sick to his stomach. So he'd settled into a life of one-night hookups and casual relationships. Some called him a serial dater.

His only commitment? Throwing himself into high-risk rescues while crossing days off the calendar until he could see his wife and kid again in the afterlife.

Right now, though, the thought of marking time with Amelia Bailey sounded... intriguing. "I may not be able to live up to the rat bastard's tantric reputation."

"He wasn't *that* good in bed." She rolled her pretty blue eyes.

"Glad to know you're willing to lower the bar for regular saps like me." He smiled, really smiled.

And she grinned back, the kind of grin that lit up a person's face, the last sort of reaction he expected to get from her here, today. Maybe she was getting punch-drunk on insanity and exhaustion. Could be that he was too. Regardless, right now he could envision one mind-blowing decompression session with this woman he'd barely met. Hell, he didn't even really know what she looked like under all the grime, just that she had piercingly blue eyes, an upturned nose, and a hundred-watt smile.

A smile that faded.

"Hugh, this is all too silly. I'm not usually so blunt."

"This isn't a usual sort of situation."

"True enough. Real life is very different. You

probably have a lovely wife and family back home, and here I am flirting with you."

And just that fast, his smile faded too. He had a mission to complete here, a woman to save. Time to quit thinking with his dick and do his job.

"No family." He reached for his gear bag. "Let me have your hand again. I need to check your vitals."

~~~

The Guardian gripped the walkie-talkie in one hand while steering the Jeep around a fallen palm tree. The Motorola transceiver was top-of-the-line, not some two-tin-can kid stuff. Very few unofficial personnel had access to vehicles and reliable lines of communication. Those with better equipment—like the radio and the Jeep—would have an edge.

The four-wheel drive jostled over the uneven road that lay in pieces like a jarred puzzle. A catastrophe like this called for special people, with specific skills and equipment to keep others from being victimized. Above all, the children had to be protected. The Guardian considered it a life's calling to remove babies from inadequate homes and provide them with better futures.

Never had that mission been more important than now.

Red tape meant nothing in the aftermath of the earthquake. Two decades of experience circumventing official channels would come in handy. Guardian troops already trained and in place would carry out orders without hesitation and with ease in the country's current lawless state. Babies wouldn't have to languish in an understaffed orphanage in this earthquake-ravaged hell while waiting for rubber-stamped paperwork.

Rows of sheet-covered dead filled a concrete parking lot outside a crumpled grocery store. The smaller forms carried the biggest punch, reminders of another lost child, a little girl whose face was still painfully clear even after so many years of grieving. The past would not repeat itself.

Anyone who interfered with the Guardian would become a casualty of war. Sad, but unavoidable. Nothing else mattered but gathering the children.

Chapter 3

LIAM MCCABE SQUINTED AT THE SETTING SUN. THEY would search into the night, but even with work lights, the operation would be tougher, slower.

The looters would grow bolder.

His eyes shifted to two security cops handcuffing the latest trash pickers. The seventh attempt today, mostly by starving displaced families. They would be escorted to one of the tent camps. The hungrier they got, the more desperate they would become.

They needed more aid—ASAP.

But for now, he would have to content himself with the one fresh set of hands and paws. He charged across the debris, determined to intercept the newest search and rescue dog handler and shout dibs. He'd informed everyone on headset that his mission was top priority, but that wouldn't keep somebody from trying to scoop her up first.

She was wiry, with a hint of dark hair peeking from beneath her helmet. She seemed too small to stand up under the weight of her gear, but she showed no signs of swaying. Her steel-shanked boots were planted firmly on the uneven ground.

Shouldering past two E3s setting up new stadium lights, Liam thrust his hand toward the woman. "Major McCabe, pararescue out of Florida," he introduced himself abruptly. "You're with me. Hope you're ready to roll."

"Rachel Flores." She stroked the neck of her black Labrador retriever. "This is Disco. We're not newbies. Been at this for over ten years. So give it to me short and sweet."

"I've got men on the pile now. One under the debris. He went in to stabilize a survivor." He pointed to the German shepherd about fifty yards away having his front paw taped. "The dog there—Zorro, I think they called him—found the scent, but he's worn out and has an injured paw."

Her deep brown eyes assessed the scene. "My dog only does live searches. Not cadavers."

"My guy is not dead."

She looked back fast, pinning him with a no-bullshit stare. "I'm not trying to get up in your grill, but you need to keep your objectivity. We have limited resources. If I spend hours searching here, then someone else goes unfound. I can't have you using me for your personal agenda, Major."

"My guy is not dead," he repeated through clenched teeth. "And my objectivity is rock solid. He's down there with a female victim and a male toddler."

"Okay"—she nodded curtly—"I'm just making it clear. Ready to roll."

He shifted into work mode, rattling off details and answering her questions as he escorted her to the dig site. Disco trotted alongside, looking like any regular house pet out for a daily walk. Until a person looked closer and realized how finely in tune the canine was to every minute gesture of his handler. How they were both on edge and prepared for anything they might face.

The death they likely *would* face.

God, he hated missions like this most of all. He'd seen so much death back during his days as an Army Ranger. Once the PJs accepted officers on their teams, he knew without a doubt where he had to be. He'd swapped from army to air force. From *hoo-uh* to *ooh-rah*. He wasn't ready to hang up his uniform, but he'd needed to shift to the saving end of the job before he burned out.

Life by life, he gained back pieces of his sanity. Cause for rejoicing. Except he'd left the wreckage of three divorces behind him. He'd liked being married, having someone to come home to, a soft woman in his life. He fell in love too easily and unwisely.

But here, on the job, he didn't doubt his instincts for a second. And his gut told him Rachel Flores would find Hugh Franco. She had to.

The alternative was unacceptable.

~~~

Every bone in Amelia's body ached as huge hands under her armpits hauled her from the crevice. Loose rocks and stones scraped along her back through her shredded silk blouse, but oh God, finally, she was free.

Lights flooded her cave, a larger space now that the rescue workers had hacked away enough concrete to pull her out. She landed on a canvas stretcher, the IV tube slapping her arm. She twisted to check Joshua—

Hands bracketed her head a second before a strap stretched across her forehead, securing her. She didn't even have to look to see who had hold of her. The past hours had even her breaths synced up with Hugh Franco.

She grabbed his sleeve and squeezed hard so he

couldn't walk away. "Hugh, please, get Joshua... don't give up on Joshua."

"They're on it." His fingers slid from her hair. "I promise."

"*You.* I want *you* to be the one. I know you've already done so much for me, but I trust you—"

His face creased with one of those half smiles that had carried her through hell. "I appreciate the vote of confidence. And all Superman claims aside, I'm a worn-out, exhausted piece of crap right now. You want someone fresh freeing the little guy. My buddy Cuervo's already going in, and he will take the best care of him. Trust me on *that*." He squeezed her shoulder. "No freaking on me now. I don't want to have to knock you out with a Vulcan nerve pinch. Okay?"

Nodding, Amelia slumped back onto the stretcher. Finally, finally daring to let herself relax as they made a jostling journey through a tunnel in the rubble so lengthy she was overwhelmed by what Hugh had done for her.

And because of him, she was actually going to get out of here. Alive. In one piece. Granted, every piece of her ached from a combination of bruises, scrapes, and immobility. But she welcomed every twinge, stab, burn that let her know she was alive. Somehow, she'd survived. She had the chance to breathe regular air again.

The end of the tunnel waited ahead, glowing. A breeze gusted inside, dank but free of grit. Strapped to the stretcher, she slid free into her second chance, like a rebirth.

Blazing lights pierced her eyes. From the sun? She'd lost track of time. But no. It was night now, with halogen spots placed all around, illuminating... *Hell.*

The beautiful tourist town was gone. So much devastation. Hotels and brightly painted shops were either broken in half or covered in a film of gray grime.

Noises, no longer muffled, assaulted her ears. The growl of machinery. Engines straining in tractors, trucks, and cranes. Shouts. Barking dogs.

And moaning masses of injured humanity.

Her gaze scanned to... oh God, a tarp on the ground with sheet-draped bodies on top. The dead. Horror and bile filled her mouth. She winged a prayer for all those lost souls, all too aware of how easily her lifeless remains could have been there, unclaimed, unknown.

If not for Hugh Franco.

Her eyes tracked back to him as he towered over her. He held one side of the jostling gurney. He'd been through a horrific ordeal himself and yet he still had the energy to haul her out, waving aside a uniformed medic trying to take his place.

Hugh shrugged off the man's hand on his shoulder. "I'm fine, Major. Surely there's somebody in this godforsaken mess who needs you more."

The major backed away, out of Amelia's limited sight line. All the same, she wondered if Hugh was hiding an injury. Why hadn't she thought to worry more about him belowground?

For the first time, she could really see him. Before now, he'd been a deep voice and shadowy savior under the hard hat. She tried to turn her head for a better view, but the strap held her secure.

Gravel crunched under Hugh's boots, his broad-shouldered body looming. He was taller than two men jogging past. In fact, he was every bit as tall as she'd thought in their cavern. The outside world and circle of lights only accentuated the breadth of his shoulders, the hard lines of his face.

A harsh shout echoed in the distance a second before she heard—

Gunfire.

Staccato shots popped in the distance. Her heart echoed in horror. Her every muscle screamed *run, run, run!* But she couldn't move.

The stretcher thumped to the ground. Hugh threw himself over her, covering her with the bulk she'd been learning only seconds earlier.

The hard wall of his chest shielded her. His body curved around her and she realized that even in the pandemonium, with bullets flying, he still thought to keep his weight off her in case she was injured.

She stared up at him, his piercing green eyes close to hers, as they'd been when he first found her. Her mouth dried up. She wanted to tell him she was okay, that she could take care of herself. He should look out for his own safety.

As a prosecutor, she stared down criminals on a regular basis in prison interrogation rooms, on the witness stand. She'd even been confronted once by a drug dealer out on bail who'd hoped to intimidate her. She'd thumbed her car alarm and kneed him in the balls—then almost passed out when a rat ran across the alley.

But hey, she'd taken care of herself then and she could do it now—if someone would free her hands. Yes, she was a wimp on the inside, but she could deal when she had to.

And she'd always had to.

Being protected felt... foreign, strangely frightening in how easily she gave over control and simply absorbed the feel of this toned man on top of her. Her pulse hammered in her ears. Her blood burned through her veins as her senses went into hyperdrive. The sliver of air between their gazes fizzed with awareness, danger, and some sort of world-stopping connection. Which was so ridiculous, given that they were both filthy, beyond disgusting, after being all but buried alive—and yet somehow that didn't matter. And she could swear she saw a whisper of matching emotion in his eyes as well.

It had to be from what they'd experienced together. She knew that intellectually. Her body, however, clung to the feel of him.

Then he looked away. Air whooshed from her lungs.

He glanced over his shoulder a second before he eased himself off her. "Just some looters. They come out in droves at times like this. Security personnel have it under control."

How could she have forgotten for a second how dangerous it must be out here in the aftermath of such a catastrophic earthquake? How vulnerable Joshua would be without his newly adoptive mom and dad. And until Aiden and Lisabeth were located, Amelia was Joshua's guardian, his protector. She couldn't lose sight of that for even a second.

"Hugh, please be sure your buddy Cuervo and the medics know who Joshua is when he's checked over, just until I can get to him." She pleaded with her eyes, her voice. Hell yes, she was shamelessly using that connection, that thread she'd sensed between them. Something shifted in his eyes when she mentioned

Joshua, and damn it, she would use whatever she could to keep that baby safe. "It's too easy for a child to get lost in this confusion. You know I'm right, and I realize you have to be exhausted. But he's a helpless baby."

Hugh's throat moved in a long swallow.

She clung to his sleeve as two medics lifted her stretcher again. "I know you've already done so much for me." She spoke faster, time running out. "I don't have the right to ask for more, and I wouldn't, except there's no one else for me to turn to. Please, can you stay to be sure?"

He shook his head slowly. "Amelia, you have to accept that the boy is d—"

"No! I realize you don't believe he's alive but—"

A cry cut through the mayhem, a lone piercing wail so different from the jaded horror all around them. The gasping sob of a child.

Joshua.

She squeezed her eyes closed in relief. He was alive. She wasn't crazy. Thank you, God, her nephew was alive. She blinked back tears and stared back up at Hugh.

Her hulking rescuer turned paler than any corpse.

—◦◦◦—

Hugh fought the urge to punch out.

The major wouldn't question him. He'd pulled his weight today. But it wasn't exhaustion nailing his ass.

Right now, he was scared shitless of the squirming kid being thrust toward him. Instinctively, Hugh took him with the sure hands of a father who'd cradled his own baby girl through colic, teething, night terrors, and scraped knees.

He forced his focus on the present. On this child. A boy, a toddler, just as Amelia had said.

Her nephew was really alive, in spite of the odds.

His chocolate brown skin had lost some elasticity due to dehydration. The kid was covered in dirt and his own feces. But his eyes were wide, alert, and staring straight up at him. The boy—Joshua—reached a shaking little fist toward him. His dry, cracked cherub mouth moved with a raspy whisper of garbled baby talk.

The weight and wriggle of him in Hugh's hands felt too familiar. Too painful.

He thrust the child at Cuervo. "Make sure they stay together. He's hers." Stuffing his fists into his pockets, he nodded to the gurney disappearing into a medical tent. "Amelia Bailey. She's his aunt, adoption completed just before the earthquake."

"Right." Cuervo secured the kid against his chest. "Will follow through. You should go back to the hooch, clean up, and sleep. You look like hell, by the way."

"Thanks. I'm outta here." He pivoted on his heel. Away from the woman.

Away from the kid smiling at him with six tiny teeth.

His throat closed up.

Major McCabe clapped him on the back. "You had us worried there for a while."

"When have I ever not come out okay?" He scanned the ruins for someplace to help, another mission to take on, the crazier the better, because sleep suddenly didn't sound like a good idea, with nightmares sure to haunt him. Better to work himself unconscious instead. A good plan. It had carried him through the past five years just fine.

"Hey." McCabe snapped his fingers in front of Hugh's face, drawing his attention back. "You can't count on that kind of logic to carry you through forever. I should have your ass for not coming out after you stabilized your patient."

"Staying kept her stable." He frowned, his jaw jutting. "Write me up if you need to, but I wouldn't change a thing."

McCabe sighed like a weary parent. "Let Rocha check you over. *Now*. We need to make sure you're not hiding any injuries."

He grinned, forcing a smile through caked-on grime so the major wouldn't realize how blown to shit his insides were. He refused to be benched. "Would I do that?"

"Yes you would. Go. It's an order."

"Yes, sir."

A light breeze parted the stifling air, welcomed for the cooling. Dreaded as it stirred the flies and the stench. Snakes and rats already scavenged through the debris. The fetid wind rolled across the uneven landscape, gathered grit and stray papers before lifting the door flap of the nearest medical tent...

His boots picked up speed toward the field hospital they'd put together shortly after landing. Triage was in place for major injuries to the left, minor to the right. Lines of wounded streamed out of both. His teammate Wade Rocha was already waiting, just as the major had insisted.

Still, Hugh checked one last time... just as Amelia's stretcher reached the tent flap. He could swear she stared back at him, held him with those intensely blue eyes. Eyes that reached down deep in his gut and twisted.

He'd only felt this connection once before in his life. The day he'd looked at Marissa's tear-filled eyes as she'd begged him to get her Siamese out of the tree. Next thing he'd known, he was hauling his ass up a twenty-foot oak.

He didn't want this.

The past few hours had proven beyond a doubt that Amelia Bailey was dangerous as hell to his peace of mind. More than ever he couldn't afford this during a mission that already put him raw and on edge.

And still... He bolted across the jutting mass of broken concrete. His eyes locked on the stretcher being carried to a drab green tent, the canvas flapping in the muggy air, stirring fat flies around.

He grabbed the arm of a foreign medic, a wiry guy with a top-of-the-line Motorola two-way radio and a clipboard. "Where will she go after you finish here?"

"There are already over a dozen makeshift hospital sites being set up in schools and churches." The foreign soldier covered the mouthpiece on the walkie-talkie and tucked the clipboard under his arm. "It's going to be a matter of which one can take them."

"I know it's chaotic right now, but if she's not going to be flown out—"

"Do you know this woman?"

So easily he could end this now. He could do what he would—and should—in any rescue situation. Ensure the appropriate personnel made a record of the pertinent information, such as her connection to the child, then move on to the next case.

He could not be personally responsible for every individual he saved. It wasn't practical, feasible, or mentally advisable, if he wanted to keep from falling the rest of the way off the deep end.

But then he'd stopped giving a shit about his sanity five years ago.

Hugh looked back at Amelia, under the sheet with only her face and one arm sticking out. "Yeah, her and the kid... They're mine."

Chapter 4

DR. AIDEN BAILEY THRUST HIS HANDS INTO THE MAN'S chest cavity and squeezed life back into the dead heart.

Squeeze. Squeeze. Pray.

"Catch, damn it, catch," the seasoned surgeon muttered with each massage of his fingers.

The canvas wall creating the makeshift operating room flapped from movement on the other side, another surgical team to tackle the insurmountable flood of injured. Aiden focused, worked, even though he'd been in the Bahamas to adopt a son, not ply his trade.

Squeeze. Squeeze. Pray.

He'd volunteered his services in the improvised hospital after the earthquake hit. His Hippocratic oath, his call to heal, wouldn't let him turn away from the masses of injured.

Squeeze. Squeeze. Pr—

Through the thin membrane of latex gloves, he felt the warm blood, the fibrous muscle, the tips of his fingers tuned in for the tiniest hint of a… throb.

His imagination?

No.

The heart expanded against his palms. Again. And again, as life returned to the waxy, middle-aged man sprawled on a stretcher in the half-standing church that had been turned into a temporary hospital. Supplies and conditions were rustic, to say the least.

NGO workers and military medics on loan from other countries brought freshly wounded faster than he could treat them. Groans filled the air, mixed with the crackle of shortwave radios. A couple of people had been lucky enough to get a cell phone connection and a rare few had satellite phones, but none of that had helped him find out what he needed to know.

So he worked. And waited. His mind filled with the worst-case scenarios. Joshua. Amelia. Helpless in the face of more than just the destruction. Looters. Worse. He understood how far seemingly normal people would go better than most.

God, he had to keep busy or his mind would explode from worrying about his sister and Joshua.

Once he was certain the patient had stabilized—as much as anyone could be considered stable in these crappy conditions—Aiden extended his hand, ready to suture layer after layer to close the gaping chest cavity. He didn't even need to look or ask. His nurse—his wife—had worked with him for five years on Doctors Without Borders missions before they'd recently swapped to Operation Smile to repair cleft palates in children. They'd known each other far longer, having met as undergrads at Auburn.

They didn't require words anymore when operating.

The terror he saw in the eyes around here, though, would require more skills than he possessed. So he focused on what he *could* accomplish rather than dwelling on the grief gripping his chest as tightly as any fist wringing life back into a dead human hull.

His sister and his son were somewhere out in that post apocalyptic hell, and there wasn't a damn thing he could do. His *little* sister was out there, the sister he'd taught to drive, helped proof her college papers, vowed to take care of since their father died. And his son... already he hadn't been there when his child needed him.

If only he and Lisabeth hadn't jumped in that cab to pick up lunch at her favorite place a few blocks away. Joshua had been napping, and they'd wanted to treat Amelia to a special meal in thanks for all she'd done for them with the adoption.

And yeah, he'd wanted some time to absorb becoming a father, something he'd never expected to happen. He'd thought he and Lisabeth had a life path in place, dedicated to helping other children. He'd needed to take in how that course had shifted.

Then the world had shifted in a different, all-too-real way.

He and Lisabeth had spent the first six hours after the quake hit searching for Amelia and Joshua. They'd tried to get back to the hotel, only to be blocked and sent to the site where survivors had been taken. Then they'd been told patients had been sent to multiple locations. Some names appeared on multiple lists, but no list carried the names he was looking for.

Still, they'd searched without turning up any leads. They'd been turned away again and again at barriers and checkpoints as martial law quickly slid into place. They were just two of thousands desperate for information.

They'd given Amelia and Joshua's names and descriptions to rescue workers, who made notes with fatalistic compassion. Lisabeth's silent tears had tracked paths through the grime that coated everything. They hadn't even been allowed near the hotel, the epicenter.

Instead they'd been shuttled to another site... this crumbling church-turned-hospital. Now nearly three days since the earthquake, he'd lost count of how many lives he'd saved—and lost.

He stepped back from his patient.

This man, at least, was alive. For the moment. He'd patched up a forty-seven-year-old father caught looting an overturned market vendor's booth for untainted food. The guy had sprinted away with a burlap sack full of bananas and pineapples, slipped on loose gravel, and fallen into a pile of rotting fish—impaling his chest on a metal rod.

Aiden flexed his fingers. He'd caught shit for saving a thief when earthquake victims waited. This place was a lawless hell full of scared, desperate people, and no doubt it would only get worse. Even if his Hippocratic oath hadn't already demanded he stitch up the man, Aiden still wouldn't have been able to turn away from a father putting his family first, defending his children, something far too rare in his experience.

Backing away from the stretcher, he left the church's social hall, which had been turned into an operating room. As he charged down the corridor, he kept his eyes off the frescoes and crosses. A helluva time to realize he hadn't been in a church since his wedding, and then only because his wife had insisted on a service in her childhood chapel back here in the Bahamas.

Pushing through double doors, Aiden retreated to the chapel's kitchen. Clean scrubs and gloves were stacked on a shelf beside the sink. Some military group called RED HORSE had dug latrines and drilled a fresh well for showers. Except on a day like this, he didn't think there was a shower long enough to wash away the destruction.

He peeled off the bloodied gloves and pitched them in the trash, *slap, slap*.

"Aiden?" Lisabeth's calm, soft voice cut through his thoughts. "Are you okay?"

"Of course, just recharging the brain." He pulled off his glasses, wiped a spot of blood off the left lens with an alcohol wipe, and put them on again.

She studied him over her surgical mask, her brown eyes turning golden yellow with concern, too perceptive after sixteen years of marriage. He looked away quickly.

Her cool hand fell onto the back of his neck. "I know you better than that. You may look emotionless to the rest of the world, but I see deeper. I know how much you hold in."

She pulled her mask down, revealing her regal face, which had stared back at him across the pillow every morning since he was twenty-two. "All of this is more than any one person can bear. We need to turn to each other. I *need* to talk to you."

He held out his arms without hesitation. "I'm here for you."

"I know that. But will you let me be here for you, love?" she said with a rare hint of British accent she'd picked up from her father. Her dad had moved to the Bahamas to teach history, met her mother, and stayed. Lisabeth had been their only child, their world, treasured.

The way life should be for a kid.

He turned back toward the sink. "If you want to help me, then ease up right now. I'm maxed out."

She slid her lithe body between him in the basin. "You can't always protect your sister. This is not your fault."

"Do *not* go there," he snapped. "Not. Now."

He already knew how fallible he was.

"Okay." She eased off in surrender, sweeping off her surgical cap and shaking free her short black curls. "Let's just sit together for a minute quietly and catch our breath."

Aiden reached for the antibacterial scrub. "No time for that now. People will die while we breathe in a paper bag. We'll talk later."

He was lying about that, but willing to do anything to get her to stop this line of questioning. Bullshit weakness. He shouldn't have caved to Lisabeth about adopting a baby from her home country. If he'd held strong, they would be home in the States now. They would be safe.

. And the child? Joshua? Aiden pivoted away from his wife before she could read the pain in his eyes. She needed so much more than he could give her. He still wasn't sure why she stayed with him, but God help him, he couldn't walk away.

He felt her standing behind him for at least five heartbeats before the soft sound of her footsteps faded. Sighing, he let his guard down and swayed, dead tired on his feet.

Through the cracked stained-glass window, he saw a military Humvee pulling up with armed guards in front and back. Most likely the restocking of medical supplies. The last convoy had been ambushed.

Typical shit that happened in situations like this. Looters. Medications would sell for big bucks in the outer regions, where help hadn't yet reached. Hell, anything could happen at times like these… Everything from drug trafficking to human trafficking.

He had a 9 mm tucked under his scrubs and he knew how to use it. Yeah, he'd made use of one of those black-market scavengers right after the earthquake hit. It had cost him his Patek Philippe wristwatch to get a weapon. He hadn't hesitated in making the exchange. No one would touch his wife.

And his sister? His… child?

Bile churned in his gut until his vision dimmed. He pushed down the abyss of memories always there waiting, threatening to swallow him. Turning back toward the sink, he became the surgeon again. No longer Aiden, husband, father, brother… son of a perverted criminal. For now, he would save lives.

But if anyone threatened his family, he wouldn't think twice about once again becoming a killer.

———

She would kill for this baby.

Amelia cradled Joshua in her arms as she had through the night, rocking her nephew in the school library that had been turned into a pediatric ward. She'd never imagined such powerful protective instincts could fire through her. But her love, her bond with her nephew couldn't be denied.

Although he slept peacefully, she wasn't ready to let go of him yet. Pressing a kiss to his smooth forehead, she breathed in the scent of his freshly washed skin and hair. Clean clothing was in short supply, so he wore only a diaper and a T-shirt that was a little too large. Bright letters spelled out *Bahamas*, with a toucan and palm tree. Apparently even the good guys were looting.

Sighing, she smoothed the cotton, tugged the hem, and reassured herself in a dozen ways that he was okay. Scrapes marked his tiny limbs, but miraculously, no cuts, no stitches were needed. Only the IV taped to his arm hinted at the ordeal he'd endured, trapped under an entire hotel.

Her body ached more than she could have believed possible, but other than bruises, scrapes, and a cut on her hand, she'd come through blessedly whole as well. The medics had pumped her full of antibiotics and a tetanus booster, then freed her to go with Joshua. She hadn't left his side since.

Two nurses—or some kind of medical techs— circulated around the room, checking on their dozen little charges, making notes on their painfully thin charts. Most of them were orphans. The rest had parents or relatives in critical condition elsewhere.

And Joshua's parents? Her brother and his wife? Amelia's head fell back as she tipped her face toward the open window. The first morning rays splashed a tequila sunrise across the parched dusty world outside.

The night had passed quickly as her nephew had been shuffled from the tent clinic to an elementary school that had been converted into a hospital. The library had tables stacked in a corner, the open floor space filled with tiny cots, basinets, even pallets, anything that could hold an injured child until better accommodations could be airlifted in. Blankets were hung up here and there for impromptu privacy. A battery-operated radio hummed softly in a corner.

The building ran off generators now. There was no air conditioner, but fans hummed lowly in the windows, the sounds and the morning world coming to life, so normal and yet strangely empty without the sound of Hugh Franco's calm reassurance.

How could she have grown that accustomed to, so dependent on, his voice in such a short time?

A hand on her shoulder jarred her from her thoughts.

"Ms. Bailey?" A military nurse passed her a bottle of water. "You need to remember to take care of yourself. You've been through quite an ordeal."

"Thank you, but really, I'm only sitting." She opened the bottle and took an obligatory sip so Nurse — she read the tag stitched onto the uniform — Nurse Gable wouldn't worry. "I just don't want to let him go."

Nurse Gable knelt beside her, warmed her stethoscope against her palm, then slid it under Joshua's shirt. A second later, she nodded. "That's understandable, after what you've experienced. But we have extra nurses coming on shift, thanks to more relief efforts coming in, so whenever you're ready, you should go to the cafeteria and get a boxed meal. Even if you bring it back here, the walk will do you good."

"I will, soon, I promise."

And the woman was undoubtedly right. The shower earlier had spiked her energy considerably. She plucked at the borrowed hospital scrubs she'd put on once she'd finished the lukewarm rinse-off in water pumped from a newly dug well—thank goodness for the military engineers. Her spray had been trickling and brief, but orgasmic. She'd been warned not to drink even a taste of what spewed from the faucet. The desperate urge to be clean had overridden any concerns about microbes possibly swimming through the chilly drizzle.

Yet nothing could wash away the scent of death, the fear of more bad news lurking under the rubble. Somehow she'd been calmer underground with Hugh than she was now. How could one person be so full of gratitude and grief at the same time?

If only she had some word about her brother and Lisabeth from one of those people with a two-way radio. Their names weren't on any of the casualty or wounded lists, but the number of dead was already so horrific... Amelia cuddled their son closer as she rocked next to the playpen being used as his bed. She had to believe they were okay. Just detained somewhere. She'd hoped the fact that Aiden and Lisabeth were medical professionals would bring them to the front, make them more identifiable... if they were even alive.

But she'd been told again and again that communication was spotty. It could take days, even longer, for different rescue sites to communicate back and forth with ease.

So much had been accomplished since the earthquake over three days ago, with so much still left to do.

How could she have been down there for two whole days without realizing that much time had passed? The doctor had told her she must have been unconscious at first, a diagnosis the monster-sized lump on the back of her head validated.

Hugh hadn't told her about the passage of time either, likely to keep her from panicking. Good call on his part. But then he'd seemed so confident throughout the entire ordeal, so in control during living hell, she shouldn't be surprised at how he'd known just what to do. And now he was off helping someone else who needed him, offering those same words, that same comfort. She needed to realize she was just a routine mission for him.

Yet still...

Even when he wasn't around to fill the space with his broad shoulders and strong reassurance, he occupied her thoughts... and even her dreams.

Her head lolled to the side as she drifted into another micronap, exhaustion tearing at her. Amelia indulged herself in the memory of his reassuring bass, the lingering feel of his hand. She invited thoughts of him to fill her, to anchor her through the nightmares.

"Amelia," his voice whispered through her head, the feel of his hand on hers becoming all the more real until...

She jolted upright to find Hugh kneeling in front of her. Green eyes held her with the same intensity that had sustained her for hours belowground.

Her brain churned overtime to make the leap from sleep to awake, the dream and real world blurring. "Is everything all right? Did something happen during the night? Are you here to see a doctor?"

"I promised to check on the kid and I keep my word. I just finished my shift or I would have come earlier."

Those bourbon-smooth bass tones had kept her alive. She couldn't forget the sound of him even if she never saw him again.

But a clear view of his face, of his body? There she found uncharted territory. She'd thought she memorized the look of him as she'd been carried out on the stretcher. But realized she'd only seen his body. His face had been covered in grime, and while his clothes were still grimy, he'd washed his face and hands.

His face wasn't poster-boy pretty. He was all man, with hard handsome angles and gleaming emerald eyes. Buzzed short black hair proclaimed a lack of vanity. And his mouth was a full but hard line that called to a woman's finger to trace, to tease into softening.

She reached for a gulp of water.

His dusty camo uniform sported a survival vest. His weapon was strapped to his hip. An angry scrape down the side of his face added to the outlaw look, like he was some kind of rogue rebel fighter. He personified everything edgy and dangerous she'd steered clear of as an adult—and strangely, exactly what she needed right now.

"Amelia? The kid?" He nodded to the sleeping baby in her arms. "What did the doctors have to say?"

"Oh, uh…" She toyed nervously with the drawstring on her surgical scrubs.

Damn, she was seriously losing her grip. She should find a free cot and just sleep as the military doctor had suggested, but she couldn't bring herself to send Hugh away.

Besides, she was suddenly wide-awake and wired.

"The doctors say Joshua should be fine, once he's rehydrated. And he's blessedly unfazed by the whole ordeal, as if he truly did nap through it all. A couple of IVs and he will be ready to eat, play, laugh, just like before."

"Good, that's really good."

"What about you? You were supposed to see the medic last night. I thought you would still be asleep."

He scrubbed his fingers along the scratch on his cheek. "We found another pocket of survivors. My help was needed. Sleep can come later."

Yet he was here now instead of resting.

She stood, placing Joshua in the playpen, careful to adjust his sleeve for the IV. With a couple of nurses watching over him and the other eleven napping babies, she could afford to step away for a moment.

"The nurse was just telling me how I should pick up one of the boxed meals in the cafeteria. Would you like to walk with me? I imagine, since you worked through the night, there wasn't much time for food."

A smile kicked into one cheek. "You guess correctly."

She pulled her eyes off his mouth and angled past, leading him into the hall packed with pallets of supplies, and the only part of the school without people to disturb. Other corridors were full of injured, but they kept the kids with the gear as a means of quarantining the more vulnerable little ones. The building was filled to capacity. She'd heard they were sending all new arrivals to another site set up at a nearby church.

Hugh marched past a mural obviously painted by the school's students, a playground scene of rainbows and palm trees. "You've bounced back quickly for someone who went through hell for forty-eight hours."

She breathed deeply, still savoring the ability to draw air into her lungs after her time in the dark and dust. Now she smelled twenty years worth of peanut butter and jelly sandwiches, a scent that no amount of hospital antiseptic could dispel. "I'm fine. I have a baby to take care of, a brother and sister-in-law to search for."

"No word at all on them yet?"

Her chest went tight. And suddenly she understood her draw to him, to his reckless look. This was the kind of man who—in a lawless world—kept people safe. "They're still unaccounted for."

"I am sorry."

More of that fear and grief howled inside her and she saw a deep understanding in his eyes. Those three words weren't the mere platitudes others offered.

"Thank you." She sucked in another breath, shakier this time as she worked hard not to think of the particular brand of hell her brother could be going through. "I have to believe they're okay, out there somewhere, worrying about Joshua and me."

"What's your plan?"

"I'm staying here with my nephew. I won't, I *can't* leave him. I'm hoping to hire help in searching for my family." She needed someone like Hugh, but he obviously already had a job of his own.

"It's not safe to stay here."

"I know." But what choice did she have? "I've heard there are looters everywhere."

"Damn straight. And worse. Black-market types thrive on situations like this. With all this food and all the drugs here, I wish there were more guards to go around. The best thing you can do is get on the first plane out. I can pull strings for you—"

"Stop." She squeezed his forearm, pausing outside the cafeteria. "I will not leave Joshua. Legally, I'm on shaky ground without his parents. It'll take a while to get me declared his guardian until my brother is found."

"You're a tenacious one."

"You're one to talk." A smile slid through her grief.

Hard muscles contracted under her fingers. Had she been holding on to him this whole time? Apparently so. *Gulp*.

Her body hummed with that same sensation from earlier, so much so, she could no longer write it off as coincidental or some general need for sex. But the feeling, the connection, was inconvenient and unwise. She felt guilty. Her thoughts should all be focused on finding her brother and sister-in-law. Instead, she was a ragged mess clutching some hunk's arm like a lifeline.

And he didn't move away.

He eye-stroked her in a way that made his answering attraction clear without crossing the line. "You clean up nice."

"You're not quite what I expected either, now that we're in the daylight." She slid her hand away, closing her fist to hold on to the feel of him.

"What did you expect?"

Someone with traditional good-guy looks—blond. All-American like her ex. Would she have reacted differently earlier if she'd known her gentle, steady rescuer had a bad-boy body and forbidden-sex eyes?

But she still hadn't answered his question. She settled on a safer lie, a last-ditch effort to hold strong against the need for an outlet clawing at her insides harder and harder with each second. "I expected someone older."

"I'm an old guy in this career field." He scrubbed a hand over his beard-stubbled face. His eyes tracked a kid crying in a wheelchair all the way into the cafeteria. The noise inside swelled out as the double doors opened.

"Age notwithstanding, you got the job done."

"I only wish we could have freed you faster." He

lifted her hand, her bandage stark white in a dull gray world. "What happened?"

"When the aftershock came, right after you found me, some debris cut my hand, but it only needed butterfly bandages. They pumped me full of antibiotics and a tetanus shot for good measure." She thought back to cupping Joshua's head. If she hadn't, the debris would have pierced his skull. She'd been granted a miracle. She just prayed there was room for another for the rest of her family.

"You should have told me." He thumbed her fingers until her fist unfurled.

"Wouldn't have made any difference. It wasn't as if I could have rolled over to give you the hand to treat."

"And you called yourself a wimp? I gotta disagree." He stepped aside to make way for two nuns carrying stacks of boxed meals toward the children's wing.

"I just did what I had to in order to survive. What you've been doing out there? That's takes bravery to a whole new level. Thank you again."

"No more thanks needed. You'll make me blush and ruin my badass image. Let's find some food."

He palmed the small of her back. The heat of his hand steadied her in a way she hadn't felt in days, then warmed her in an altogether different way. An inappropriate way, given what was going on in this corner of the world. She stepped ahead, moving with the line inside.

The room was packed, not a seat in sight, hollow-eyed survivors filling the space and eating the boxed meals with a dazed-automaton motion. Even the small stage to her side was crammed with people eating while sitting on the floor around an old upright piano.

Her feet stilled. "The children break my heart the most. They should be playing outside, singing in music class"—she skimmed her hand along bins of stacked instruments on the steps leading up—"or even grousing about a spelling test."

"The kids are always the hardest." He scooped a guitar from an open case.

"You play?"

"I do." He slid the strap over his head. His fingers worked along the strings as he twisted the tuning pegs.

Heads turned in his direction in a wave of increasing attention. One child, then two, then small clusters, moved toward him. He grimaced, before shooting her a wry grin. He shifted from tuning to a song. Before she could process the shift in *him*, Hugh was strumming through "Be Kind to Your Web-Footed Friends."

Surprise tingled through her. When children looked up and began migrating toward him, he started singing. No self-consciousness. Just pure rich tones smoothing tension from the room as tangibly as a hand sweeping over a wrinkled sheet.

A small mosh pit of little fans gravitated toward him. He segued into "If You're Happy and You Know It," which should have seemed grossly ironic, except the children were smiling and clapping along. One of the nurses reached into a box and began passing out classroom instruments—finger cymbals, blocks, tambourines, castanets, and some rattles she didn't recognize. An older man left his food to help pass out the instruments to the children, his stoop-shouldered walk growing taller by the second.

Hugh's ease with the children couldn't be missed or

faked. Her heart squeezed, hard. Watching him with the kids, how could she not think of her own dad right now? No matter how hard she tried to push back memories of the way her father had betrayed his family, purely emotional times like this brought the loss crashing forward. Her father had taken that purity and exploited it, seducing her teenage friends.

Part of her trusted the world far less because of that. Another part of her couldn't help but celebrate true honor when she came across that rare commodity.

Like now.

Clutching her boxed meal to her stomach, she turned away sharply. But with every step back to the nursery, she strained to hold on to the echoing drift of Hugh's voice.

Liam McCabe had stayed in some nightmarish shit holes over the years, but as far as living quarters went on a scale of one to ten? This place rated a negative two.

A tent in a field would be better—not to mention more stable—than a beach cottage on a crumbling bluff.

Although considering that much of the region was currently homeless, he probably shouldn't complain. As long as the two-room shack with a cracked foundation didn't slide the rest of the way into the ocean before he finished taking his shower, he was cool.

He turned off the faucet, gathered up his toiletries, and tossed them into his travel bag. Snagging a towel off the stack, he swiped the inside of the shower stall down, cleared his beard shavings out of the sink, made sure he'd flushed the john. All three of his marriages may have failed, but he'd picked up a few friendly housemate habits along the way.

His exes may have been right in calling him an immature son of a bitch, but by wife number three, he never forgot to put down the toilet seat.

Now that the cottage bathroom was cleared, time to hotfoot it out so the rest of the team could clean up. The place had running water and a stack of semiclean bedrolls. Even if the hundred-year-old structure reminded him of a haunted house carnival ride. The floor shifted under his feet every other step as he tied the towel around his waist.

At least it was private, a place to decompress from the hell they'd seen over the past eighteen hours.

He tugged open the warped door leading into the living area. The other seven PJs tasked for this mission were scattered out in the two rooms, quiet, letting the weight of the job roll off before they returned for more tomorrow. An evening muggy breeze drifted in through the open windows, doing little to ease the heat. Grimy uniforms aired out, hung over chairs and nails hammered into the wall, while the team cooled down wearing their boxers or a towel.

Franco—who'd already showered—sat on his bedroll, back against the cracked wall… with a guitar?

Liam tossed his shaving kit on a cot. "Where'd you pick up a guitar in this place?"

"Local school," he said without missing a beat in a vintage Clapton tune. Good stuff, with the deft touch that had earned Hugh the nickname Slow Hand. The guy was so into his music, he even had some kind of musical staff tattooed on his chest.

"And you were there for a concert gig or what?"

"Checking on patients. Folks there loaned me the guitar." His head went back against the wall, eyes closed as he played—and sent an unmistakable message of *conversation over*.

Not surprising. Missions like this sucked the stuffing out of anyone. At least Franco was finding an outlet with the music.

Liam scanned the rest of the room, monitoring the mood of his team. Dupre worked a Sudoku puzzle book, his foot tapping in time to the beat. Bubbles cleaned his weapon—dropped the magazine, peered inside, switched on the safety, and so forth as he went on autopilot, going through the motions. Routine was a great calmer.

Securing the knot on his towel with one hand, Liam jerked a thumb over his shoulder with the other. "Bathroom's clear. Next."

The newbie guy—Fang—shot off the rocking chair and bolted toward the bathroom without a word. The rocker slammed back against the wall, showering plaster on the slate floor. The call sign *Fang* was actually an acronym for *Fuck, Another New Guy*. Once some other newbie came into the squadron, the current Fang would get a permanent nickname. The old Fang—Marcus Dupre—had become Data due to his computer/math-geek ways.

Frowning, Liam turned to Data, Fang's teammate this mission. "Is he doing okay?"

Sprawled on the rattan sofa in military-tan boxer shorts, Marcus Dupre set aside his *Sudoku Supreme* book. "Have to confess today was a tough one, even for someone like me, who's been around for a while."

Marcus had been around for all of eight months.

Not that Liam saw the need to point that out. Normally he wouldn't pair up a new Fang with a recent Fang, but Dupre was rock solid. And while Liam had tried to direct the two of them toward what appeared to be the lighter rescue, sometimes seriously bad shit just happened in this job.

Liam dropped into the rocker, tossing his toiletries case on the floor beside him. "Wanna talk?"

The Clapton tune from Franco's guitar segued into a mellow Jimmy Buffett riff.

Marcus shrugged. "Not exactly the mission for a fresh-faced Ohio farm boy like Fang to get his feet wet. While we were down there..." Pausing, he scratched his neck, his collar bone, the back of his neck, as if he couldn't scrub off the itch of memories even after a shower. "We had to cut through a dead woman right down the middle to save her teenage daughter."

The guitar music faltered, then slowly restarted, the only sign that anyone else was listening in. The images, the smells... Liam didn't have to work hard to know exactly what that must have been like.

"Shit." Liam glanced at the bathroom door, running water echoing from beyond the thin panel.

The kid hadn't looked right all evening, but surgically sawing through a dead body to reach a live one? That would leave crazy horrors clogging the brain, impossible to block or forget. And the stench. God, the smells that clung to the air even now like rancid meat in a septic tank.

This kind of day packed a punch for even the most seasoned warrior.

His gaze shifted to Franco, pouring his attention into classical music now. Bach, maybe? Regardless, his "stand back" vibe came through loud and clear as he picked away faster and faster on the well-worn acoustic.

Liam had spent so much time in marital counseling he should have received some kind of honorary certificate for having processed the gamut of psychobabble. Although it didn't take a PhD to see the emotional carnage rattling around inside Hugh Franco.

The floor creaked a second before Cuervo stepped out of the bedroom. He stopped at the counter in front of a box of MREs—meals ready to eat. "I see the catering staff is as high-end as ever."

Bubbles grunted without looking up, moving on from cleaning his gun to sharpening his survival knife.

Cuervo tossed back a handful what looked like generic M&Ms. "Somebody's a Debbie Downer."

Gavin "Bubbles" Novak never laughed and rarely talked. Whoever had given him that call sign had a serious sense of the ironic.

Cuervo held out his hand with the rest of his candy. "Want some? They're yummy."

Bubbles eyed him for three slow blinks before saying, "You're a sick puppy."

"Laugh or lose my cookies?" Cuervo chewed thoughtfully, then nodded. "I'll go for laughter. Gets a person through the day, right Major?"

Liam just smiled. Usually he did agree with that mantra, but today was harder than most. The responsibility of leading his team, keeping their heads on straight, weighed heavy on his shoulders. There weren't many opportunities for him to blow off steam these days. But this was the only life he knew, the path he'd chosen at the expense of everything else.

He eyed his team, his family, his kids to keep safe.

Cuervo snapped Hugh Franco's leg with a towel. "Practicing up your tunes for a hot date, Franco?"

Cocking one eyebrow, Hugh caressed his way through the notes. "This just happens to be Bach's Toccata and Fugue in D Minor. It's called culture. Give it a try sometime, bro."

"Has everyone lost their sense of humor?" Cuervo pitched back the rest of the candy, his wiry frame not showing the least sign of his junk food habit.

"I must have left it in the pile of mangled corpses." Franco's fingers picked up speed on the neck of the guitar, emotion damn near pouring from the strings.

Cuervo took the hint and dug around in the MRE box without commentary. His sugar high would send him pacing around the room, but eventually he would crash.

Quiet settled over the room long enough that Liam considered snagging a bedroll of his own and heading to the other room. The next shift would come around soon enough, with a new level of horrors as the chance of finding survivors decreased.

With a final check-in look at Marcus Dupre and Hugh Franco, Liam shoved to his feet. The floor predictably squeaked under his feet. The room seemed to tip sideways, but God, he was so tired he'd probably gone a little loopy. His shower sandals slapped the scarred wood floor. He leaned to grab his gear and bedding—

The ground rumbled. Unmistakably.

Another earthquake, or at the very least a kick-ass aftershock.

Curses bounced around as fast as feet hit the floor. Fang shot out of the bathroom, wrapping a towel around his waist without missing a step. The front door clogged as they all angled out sideways until they burst through. Liam scanned the cottage fast, finding all out, and followed them to the cobbled road.

The ground stilled as quickly as it had stirred.

Just another aftershock.

But apparently the whole damn town had been just as afraid. The side street was chock-full of locals and relief workers. Except they were all dressed and staring gape-eyed at him and his team.

Hugh Franco held his guitar in one hand, securing his towel with the other. Fang's knot on his hip slipped and he grabbed for the edges frantically. Marcus covertly checked the fly of his boxers.

Cuervo's mouth twitched with a laugh that Liam could feel welling inside himself as well.

Ah, to hell with it.

He let the laughter rumble up and free, hopefully carrying some tension out along the way. He flattened a hand to a half-uprooted palm tree and shook his head as Fang jogged inside again, his flapping towel flashing half a butt cheek.

No doubt, Fang was going to have a stripper-style call sign by morning.

Some of the tension unkinked in Liam's gut and he straightened. "Okay, everybody, let's close down this peep show and catch some Z's."

He pivoted on his heel, a deep dog bark giving him only a second's warning that he was about to bump into—

Rachel Flores.

"Lose your clothes, Major?" She stood beside her black Lab, leash in hand. Her grimy cargo pants and body-hugging T-shirt declared she was still working.

Her dog started sniffing the edge of his towel suspiciously, all seventy pounds of pooch tensed, hackles rising along the canine's spine.

"It's not my clothes I'm worried about right now, ma'am. Think you can get your dog to let go of my towel?"

"Disco?" She thumbed some kind of clicker in her hand and the dog dropped to his haunches. "Good boy."

"Thanks."

"And Major?"

"Yeah?"

"You may want to invest in a larger towel." She clapped him on his bare shoulder matter-of-factly before striding past, toward the cabana next door.

Her touch lingered on his bare skin. He stood rooted to the spot for a solid five seconds, watching her walk away, her thick ponytail gathered high and haphazardly on top of her head. Wavy brown hair swished with each step.

Movement from the cottage door tugged at the edges of his attention, even as he kept his eyes glued to the no-nonsense twitch of Rachel's hips. Franco charged back out again, no guitar this time, but fully clothed. He ran past in camo pants and a fresh brown T-shirt, yanking on his survival vest.

"Going somewhere, Franco?" he asked distractedly.

"I'll be back in an hour, sir." Without giving Liam a chance to protest, Franco jogged away, weaving through the milling crowd.

And it didn't escape Liam's notice the brooding sergeant was heading toward the half-demolished school that had been converted into a temporary hospital. The same place he'd said he picked up a guitar earlier...

He should have known Franco would track down Amelia Bailey again.

Women. It was always about the women. His focus went right back on Rachel Flores, slipping inside the next-door cottage.

He'd been searching for a way to wade through the tension of the day. Then just a few words from that woman and the load on his shoulders felt a little lighter. Damn. He studied the tracks left by Rachel in a layer of dust on the street, dog prints in perfect sync alongside.

If he closed his eyes, he could still see the twitch of her hips, the tangled mass of hair whipping around in the breeze. Only a day and he already had every inch of her hot body planted in his memory as firmly as he could hear her voice, see her smile. All that relationship counseling about taking his time and thinking things through when it came to women hadn't made a bit of difference.

He was already halfway head over ass in love with Rachel Flores.

Chapter 5

HUGH STOOD IN THE DOORWAY TO THE TEMPORARY pediatric ward, staring at Amelia like a junkie jonesing for crack.

His need—a gnawing hunger—to see her again wasn't healthy. Coming back here definitely wasn't smart. But the second that aftershock had hit at the half-wrecked cottage, he hadn't wasted a second. He'd only thought of getting dressed and hauling ass to the hospital to check on Amelia.

And now he'd found her. Alive. Safe. Mission accomplished.

He should leave. Should. But didn't.

Instead he kept his boots planted, taking advantage of the fact that the medical techs on duty with their shortwave radios and walkie-talkies wouldn't question him being around so late at night, since military presence was a given in these circumstances. So the nurses went about their business while he soaked up the sight of Amelia bathed in the glow of a low lamp.

She slept in a teakwood rocking chair, the kid snoozing against her chest the same way he'd found her the day before. He averted his eyes from the child and back to Amelia. She wore standard-issue green surgical scrubs and a pair of plain white gym shoes that had undoubtedly come from one of those hundreds of empty pallets. And still nowhere near enough gear had been shipped in yet, even four days after the earthquake hit.

Just like when he'd seen her at the hospital before, her hair streamed over one shoulder, sleek and damp. She was a blonde. He hadn't known that when they were underground and covered in dirt. He hadn't really thought about how she looked then, just seeing—admiring—her determination. Such calm in a crisis didn't come around often. He couldn't even count the number of times the person he'd been sent to save had freaked out. In the water. On a sheer cliff. In the desert. On a helicopter rescue cable. He usually came out with more bruises from being thrashed by the victim than from the actual rescue work.

Not with Amelia though.

Her spirit drew him, and he couldn't deny the surge of attraction he felt from just looking at her. She was... beautiful. Stunning, even, in a delicate way so contradictory to her tenacious spirit that it made her even more appealing.

A fresh surge of protectiveness hummed through him, tinged with something else. Something he recognized well. He wanted her. So much, the force of his ache to be inside her threatened to drive him to his knees.

He slumped against the door frame. Seeing her again hadn't reassured him in the least, only stirred up a whole new tangled mess of thoughts—along with the undeniable urge to touch her hair and see if it was as soft as it looked. Find out how it would feel splayed over his shoulder while she sprawled naked on top of him.

The way she'd left the cafeteria without saying good-bye should have kept him away. Their time together was over. Mission complete. And yet he'd still been unable to scrub thoughts of her from his mind. Normally music offered him an escape, and now she'd invaded even that corner of his life.

Which brought him right back here. Searching for closure? A wise man would. But then he wasn't known for his levelheaded thinking.

Already making his way into the library-turned-infirmary, he absorbed the look of her, relaxed in sleep. His eyes fell to the plump curve of her naturally pink lips. The floor seemed to vibrate under his feet and he knew there was no aftershock this time. The humming came from deep inside him.

Shit. He was screwed.

"Hello, Amelia."

Hugh's voice whispered through her mind so tangibly, she could have sworn he spoke from inside her dreams again. And if so, she wanted to stay asleep a little longer, even as reason intruded. Images of him in a hammock at her Alabama condo didn't make sense but felt so right. Just lazing in her backyard, soaking up the clean air, the bright sunshine...

And munching on a huge hamburger.

Okay, now she really knew she was dreaming. Her stomach grumbled.

"Amelia?" Hugh said again, louder this time, from behind her.

Joshua stirred against her chest before settling his cheek into the curve of her neck again with a baby sigh and a bit of drool. Blinking through the layers of foggy sleep, she secured her hold on her nephew and looked over her shoulder.

As if conjured from her dreams, she saw Hugh waiting a few feet away by a shelf of reference books. She blinked fast, and sure enough, he stood a hand stretch away. His face was cast in shadows, the lights dimmed for the dozen sleeping children.

"What are you doing here again and so late?" she whispered as he moved to her side. "Is something wrong? Did you find out something about my brother and his wife?" Her throat closed up.

"No, I just—"

Nurse Gable shushed them both as she patted a sleeping baby girl on the back.

Amelia smiled an apology before turning back to him. "Let's talk outside in the hall."

He nodded and sidestepped the vigilant nurse on his way toward the door.

Slowly, Amelia stood, careful not to wake Joshua as she returned him to his playpen. Kissing her fingers, she pressed them to his forehead and swept a hand over his tight curls before turning back toward the open room.

And the man who'd filled her life so completely so quickly.

Hugh had come back. The first visit she could chalk up to curiosity and following through on his mission. The fact that he'd come a second time moved her more than it should. She'd sworn never to let a man's presence matter so much again. Damn it all, she felt too vulnerable, too exposed and raw after her ordeal. That had to be the reason for her out-of-control reaction to this man.

She stepped into the hall where he waited, the brighter

lights bringing into sharp focus his face—his eyes that burned with a wild and untamed look. Her stomach took a tumble.

His gaze held hers for another of those lightning-crackle moments, which felt all the more powerful in the night quiet of the hospital.

She wished she'd brought her water bottle to wet her dry mouth. "Why are you here? Did you find out something about my brother?"

"I'm sorry, but no."

Disappointment stung, then shifted to confusion. "Then why are you back?"

"How much longer are you stuck in here?" He crossed his arms over his chest, big, unapproachable, and all the more confusing.

"I'm no longer a patient." She crossed her arms defensively as well. "The doctor said Joshua can leave in the morning. I begged my way into the nursery so I could stay with him."

"They probably welcome the help."

Silence stretched, broken only by the occasional whimper from a baby or the subdued shuffle of distant feet. Finally, she blurted, "Why are you here in the middle of the night?"

"Why did you walk out of the cafeteria without saying good-bye?"

She blinked in surprise. "You're here because I hurt your feelings?"

"I wouldn't say that."

"Then what would you say, exactly?" She stepped closer, frustrated by whatever game he was playing but unable to walk away from him again. She clenched her fists by her side to keep from reaching for him. To keep from indulging in the crazy need to find out if his chest was as solid as she remembered from when he'd covered her body during the shooting.

He scooped up one fist, his thumb sketching over the bandage on her cut hand. "I'm here because I owe you an apology."

Now that wasn't what she'd expected to hear. "I'm not sure I understand."

She didn't pull away. Yeah, it was silly, but she needed the comfort of human contact. Of contact with *him*.

"It's the real reason I'm here, I guess. Unfinished business with you."

Unfinished business. The two words hung in the air between them, filling the space with possibilities until she could have sworn their bodies shared a link.

His dark eyebrows pinched together and a shiver skipped down her spine, pooling in her stomach. They weren't flirting exactly, but she was fast realizing they were engaging in a dance of sorts here. She was not alone in feeling this draw, in needing something tangible to hold on to in a world turned upside down.

"Hugh? And this unfinished business would be?"

"I apologize for doubting you earlier when you told me Joshua was alive."

She exhaled hard and hadn't even known she was holding her breath. "I imagine you've seen so much in your job, you would get jaded. The worst-case scenarios would be more vivid for you."

"You could say that. I'd think your job would do the same to you."

"Sometimes... Mostly when it comes to trusting

adults with a history of larceny, armed robbery, and so forth, but you get the idea. I could have just as easily been wrong about Joshua." The truth of that clogged her throat for a second. "Reality was questionable down there. I had no idea I was trapped for two days—which you were wise not to clue me in about, by the way. My mind obviously was playing tricks on me so I wouldn't panic."

Was her brain toying with her now? Leading her to imagine what it might be like to explore every inch of that muscled strength that had saved her today.

"Your mind was doing its job helping you survive, and if your brother is half as tough as you, I predict he will be fine."

"You have a way of instilling confidence. That's quite a gift. You pulled me through in more ways than one." A big battery-operated clock ticked behind her, stirring fear of passing time and how soon he would walk away. Every second that passed reminded her of the precious gift of being alive tonight. With him.

Thanks to him.

"It's my job."

Her eyes fell to his survival vest stretched across his broad chest.

"Somehow I don't think it's in your job description to shoot the breeze under tons of rubble. You could have left once you found me and put in that IV. You didn't need to come here to check on us. And you definitely didn't have to give up sleep to sing to a cafeteria full of children."

"What can I say?" He shrugged, his green eyes glittering in the dim night. "I'm a softie."

She snorted her disbelief. "Hardly." Although the way he'd pushed aside the exhaustion from his face to distract traumatized children with songs had been mesmerizing. She didn't trust easily, especially not after her father and her ex, but she desperately wanted to believe in what she'd seen in Hugh then and now. "Was the story about the Siamese cat and the little girl next door true? Or were you just shooting from the hip with stories to keep me calm?"

A flash of something shadowy whispered through his eyes.

"The story was true." He released her hand and fished in his pocket. "I should leave, let you sleep. If you need anything, there's a number here where you can reach me. Hopefully, cell phones will be working more reliably soon. And if not, just go to any of the military personnel and they'll be able to track me down from this info. I'll be on the island working for at least a week, maybe longer."

"Thank you. That's generous of you." She took the folded paper from between his fingers. Was it her imagination or had he held onto the doubled-over slip for a second longer than necessary?

She thumbed open the paper. His handwriting was dark and angled, as if he pushed through the words hard and fast. He'd written a phone number and a local address.

Her jumbled emotions didn't know what to make of this. Part of her still believed they'd shared a unique connection during their time together, and another part doubted herself on any number of levels. She only knew one thing for sure, she needed closure with him after all they'd shared underground. Maybe that's what had brought him here as well.

"Don't take this the wrong way, Hugh, but is it okay if I hug you?"

"A hug? Uh, sure."

He looked so uncomfortable, she almost lost her nerve. She closed the last step between them and wrapped her arms around him. God, he was so much bigger than she'd even realized. Her head tucked under his chin and her arms couldn't make it all the way around his back. And he smelled so damn good, like Dial soap and vital man. He palmed the middle of her back, but other than that made no move closer. Somehow that turned her on all the more. She could hear his heart beating faster. The heated gusts of him breathing harder steamed through her damp hair. He was every bit as moved—hell, as turned on—as she was. Yet still, he restrained himself.

That honorability stroked her as firmly as any bold touch.

She inched back but didn't let go of him. She couldn't. Her brain clamored for the ultimate outlet to the frenzied storm inside her. And with an answering lightning crackle all but radiating off him, her words from their time together underground, about missing sex, came roaring back to fill the wake of her adrenaline letdown. What would it be like to grab him by the shirt-front, haul him into the nearest private nook, and give herself a temporary respite from the worries, the fear, the horror of the past days? Something dark and wild in his glinting green eyes said he could deliver everything she needed and more.

Was she making a fool out of herself even thinking these thoughts and holding on to him this way, this long? And if so, what the hell did it matter? She wouldn't see this guy again once she left the Bahamas.

Right now, she was overwhelmed and confused and needing to take charge of something in her life. She needed to feel alive, as tangibly strong as the beat of his heart against her chest, a reminder of his health and vitality, the sheer force of his will that had driven him to find her. To stay with her.

Without him... She shuddered. Words weren't enough to express what she felt for him.

It wasn't just gratitude that flowed through her veins right now. Her whole body hummed with a primal need to celebrate the moment and the man.

"Hugh?" Her fingers moved restlessly along his shoulders. "About that thing I said when we were stuck together, about how I miss..."

"Sex." He chuckled lightly against her hair before stepping away. "Hey, I know that was just the stress and the situation talking."

She looked up and met his glittering green eyes boldly. "What if I was serious? What if I'm hoping you feel the same way?"

He went still, his slow blink the only sign he'd heard her. "I would worry that I might be taking advantage of a vulnerable woman. I would be concerned you are mixing up feelings of gratitude with something else. That you're in need of an adrenaline outlet."

Possibility hummed through her veins. He wasn't laughing. He wasn't leaving. He was only spelling out questions about her motivations, more concern for her.

"I have to cop to the adrenaline thing. I could definitely use an outlet for all I'm feeling. And yes, I'm grateful, but I'm also grateful to your friend who pulled out Joshua, and the doctor who took care of my hand. But believe me, I'm not imagining what sex would be like with them."

His eyes flamed at her words, but he stayed silent, apparently not yet completely convinced she knew her own mind.

"What if I assured you I am completely aware of what I am saying, of what I need more than anything? And right now I want to have life-celebrating sex with you."

Straightening, he towered over her, his eyes glowing with unmistakable heat. "I would find the nearest supply closet and take you up on that offer faster than you can say 'Let's get naked.'"

Chapter 6

His body in overdrive, wanting, needing to be inside Amelia, Hugh kicked the supply closet door closed and turned the lock. For extra security, he yanked a trash can across the room and jammed it under the knob.

The place was private, quiet, a hall away from the staff. Even the antiseptic scent of cleaners burned off the hellish stench outside their haven. He hadn't come here expecting this, but he also couldn't think of anything he wanted more than to be here with her.

Inside her.

His eyes adjusted to the dark just as she yanked a string overhead. The single bulb flickered to life inside the eight-by-ten closet full of shelves that had been stocked full of hospital supplies, with a small utility table wedged in a corner. Amelia stood in front of him in her borrowed scrubs, her hair still damp.

His hand gravitated to stroke a strand, finding it even silkier than he could have imagined. Everything about her was so damn delicate, he had to remind himself this woman was tough. He'd come here to check up on her, just to lay eyes on her. He couldn't trust anyone else's word. And now it appeared he was going to lay more than his eyes on her. If he had his way, he would explore every inch of her body with his hands, his mouth.

And she was in his arms again, not just to hug but to hold on, to caress and explore his body. He angled his head toward her just as she arched up on her toes, her face tipped. Mouth to mouth they met, tasted. Her tongue explored just as fully as his did. She tasted like toothpaste and coffee. Her hands scaled along his back, shoving his survival vest to the ground.

His mind shouted this was a damn stupid idea in spite of everything she'd said. She was still reeling from the trauma. He wasn't all that steady either. During that aftershock at the beach cottage, his mind had filled with images of Amelia and the kid trapped again, needing help, calling out to him. He'd been off like a shot to check up on her. And yeah, he knew this was tied up in the past.

She yanked his T-shirt free of his pants.

Any rational thoughts made a double-time retreat. Air whispered over his back, followed by her touch. He traced the hem of her surgical top, hesitating, his conscience kicking him in the ass.

Her cool fingers slid up his spine, her clipped short nails digging into his back. "Stop thinking. I know what I'm doing. I want this. I need to be with you, to forget about all of those horrors that I'm helpless to fix."

How she'd read his mind, his doubts, his own howling frustration, he didn't know. Still, he had to be sure, to protect her, even if only from herself.

He smoothed back her hair with a hand that shook harder than a newbie on his first mission. "You're mixed up because I rescued you."

"What about you?" Her fingers crawled up his chest to caress his neck, her body melding with his in an unmistakable invitation. "Are you mixed up? Should I be protecting you?"

Blood supply to his brain was seriously compromised, since it was all surging south. His erection throbbed against his fly as he tried to sift through her words. Had she somehow found out about—God, he couldn't even think of their names right now. "I'm not sure I know what you mean."

"Do you sleep with the people you save very often? Enough that you can be so sure of what I'm feeling?"

Her words flicked cold water on his libido, not totally dousing it but definitely giving him enough of a wake-up call to clear this up. To make sure she understood how she affected him in a way even he wasn't sure he understood yet. "I've never slept with anyone even remotely tied to one of my military rescues, and if you don't believe me on that, then we need to stop this right now."

"If you're sane"—she traced his ears lightly, intimately—"then why are you trying to push me away, unless you think I'm a needy nutcase who doesn't know what she's doing?"

The surety in her voice fed the hunger searing his insides. "I'm only asking you to be certain. I don't want you to have regrets or add to the fallout from what you've been through."

"I am thirty-one years old, and I know my own mind." Her feathery touch skimmed over his temples, down his cheeks to circle his mouth. "I want to have sex with you, no strings, just now. Together. To affirm the fact that we both came out of this alive. To find some closure. To feel good again."

She sounded clearheaded and decisive to him. Fair enough. And the way she'd started nipping his bottom lip...

He swallowed hard. "So you trust I have the ability to make you feel good?"

"Very much so," she said with an intensity echoed in her sky blue eyes, "and I can't wait for you to prove me right."

"Okay then." He sealed his mouth to hers, his arms locking around Amelia as she twined hers around his neck.

She kissed him again, more knowingly now, more familiar. He plunged his fingers into her hair, absorbing the texture, memorizing the feel of her. Burning to see every inch of soft feminine flesh.

Bunching up her top, he inched the fabric higher between them. She covered his hands with hers just below the gentle curve of her breasts.

"Everything's borrowed from the rescue supplies," she gasped breathlessly. "I'm not wearing anything particularly seductive under there. Just a generic sports bra."

Keeping his eyes locked on hers, he eased the top the rest of the way up, breaking eye contact only for the instant it took to sweep the shirt the rest of the way off.

And then he absolutely could *not* look away. "You make white cotton look sexier than any lace."

The horror of the past hours faded as he drank in the curves of her breasts hugged by the fabric, her nipples beading in obvious arousal. Then he saw the bruises purpling her ribs, another mark on her shoulder. No doubt, there were plenty more dotting her all over after what she'd been through. He reached toward the largest on her side.

Grasping his wrist, she redirected his palm until it

rested over her breast. His fingers massaged reflexively into the softness and she moaned softly in response. *Encouraging him*. He peeled the bra up with precision, deliberation, savoring every damn second. Her eyes sparked the hottest blue flames back at him, warning him she was every bit as on fire as he was. She stroked under his T-shirt and palmed her way up his chest, scrunching brown cotton in her hands until she cleared his head and flung away the military-issue tee.

He hauled her against him.

Skin to skin.

Bare breasts to his chest.

Hips to hips, with too many barriers between them. And one very important barrier missing.

He pressed a kiss to her forehead. "I need for you to wait one second."

"Why?" she gasped.

"I need to get a condom."

"You carry them with you to earthquake rescues?"

"Believe it or not, they're part of the gear in a survival vest—the most efficient way to carry water."

"Water carrier? Like a balloon? You've got to be kidding."

"Afraid not." He knelt, scooping his vest off the floor. "But I'm really not in the mood to discuss survival training right now."

"Me either." She tugged his vest from him. "And I have a better idea than you using up the 'water *jugs*' stored in your vest."

Amelia pointed past his ear.

He turned to look at the metal shelves behind him and found… an industrial-size box of condoms. "Holy crap.

Somebody's got ambitions. Although if we were out of this hell and had a long weekend, maybe…"

She yanked the box from the shelf. "How about you stop bragging and start proving?"

"Roger that." He took the carton from her, tore open the top, and dug around inside.

"Hurry," she demanded. She shoved the box back on the shelf quickly, toppling it sideways. A half dozen rained from the box onto the floor.

But he had one firmly in hand. Urgency hammering through him, he slapped it on the small corner desk behind her, put his gun safely aside on a shelf, and devoted his entire attention to Amelia.

She met him kiss for kiss, touch for touch. His hands dipped inside her pants, cupping her bottom, lifting her more fully against him. The soft pressure of her rocking her hips against his hard-on threatened to send him over the edge.

He dipped his head, taking her nipple in his mouth. Her gasp, then purring moan, sent a fresh bolt of lust shooting through him. She sagged in his arms and he secured his hold, shifting his attention to her other breast, licking, nipping, teasing. Her head fell back and she mumbled breathy encouragement, urgent requests for *more*.

He completely agreed.

Distantly, he heard a rattle beyond the door, low voices. His body tensed until the sounds continued past their locked haven.

Amelia rubbed her cheek against his. "No more waiting."

Her fingers worked the fly of his pants until she freed him. For two labored breaths, she held him, her fingers enclosing him like a cool silken glove. Then she stroked and he lost his footing for a second.

He braced a hand against the table behind her. Her lips curved in a knowing smile that she grazed along his neck, up to nip his earlobe.

Reaching behind her, she groped along the table until she located the condom. She tore it open with her teeth and sheathed him quickly, efficiently. So *very* thoroughly. The caress of her hands down the length of him threatened to undo him right then. He reined himself in, reminded himself of all she'd been through—

She bracketed his face with her hands and stared straight into his eyes, her shoulder-length blonde hair a tousled, sexy mess around her face. "I don't want tenderness and I don't want some sort of fake romanticism. We both know what this is about."

"You're—"

"Tired of talking." She urged his head to hers and kissed him, full-on and full-out, demanding with her mouth and her hands.

He'd been planning to say she was bruised and exhausted from her ordeal. That this was crazy and they needed to be levelheaded.

Sanity be damned. If this was insanity, he was all in. Literally.

Nudging down the pants of her scrubs, he cupped her butt again, lifting her, settling her on the edge of the desk. She wrapped her legs around his waist, her heels digging in, urging him forward until…

He pushed inside her.

Teeth gritted, he held still. "Okay?"

"More than okay, but I could be better if you would…"

She dug her heels into his ass and urged him closer. *Deeper*. Her eyes stared back at him in the dimly lit room, the same sweet blue drawing him in as completely as her body held his. He thrust and her forehead fell to rest against his, her sigh filling the air around them.

The tension that had begun building since the first time he saw her, that had only continued and increased, grew teeth inside him. The need, the hunger, gnawed at him, demanding he move inside her, meet the wriggle of her hips in just the right way to take her as high as she took him.

Growling, he kissed the curve of her neck, up, up, until he took the lobe of her ear between his teeth the way she'd done to him, guessing she'd done something to him she liked for herself. Her purr of pleasure rewarded him, and damn, making her feel good made him feel even better. She rocked against him and clawed at his back as the table inched backward, ramming the wall, rattling the bottles on the shelves with each thrust. She buried her face into his shoulder, muffling her cries of pleasure from anyone who might pass by their closet.

A closet, for God's sake.

He wanted to take her again in a bed, in a shower, anywhere more civilized than a fucking broom closet in an earthquake zone. He wanted to stretch her out naked and taste every inch of her again and again until she came apart. And damn, damn, *damn*, he was the one coming apart as he pounded inside her.

Still, every time he tried to go slower, easier, she demanded more. She writhed against him, faster, breathing in his ear how close, so close, she was.

Her orgasm squeezed around him, harder and harder

in a velvet vise. He thrust harder and faster, finally free to give in to his own release. The tension uncoiled, expanding, pulsing through him as he came and came again inside her. The force of it convulsed his arms around her, damn near buckled his knees like the demolished world around them.

And before the haze of pleasure faded, he felt her pulsing again. Her teeth sank into his shoulder and he reveled in the pain brought on by the satisfaction *he* gave her.

A light sheen of sweat slicked his torso, sealing their bodies together. He stayed inside her, knew he should pull out, clean up, say something... nice?

Damn, he was the king of postcoital platitudes after his dead-end relationships of the past five years. He knew dozens of ways to reassure a woman she was sexy and rocked his world, but he understood she needed someone different.

Then he could walk away with a clear conscience to hang out with his memories. His grief.

Yeah, that was a screwed-up cycle, but he didn't know any other way to live without becoming a monk. Not an option.

Right now, *really* not an option.

So he scrounged for those words to give her, to somehow make sense of what they'd done.

She placed two fingers along his mouth. "Don't talk." She pressed her lips to his tenderly, briefly. "Don't mess this up with words or half-meant promises that will feel awkward when we're both clearheaded. This is what it is—an incredible culmination—and I thank you for that. It's something I suspect we both needed and now it's done."

Before he could pick his jaw up off the floor, she'd gathered her clothes and dressed. She rested her cheek against his back for a heartbeat… and left.

The door closed softly behind her.

The silence echoed around him, the scent of her, of them, and sex mixing up with the disinfectant in the air. She'd actually walked out on him. She hadn't even given him a chance to roll out some face-saving words for both of them.

He yanked up his pants, tugged on his T-shirt, and shrugged back into his survival vest, wondering why in the hell everything still felt so off-kilter. She'd said everything he should have wanted. Exactly the sort of words he'd spoken to women over the past five years. Sex. Just sex. No commitment or messy emotions. He'd seen she and the kid were okay. And all crazy sex aside, she'd still given him the free and clear to walk away. Except for the first time in five years, he didn't want to walk, he didn't want to forget.

And that scared him shitless.

~~~

She would never forget him.

How could she?

He'd saved her life—not to mention just given her earth-shattering sex, making her forget she was in a broom closet, for crying out loud. She'd learned one thing for sure. Her ex had been right in dissing their chemistry, because she'd never felt anything like this during her entire marriage.

Her ex was a serious dud in comparison to Hugh.

What if she'd met Hugh Franco during a true

Bahamas holiday? Maybe she could have indulged in more than one impulsive encounter in a broom closet. But life wasn't normal even when it *was* normal. She had a crummy marriage behind her and a dead father who'd left his kids with a crappy legacy of heavy-duty baggage.

All that aside, she had practical worries and concerns in looking after whatever family she had left. Tears burned to be set free but she held them back. She'd been selfish enough stealing the past twenty minutes for herself.

Time to focus solely on Joshua and finding the rest of her family.

She rounded the corner to the quiet pediatrics hall, weaving past crates and stacked supplies. The corridor was deserted, other than one nurse or doctor walking away with a toddler, the little guy sleeping on her shoulder.

The baby wriggled awake, eyes blinking wide and staring down the long hallway, straight at her. Something stirred inside Amelia. A sense of recognition.

Joshua.

She wasn't sure how she could be so certain after only spending such a short time with him. But his little face seemed imprinted on the back of her eyelids… even deeper on her heart.

Why was the nurse taking him away? Was he sick after all? Or was it a doctor? The unfamiliar woman wore surgical scrubs like everyone else, her cluster of thin braids gathered into a low ponytail. A two-way radio was clipped to the waist of her pants.

Amelia raced down the hall, her borrowed tennis shoes squeaking against the tiles. "Excuse me."

The woman didn't turn, didn't seem to have heard her

at all. But her feet moved faster… Amelia's heart sped with the first inklings of fear.

"Ma'am? Stop, please or I will find a guard."

The woman turned slowly, holding Joshua so tightly he began to squirm. "Yes?" she said with a local accent. "What do you need, Doctor?"

This woman thought *she* was a physician? Amelia looked down at her own surgical scrubs. With medical personnel from different groups working together, it wasn't unusual not to recognize the staff, and they were all wearing the same clothes stacked up beside the tarp shower stalls outside.

Still, alarms jangled in her head. The woman's body language seemed *off*, and anyone could have picked up a set of the surgical clothes. "Is something wrong with him? Where are you taking him?"

"To give him a test. I am a nurse."

Then why hadn't she been told? And why was the woman who called herself a nurse wearing leather sandals? "In the middle of the night?"

The woman paused, then said, "There are no set hours during a crisis. Now if you'll pardon me…"

Amelia walked closer, faster, holding out her arms. "Let me carry him so he won't be frightened. He's more familiar with me."

The woman's body tensed, her eyes going hard. "I think not, since I am his mother."

Shock rooted her feet to the floor. That couldn't possibly be true. Could it? "Your baby?"

"Yes, this is my son. I thought we had lost him in the earthquake, but see now?" She cradled the back of his head possessively. "He is fine. Is he not, Doctor?"

This woman's timeline just didn't add up, since Aiden and Lisabeth had already adopted Joshua before the earthquake. Amelia considered calling the woman on the lie right then and there, but the woman was holding Joshua in a fiercely tight grip. Risking a scene, anger, and God knows what else didn't seem wise.

So, what to do?

She sifted through all the information coming at her when her balance was already seriously compromised from her encounter with Hugh. Guilt swamped her. If she hadn't indulged herself so selfishly, she would have been with Joshua. None of which she could change right now.

Shoving aside the distracting guilt, she narrowed her focus, calling up her prosecutorial skills to get to the bottom of what was going on with this mystery woman—if she could possibly be Joshua's real mother. "If you're his mama, then why did you pretend to be hospital personnel?"

"Because of your paperwork." She picked at her scrubs nervously.

Instincts shouted that the woman was holding something back—and she had Joshua in her arms, which made confronting her more than a little problematic. Amelia looked around for help in the deserted hallway. *Crap*.

The case file on Joshua stated his mother had died and his father had taken him to an orphanage. She had no reason to doubt the adoption agency. She had been laboriously thorough in researching them, knowing there were definitely some suspicious operations out there.

But she'd heard horror stories of babies being stolen

from their mothers. Or mothers persuaded to give up a child for money or a so-called better life for the baby.

Or the woman could be grief stricken, mistaking Joshua for her own lost baby. In which case, she would be unstable. Volatile.

Joshua whimpered, reaching out a chubby fist. Amelia's heart twisted with love—and fear. She gauged the distance between them and decided to continue to bluff rather than risk an all-out confrontation.

"Actually, he is not okay. That's why he had the IV in." Oh God, the woman must have pulled out the needle. Where were the nurses? Why hadn't someone stopped her? "You need to give him to me now so I can get him hooked up again."

She kept her voice low and calm, her body language as loose as possible with every cell within her screaming out in protest.

Amelia held out her arms. "I'll be careful with him and have him right back to you. In fact, you can stay with us if you would like."

And, please God, they would find some other hospital staff, maybe even one of those guards carrying around a big machine gun. Or better yet, this would be the perfect time for Hugh to come around the corner—unless he'd already left through another exit to avoid her. He could already be long gone.

The woman hugged Joshua closer with one arm and called over her shoulder. "Oliver?"

Another person? The time had come to act before the odds went against her. She needed to grab Joshua and start screaming bloody murder.

As Amelia lurched forward, a man stepped from

behind a stack of pallets and shoved the woman and Joshua behind him. He wore dirty camouflage with patches from some other country, his red hair slicked back, and long, for someone in uniform.

Amelia opened her mouth to shout—

A survival knife gleamed in his fist, jagged blade kissing her neck. "The boy belongs to us now, and if you want to keep your pretty face unscarred, you'll shut up."

The other woman peered around his shoulder. "What are you thinking, Oliver? The Guardian gave us our orders. Get the kid and get out. Now kill her, and let's go."

Oliver's grip on her arm tightened while he stroked back her hair with the blade. "The Guardian understands the importance of a profit margin to keep a business going, and this woman's worth almost as much as the baby. The blonde bitch? She's coming with us."

Chapter 7

A DISTANT SHRIEK ECHOED DOWN THE CORRIDOR, stopping Hugh in his tracks as he stepped out of the closet. A cry of pain? Certainly not unheard of in a hospital. He moved deeper into the hall, peering around a corner. A solitary nurse in an open office filling out charts merely lifted her eyes for half a second.

The hall was all but deserted, just as it had been when he stepped from the closet after shaking off the shock of Amelia's rejection and hauling back on his clothes. Most everyone was asleep, and no new patients were coming to this full-to-capacity makeshift school-turned-hospital. He jogged past the gymnasium crammed with beds sectioned off from one another with extra wrestling mats and uneven bars.

Hugh shrugged away a crick in his neck and pushed through the front door into the warm haze of post-earthquake dust. He must just be on edge because of the impulsive, crazy-as-hell hookup with Amelia. What had he been thinking? One thing was clear. They both needed space to get levelheaded again. Then he would contact her and… What? Hell if he kn—

Another shout echoed. Louder, rippling through the quiet night. The scream ended abruptly, as if cut off. And God, his head must really be screwed up, because he could swear that sounded like Amelia.

Crazy or not, he had to check it out.

He scanned the dark lot, a mess like the rest of the area. Cars lay on their sides, some crashed into each other, the asphalt cracked. None on the lights worked. Two poles had fallen on top of a storage shed and corner of the school. Still, there was no activity other than a couple of displaced cats scurrying under cars, no doubt in search of the rats that had already started scuttling through the aftermath.

Which only left the back of the schoolyard to search.

A deep gut sense of premonition drove him forward. He broke into a jog, his boots pounding along the cracked asphalt, onto the soft earth. When he rounded the corner, he would probably find another cat shrieking or someone laughing. The scream had to be his imagination. Everything inside him was a jumbled-up shit pile of the past and present melding together since he'd rescued Amelia and the boy.

The back lot resembled the front, a broken mess. More rats scampered. A kitten screeched beyond the tree line. Could that be what he'd heard?

Footsteps echoed from the far end of the lot, past the cars and a spindly fallen palm tree. He squinted through the darkness lit only by a half moon above. Damn, but it was dark. He would give his left nut for NVGs right now.

He picked his way across the lot, sidestepping an upended trash bin, hurtling over the downed tree. Foreboding buzzed in his ears like the distant rumble of crashing waves on the shore.

His eyes homed in on a glow ahead, lights inside a van with back doors open. The light dimmed with a couple of people blocking the opening. He charged ahead, his gaze locked in for some clue about what was going on, as the lighting shifted over the group. The glow flickered over long blonde hair, a female face…

Shit.

About fifty yards away, Amelia was draped over some man's shoulder in a fireman's carry. A woman beside them held a baby that looked too damn much like Joshua for his peace of mind. He didn't know what the hell was going on but it couldn't be good. The silent pantomime of the whole absurd scene sealed the deal.

Hugh drew his weapon. "Stop. Put the lady down now and pass over the child."

The woman holding Joshua spun sharply, her face cast in shadows. She held the baby in front of her like a shield, damn it.

"Oliver." The woman's voice carried softly on the briny breeze. "Get the van started."

The man—Oliver—threw Amelia into the van, diving in after her, and there wasn't a thing Hugh could do about it with Joshua in the line of fire. He ground his teeth and assessed his options. For every step he took toward them across jigsawed asphalt, the woman backed away, closer to the grimy white van, until she hit the bumper. She ducked inside just as the vehicle's engine roared to life.

Waiting time was over. Hugh bolted forward. The doors slammed shut. He ran full-out, eyes trained on the taillights glowing like red snake eyes in the night. He only had a split second to make his move, to—

Jump!

He hurtled through the air. Arms extended, he willed his straining body onward. A roar ripped from his throat with the effort. He slammed against the back of the van, grunted, grappled on top for a hold. His feet braced on the rear bumper. Shit... This looked easier in the movies.

The van peeled around a corner, damn near on two wheels. Hugh slipped sideways, almost off. His heart pumped like revving pistons. He slapped the side, found a firmer hold on the luggage rack.

His brain raced as fast as the tires. No way could he make it to the front. He didn't stand a snowball's chance in hell of climbing along the top. And if they hadn't already figured out he was holding on, they would soon. It wouldn't take much to jar him loose—or ram him against a brick wall.

He needed to open the back and fling himself inside. After that?

Well, he would wing it from there. Letting the van drive away wasn't an option. Given the island's current state of disorder, locating this vehicle later would be all but impossible. And he couldn't let himself think about what would happen to Amelia and Joshua in the meantime, if they even lived.

Now, he just had to wait for the right time to make his move.

Amelia braced her feet against a crate in the van as the vehicle squealed around a corner. She clutched Joshua to her chest, struggling to keep her balance.

Thank God, their kidnappers were letting her hold him. Although that made it impossible for her to open a door and leap out onto the pavement, which may have been their intent. Not that she would have left without Joshua anyway.

She leaned against a spare tire, the road bumpy, her butt jostling painfully against the floor as the guy drove, the woman parked in the passenger seat. The smell of oil and tropical fruit hung in the air. She scanned the packed space, glass rattling, and found boxes labeled as water and juice.

So much had happened so fast. She'd barely had time to process the violent shift in her life. Why the hell had she been so proud and stubborn in walking away from Hugh out of some crazy fear he would walk away first? The man and woman had escorted her out of the school/ hospital at knifepoint. As she'd walked down that hall and into the parking lot, she'd known that once she landed inside the van, her chances and Joshua's would be reduced dramatically.

Swallowing back fear of the blade nicking her neck, she had screamed and screamed again—just before the man backhanded her so hard she'd lost consciousness for a few minutes.

She'd woken again as she'd been thrust in the back of a van. Seconds later Joshua was shoved into her arms. She'd barely regained her balance before they roared out of the lot, tires squealing.

Her hands shook as she took reassurance from her nephew's steady breaths. She struggled to stay calm, but her reserves were already depleted. Her body just wouldn't pony up any more energy. For now, she kept her ears tuned in to the couple in front, hoping to find out something, anything, that could help her escape. Thus far, she'd only learned their names were Oliver and Tandi.

Were they low-level opportunists, preying on the current crisis? Or did they have deeper ties to some kind of illegal organization from earlier, before the earthquake? Either way, the odds were not in her favor or Joshua's. Exhaustion and defeat left her on the edge of tears.

A thump on the back of the van startled her already-jangled nerves.

Oliver looked over his shoulder sharply. "What the hell?"

Tandi pulled a gun from the glove box, a pile of papers showering out along with the weapon. "Drive faster."

Amelia curled protectively around Joshua, angling her back toward Tandi, toward the gleaming gun muzzle.

One of the back doors flew open. A gust of night air rolled inside before a body blocked the opening. Amelia gasped, looking closer at...

Hugh? Oh God, it was really him. Here. And filling the opening, muscles bulging in his arms as he clutched the sides.

Tandi shouted, "Swerve, Oliver. Jerk the van around. Do *something*."

The woman squeezed off a shot into the back. The bullet ricocheted inside the metal cavern. Amelia screamed, huddling her body around Joshua.

Liquid spurted from one of the boxes. Her ears rung. The acrid gunshot scent stung her nose along with an increasing fruity smell. To hell with covering her head. She cared only about Hugh and Joshua.

Big and alive and unharmed, he still clung to the back even as the van lurched.

Oliver back handed Tandi. "Stop shooting, bitch. You're going to kill us all. I've got this."

The van swerved again, so fiercely she feared the vehicle would roll. Oh God, she didn't know what to do. If Hugh fell off, he could die. If he made it in here, he could die as well... The determination on his face, tendons straining, declared he wasn't giving up. Either way, he would die trying.

And for Joshua, she had to take whatever help she could.

She risked letting go of the baby for a flash, setting him on the floor behind a toolbox. She grabbed a handle bolted to the side, then flung out her other arm toward Hugh. She reached, fingertips grazing him, van swaying.

"Damn it," Tandi shouted from the front. "He's still hanging on. Oliver, we have to do something."

The woman started to climb over the seat. The van jerked, fishtailing on the deserted road. Tandi fell back in her seat with a shriek. Hugh was flung sideways, but he held strong.

Amelia chewed her bottom lip until she tasted blood. Joshua cried. In pain or fear? She felt torn in half, making life-and-death decisions in an unimaginable situation. Things were happening so fast, she had only a split second to act.

Her fingers hooked onto Hugh's vest, gripped, hauled. Her arms stretched in the sockets, screaming until she wondered if she might literally be torn in half. She vaguely registered Tandi shouting again at her or Oliver. Amelia tugged harder until finally—

Hugh catapulted inside. He landed hard on top of her, her nose pressed into matted tan carpet fibers.

Tandi shouted from the front again. "Who the hell are you? Where did you come from?"

"Shit," Oliver cursed.

Amelia just held onto Hugh with arms that shook from relief as much as the exhaustion.

Tandi pointed her gun toward the back, in spite of Oliver's warning. "One move from either of you, and I'll let shots ricochet right into both your heads. Got it? Answer me, damn it."

"I hear you," Amelia answered fast.

"Uh-huh." Hugh stayed on top of her, his arm curling around to include Joshua.

He was here. Actually here. She could hardly wrap her brain around the fact, but finally, there was hope again.

The van screeched to a stop. The back doors slammed closed from the momentum. Hugh grunted.

"No, Oliver," Tandi screamed. "Go! Go! They'll jump out and the Guardian will kill *us*."

Oliver cursed again, and the van lurched forward. Tires squealed along with the sound of spewing rocks as the van peeled out.

Tandi leaned over her seat, silver gun in hand and pointed at Hugh. "You picked the wrong day to be a hero, big guy."

Lisabeth Bailey was used to long days in her job as a surgical nurse. But what she'd been through in the aftermath of the earthquake surpassed anything she'd ever experienced.

She tossed the bloody scrubs into the laundry—not that clothes were getting washed, with the water shortage. Since the church was now overflowing with injured, the military engineers had set up tents outside for showers and latrines. The canvas walls flapped in the light wind that rolled in from the beach carrying the fetid odor of rotting garbage and decaying corpses. She pressed the back of her wrist against her mouth while she swallowed down bile. Strong smells were tough enough to handle in a normal situation, but this place reeked.

The garden paradise she'd loved since birth had been obliterated in a few earth-shattering seconds. Nothing about the current wreckage resembled her childhood island home, her last connection to her parents, who'd died while she was in college in the States. The loss around her, the grief and the heartbreak, festered inside her until it was all she could do to keep from vomiting during the surgery.

But her help was crucial, especially in these early hours while relief personnel and supplies were still en route. Airplanes overhead promised the arrival of more aid, but they were also faced with the shortage of nearby landing space... then ways to transport the goods and people to the critical areas.

Wind parted two tarps and revealed a bulldozer in the distance alongside a woman and man digging with shovels. The couple moved like automatons. They'd been picking through the rubble for as long as she'd been here. Looters would have left long ago. Their search was more personal. But after this much time, their odds of finding a live family member were growing slimmer.

Her gut grumbled again.

She dipped a finger into a small jar of menthol and thumbed a streak under her nose. She tipped her head back and inhaled. Exhaled. In and out, until her stomach settled. She huffed a spiral of hair off her brow.

Exhaustion steamrolled over her. She'd been on her feet for nearly five days, already exhausted when they'd arrived, racked with indecision over what to do about the adoption.

Then she'd met Joshua and fallen in love with his sweet face. Even now, she remembered the feel of his baby-soft cheek against hers. In that moment, she felt the connection, the bond. He'd become her son. She couldn't do anything to jeopardize that.

Except now he was missing, probably dead.

Could this be God's justice for her selfishness in wanting it all?

Sagging forward, she grabbed the rim of the rubbish bin. A mess, just like her life. She wanted to believe she hadn't deliberately allowed herself to get pregnant. She'd only found out for sure with a pregnancy test taken during their layover in Miami on the way here to get Joshua.

And she hadn't even begun to figure out how she would tell Aiden.

Persuading him to adopt had been tough enough. She never would have won the battle to have a biological child together. He had such immovable reasons for that decision, he would never change his mind. But they'd reached an understanding with the adoption. They'd done everything possible to prepare, taking into account the special needs that could come with international adoption. They had support and resources in place to guide them through.

But in all her preparations, she'd never taken into account one possibility.

Her hands slid over her stomach. Aiden would

figure it out soon enough on his own. He was a doctor, for heaven's sake. He likely would have noticed the signs already if he hadn't been so distracted by the adoption.

She loved Aiden, always had since she'd they'd met at Auburn University. After graduation, she'd opted to stay in the States rather than returning to the Bahamas. Her parents had died in a boating accident. She'd felt anchorless. So she'd followed Aiden to medical school, no great sacrifice, since she loved him.

And now she'd risked losing him. Tears burned behind her eyes for him, for herself, but mostly for Joshua, the child she already loved as much as the one she carried inside her. The child inside her that Aiden would never accept.

A hand settled on her shoulder and she almost jumped out of her skin. She looked back to find her husband standing behind her and she relaxed, sagging with relief. Aiden's blond hair was spiked wildly from the hours of work and lack of a good shower. More than that, exhaustion carved strain lines in the corners of his pale blue eyes behind round glasses.

He was handsome in a lanky, rawboned kind of way of a man who forgot to eat. He didn't have time for recreation, so his face was burned from their time in the sun here.

Concern dug trenches in his scorched forehead. "Are you okay?"

She smoothed a hand over his brow, his angular face so dear, so familiar. "I'm only tired. What do you need?"

"I've got some good news, finally." He cupped the back of her neck, his thumb stroking her hairline as he'd done a million times. "They've found Joshua and Amelia. Alive."

Tears rushed to clog her throat and eyes. Days of stress and grief exploding inside her as she finally, finally could let her emotions roll free. She started shaking and Aiden kept stroking, comforting. What was he holding back?

"How, Aiden? Where? What happened to them?" She shot to her feet. "We have to go to them. Now!"

His hands fell to rest on her shoulders, holding her still. "They're at a makeshift hospital located in a school the next town over. He and Amelia both are listed on their admissions roster as patients. There aren't any specifics on their condition, and it's going to be tough getting past the roadblocks."

"But they're alive?" She grabbed his arms and held onto her anchor. Some called him emotionless, but she knew her husband better than that. He was just reserved. Stalwart. Strong. He had to be, to tamp down the horror she knew sometimes threatened to pull him under.

He squeezed her shoulders. "They *are* alive. And I promise you, nothing will keep me from our son and my sister."

Hugh had the best rescue and survival training in the world, and still he wasn't sure yet how the hell he would get Amelia and the child out of the back of this van alive. For now, he focused on minute-to-minute safety until a larger plan could form. He positioned himself closest to the front, with Amelia and Joshua on his other side, his arm locked around her shoulders. If he were alone, he could take out the man and woman. It might cost him a knife wound, or cause him to take a bullet, but the odds were good enough for him.

But having others in the line of fire was a game changer.

Apparently they didn't want to risk stopping in the city. His guess? They would kill and dump him later. They'd already taken his cell phone, radio, and weapons. They'd tossed the phone and radio out the window into a bog, which ruled out anyone finding them through the GPS tracker on either device. Tandi had kept his pistol and knife well out of his reach, of course.

The thought of what people like these would and could do to Amelia, especially with the country in such a lawless state... He fought back the wave of blinding rage. He needed to stay clearheaded and calm, nothing clouding his instincts, to have even a chance of getting them out of here alive.

The van hit a pothole, jostling his shoulders against the metal side. Crates bounced and settled. If one of those fell from the top, it could do serious damage. He inched along the floor, doing his best to place his body between Amelia and any threat, but shit, everywhere he looked red flags blared. A knife. A gun. Fifty-pound crates tottering in too-high stacks.

And kidnappers with God only knew what agenda.

"How are you here?" Amelia whispered urgently. "I don't understand how you found us."

Part of planning an escape hinged on keeping Amelia calm, so he figured it was worth the risk to talk. "I heard you scream as I was leaving." He pushed back the hellish memory of the moment he'd realized that cry of panic had come from Amelia. "There wasn't much time to catch you. I was trying to pull a James Bond with my entrance, but that whole hanging-onto-a-moving-vehicle-and-punching-out-the-driver thing doesn't work quite the same way in real life."

Tucking the restless toddler closer to her, she managed a wobbly smile. "Looked like you accomplished more than anyone else could, outside the movie world." She leaned closer to him. "They call each other Oliver and Tandi. They wanted to kidnap Joshua. I caught them trying to take him from the hospital."

"Okay, that explains a lot. You're doing good, Amelia. You're doing good."

He glanced at their captors up front, and while the woman kept her gun trained on them, she hadn't tried to tie them up and she hadn't squeezed off any more wild shots. They seemed more concerned on putting distance between them and the school. Actually the smarter plan, because if they'd stopped to tie him up, he could have disabled that person and gotten the weapon before the other could blink.

Meanwhile, he'd been taking note of the landscape as best he could out the front windshield to guess their location. Not much to go on, though. Just a sense that they were driving east, deeper into the jungle. The van wove off the road as Oliver steered around another fallen tree.

Pulling in his focus, drawing on training, Hugh stared around the crowded van at the supplies—water and juice. Took in Oliver's uniform. He had some sort of paramilitary look to him, the patches in an indecipherable language. Eastern European, perhaps? Except he didn't have an accent. From the look of the back of the van, it seemed they'd been able to enter the epicenter of the earthquake site by appearing to deliver supplies. The uniform had most likely been stolen.

Hugh inched closer to her, keeping his voice low. "Fill me in on the rest. Think in terms of details. Anything could be helpful."

She jostled Joshua until the baby started to settle, his eyelids growing heavier, thank God. "After we uh… well, as I was walking back to Joshua, I saw a woman trying to sneak him out of the hospital. She claimed to be his biological mother."

His eyes shot to the front of the van, assessing the woman with different eyes. "He was *taken* from his parents and put up for adoption?"

"That's what I thought at first," she said softly, quickly. "Then she said she'd lost him during the earthquake, which of course isn't possible, since he'd already been adopted by Aiden and Lisabeth by then."

A chilly certainty jelled in his gut. "She was lying."

"I even wondered if she might be a grief-stricken mother mistaking Joshua for her real child, but then Oliver stepped out with the knife. I realized they were kidnapping Joshua." She shuddered. "They made me come along—not that I would have left him."

The pieces all came together and the final picture couldn't be any worse. "You have to understand what they must want with him."

She nodded tightly. "They said they have customers for both of us. We have to get away before this van reaches its destination. Tell me what to do."

Yeah, he agreed, and he would do his damnedest to make it happen. Although even for a guy who was willing to go all the way to the edge, options seemed slim to none.

And the unwavering confidence in her eyes stabbed him clean through. "You do realize I'm not actually Superman, right?"

He knew his own fallibility too well, felt it all the stronger at times like this, when the stakes were so intensely personal.

Amelia cupped the back of Joshua's head and stared straight at Hugh, her jaw set stubbornly. "I also know you don't quit. So stop worrying about not getting my hopes up and let's start planning."

From the back of the van, Amelia watched her kidnappers, determining what little she could from the green glow of the dashboard lights. She made her living off noting the tiniest details and gauging expressions from witnesses. But it had never been more important than now to get things right. She kissed the top of Joshua's head as he slept in her arms, his gentle baby snores so sweet, her heart squeezed.

Eyes front, she reminded herself.

Oliver's rough handling of the van, his sharp stops and starts, and a dark hint in his voice left her certain he was the kind of remorseless criminal out for profit. She'd seen dozens of henchmen just like him cycle through the justice system. The worst were those who took advantage of children. She pushed back distracting memories of the first time she'd seen that evil in her own father's eyes. Memories of his arrest. Of his suicide.

Grappling for focus, she shifted her attention to

Tandi—currently talking on a two-way radio with some-one she called the "Guardian." Tandi appeared to have more layers to her motivations than Oliver. The voice on the other end was muffled, either a deep woman's voice or higher-pitched man's voice. Tandi's hands drifted with a butterfly gentleness as she juggled some kind of walkie-talkie with an earbud.

The woman had winced when Amelia couldn't bite back a cry of pain when Oliver's driving slammed her against a crate. And when she'd fired the gun into the back, the shot had been so wide that Amelia suspected it had been a scare tactic.

Could Tandi be the weak link? Persuadable? Because without question, they couldn't wait for the van to arrive at its destination to make a move.

The fact that they could communicate and drive about so freely in this time of limited resources and access sent a fresh bolt of fear even deeper inside her. This wasn't a spur-of-the-moment, low-level operation. These two had serious, deep-rooted connections.

Pressing an earbud more firmly in place with one hand, Tandi grabbed the dash as the van bucked and shimmied along the narrow road winding through a thick forest lit only by the twin band of headlights. "We have the cargo as promised, plus a bonus soul. A woman. We may have been mistaken in thinking the boy had no family. The woman claims he's with her, that her family adopted him. There's also a possibility the hospital mixed up records in all the confusion, sending us the wrong information."

Quiet echoed as Tandi listened to the answer, gnaw-ing her bottom lip.

Tandi nodded tightly, continuing, "We had to make a split-second decision." Frustration leaked into her voice. "If I gave her the child back, we ran the risk of her sounding an alarm and giving a description of me."

Tension tightened her mouth in the look of someone getting a serious chewing out. The more Tandi tensed, the more Amelia knew they had to put Hugh's plan into action as soon as possible.

Although Hugh's whispered instruction from earlier scared her to the roots of her highlighted hair. When he gave the signal, she was supposed to hold Joshua tight and roll behind a stack of crates while Hugh took out the pair up front. A pair with a knife, a gun—plus the gun and knife they'd taken off Hugh.

And he claimed he wasn't Superman?

The van rattled over another pothole, slamming Amelia against Hugh. His body was a sheet of sheer muscle, his emerald eyes flat and focused. He'd gone somewhere in his brain, shifting. This was a different sort of rescuer than she'd been with underground.

Shivering, she tucked Joshua closer and trained her attention on Tandi.

"Oliver and I thought it best to bring her with us. Better for her to disappear in the confusion from the earthquake than for her to tell people what she saw. If we'd left her behind she could bring undue... *attention* to us and to our operation."

Snarling, Oliver yanked the cell phone from her. "The decision was mine and it's a good one. Do you want the woman brought to you alive or dead? It doesn't matter to me either way, as long as I get my money for the kid."

Why weren't they mentioning Hugh? For some

reason they were keeping him a secret from their boss. Most likely to cover their asses for screwing up.

And oh God, that could only mean they intended to kill him, to dump his body before they reached their destination. She fought back the urge to scream. She burned to launch herself on them both and claw out her rage over how cavalierly they regarded life.

Hugh's life.

Oliver caught her eye in the rearview mirror. "It's your lucky day, lady. You get to live."

Again, no mention was made of Hugh. Her hand slid from under Joshua's legs and clutched Hugh's wrist. The warmth of his skin, his pulse, under her fingertips felt so vital, she had to believe he would make it through alive.

Dread, fear, and a surreal haze thickened the air around her until every breath felt heavier, tougher. She wanted to freeze time, capture this moment and the three of them—Hugh, Joshua, and her—in a safe bubble. Because once he gave the signal there would be no turning back. That vital pulse under her fingertips could be gone forever, with the odds stacked so horribly against them.

There had to be another way, another option, another plan. Her brain raced for some other way—

Hugh's hand curled into a fist a second before he whispered, "Now."

Chapter 8

HUGH LAUNCHED FORWARD, EYES ON THE GREEN GLOW of the dash lights. He didn't want to think about the inevitable wreck.

Rushing the pair up front was his only option. At least he had the reassurance Amelia would do everything possible to keep the baby safe. But he could not let them get to this "Guardian" person.

His arm swept a stack of crates like a battering ram, toppling them onto Tandi. The van veered hard. He landed on the driver, arm around Oliver's neck. A low-lying branch slammed into the windshield. Glass shattered. Oliver clawed at Hugh's cheek, his voice garbled.

Hugh squeezed his forearm harder along the windpipe of the bastard who'd kidnapped Joshua and Amelia. The criminal who'd leered at Amelia, not even bothering to hide his lecherous plans. He wanted to kill the bastard. No one would blame him. This was a kill-or-be-killed situation.

But Amelia sat in back. She didn't need to see that side, the violent side of him that seethed like the assholes she put in prison. He would hold tight, squeeze just long enough to knock him out—

Oliver stabbed back with a knife from nowhere. Hugh jerked, the knife grazing his leg in a fiery swipe. The car swerved. Hugh adjusted his hold and resorted to a Vulcan nerve pinch—fast and effective. Oliver slumped forward, foot ramming the accelerator.

Shit.

Hugh's hands shot forward to grab the steering wheel. The van rocked, catapulting over a ditch.

"Brace, brace, brace!" Hugh shouted to Amelia.

"I hear you," she shouted back just as the van went airborne. Time seemed to freeze for those three seconds before —

The van rammed a palm tree, flinging Hugh forward. He forced himself not to tense, to roll with the momentum rather than fight it. Pain exploded through him as the vehicle settled. Wrapped around the dash, he willed the world on the other side of the fractured glass to steady. But the spinning landscape just kept right on whirling like a kaleidoscope.

He looked left and right fast to make sure no one would come gunning for him. Tandi lay slumped against the door, her eyes wide, vacant, sightlessly dead. Blood trickled from the corner of her mouth. Oliver… still unconscious.

A scream boomeranged around the tinny cavern. A baby's cry. The kid. Joshua was alive.

But Amelia?

"Amelia," Hugh barked out, his voice more of a breathless croak, since the wind had been knocked out of him.

Hugh pushed away from the dash, careful to test his arms and legs. "Amelia, answer me, damn it. Are you and the kid okay?"

Panic replaced the pain, quickly, fiercely, and so intensely, he was rattled all over again by how fast the woman wrecked his professional distance.

He staggered toward the back, the baby's cries increasing to all-out screams. Hugh grappled along the side for balance. His eyes locked on the slim long legs stretched out from behind the boxes where he'd sent her to curl up around Joshua.

His gut knotted.

He rounded the boxes. Amelia lay on her back, eyes closed, her arms still locked tight around Joshua. The toddler shrieked and squirmed in her hold, his tiny arms and legs flailing.

Hugh dropped to his knees beside her. "Amelia? Amelia, answer me, damn it."

He cupped her face, patting lightly. The light was too dim for him to assess her fully, the moon giving way to the early-morning sun fighting to slice through the night.

"Amelia," he said louder, snatching up her wrist to check her pulse. Steady. Strong. He almost sank back on his ass with relief.

She groaned. He straightened, staring at her face. Her nose scrunched.

"That's right, Amelia," he said. "Wake up. You're okay. The kid's okay."

He patted the baby's back awkwardly.

She crinkled her nose again, her eyes fluttering open. "Hugh? Do you smell smoke?"

Shit! He should have thought of that. He looked in front fast. The first rays of sunrise illuminated the smoke spiraling from the engine crumpled against the tree.

The scent grew thicker inside the van, mixing with the unmistakable stench of leaking gasoline. Hugh scooped the kid under one arm and yanked Amelia up with his other hand. He kicked the back doors of the van, exploding them open.

"Amelia, run!"

Liam was losing his shit fast.

He charged up the front steps of the stucco island school, now a temporary hospital and the last known location for Hugh Franco.

Where the hell was he?

Franco had raced off to check on the Bailey woman seven hours ago and still hadn't returned. He wasn't answering his phone or shortwave radio. Communication was sketchy with phones, but no comm through the radio?

Something was wrong. He could feel it deep in his churning gut. Franco has said he would be back in an hour—and that deadline had long passed.

They all had to log back in to work the next shift in three hours, which didn't give Liam much time to search. He should be sleeping. Should be. But knew he wouldn't even be able to close his eyes until he got rid of this sick feeling he'd had too many times during his prior days in the Army, times when he'd lost a fellow ranger.

Franco would probably come racing in at the last second and they would laugh their asses off at Liam for acting like a fucking mother hen. At least that's what he told himself as he ran like a maniac up the steps into the hospital housed in the local school.

It wasn't as if he could report the guy to the cops to investigate. The police had their hands full, as did every other individual here. Except Franco wasn't answering his phone or pager, which of course could have been due to the jammed channels. Communication was still iffy and likely wouldn't get better anytime soon.

For now, Liam had three hours to figure out what had happened to Franco before the next rescue shift.

He tugged open the heavy wooden door and stepped inside. The light was dim, mostly filtering through the window and from bulbs running on minimal power from generators. The air was thick with an antiseptic scent and pained groans. Hospital "staff" rushed down the halls, in and out of rooms, wearing scrubs and camo.

He eyed the harried personnel and chose the least frantic of the bunch, a reed-thin woman removing the lab coat from over her camos. "Excuse me, ma'am?"

She turned and he took in the army insignia on her uniform and her name tag. A nurse, a lieutenant. "Lieutenant Gable, a minute of your time?"

She turned impatiently, took in his uniform, and her face shifted into a smile. "What may I help you with, Major?"

"I'm looking for a patient here, toddler, about a year old, named Joshua, a local boy recently adopted." He stepped closer as he sidestepped to make way for an NGO worker pushing a cart of MREs and a crate of bottled water. "He would have been brought in with his aunt from the U.S., Amelia Bailey."

Her brow furrowed with deep thought, Lieutenant Gable stuffed her hands in her pockets for a moment before nodding, "Right, right… I remember them, sweet lady and kid. Very lucky to be alive. They're not here any longer. They must have checked out while I was on a break."

Damn. Not unexpected, but frustrating all the same. "Anything else?"

"She had a military friend who came by a couple of times. I assumed he arranged a place for them to stay."

Something didn't sound right. "In the middle of the night?"

"We are in such desperate need of beds, when somebody can leave, we're glad to have the space. Surely you understand."

"Of course. Sorry." These weren't normal times. "A military friend? Male?"

"Definitely male and close friends with the woman. That's all I know, Major. We've been very busy here." She swept back a straggly strand of gray-streaked hair with a shaky hand. "I really need to get back to work."

He backed up a step. "Thanks for your help."

As the lieutenant jogged away, shoes squeaking, he stood in the middle of the two-way traffic in the hall, wondering what the hell to do now. He always had a plan of action, marching orders. But now? He didn't have a clue where to even start looking.

Where could they have gone from here? How was he supposed to even know which way to search? There weren't any bread crumbs or red arrows pointing the way.

But there was a scent.

The world seemed to slow around him and take shape as an idea came to him, one that made him a little more pumped than he should be feeling, given the current state of hell on earth around them.

But what if Rachel and her search and rescue dog could work another miracle here?

He couldn't pull them off an active search for someone trapped in the debris. Although if she could give him half an hour to just point him in the right direction...

Pivoting on his heel, he jogged back out the door, down the steps. Once outside, the sun just climbing on the horizon, he broke into a run. His military uniform would get him past any roadblocks or checkpoints. Even with the debris, he could make it to Rachel's quarters in under ten minutes.

No one looked twice at him running through the street like a madman. Nothing seemed unusual here anymore—well, other than running out in the street half-naked, wearing nothing but towels.

Had that been only a few hours ago?

This couldn't be happening. He couldn't be losing a man on his team. Yes, he understood it happened. Hell, it had happened far too often during his combat days as an Army Ranger. But he was in charge now. He controlled the missions and they focused on rescue, not combat. He refused to lose another brother-in-arms. And yeah, that made him overreact sometimes.

Like now, chasing down a missing team member who was probably just off trying to impress a woman. Except Franco never, never dated women with children since his wife and daughter died. Which brought Liam to his real fear—that this latest rescue had pushed Hugh over the edge. A dark thought, sure, but then morbid conclusions had a way of chasing him.

People thought Liam was a lighthearted son of a bitch who did a helluva Chuck Norris impression. He was just covering up the fact that his insides were so scarred up from burying fallen comrades he'd become like that old Charlie Chaplin tune his mama liked to sing through her cancer treatments, "Smile, though your heart…"

Shit. He cut the morbid thoughts off short. Morose garbage never saved anybody and it wasn't going to find Franco for him.

Although if Franco was off kicking up his heels, playing house with the Bailey chick and her nephew…

Yeah right. The chances of that happening were next to nil. The only thing Franco avoided more than commitment was kids.

He sprinted past his lopsided quarters, the cottage still hanging out on the edge of the cliff at pretty much the same scary-ass angle as before. Stopping at the next house, a yellow and green little place with porches all the way around, he tugged his camo top smooth again. The door was covered with plywood over where a glass panel must have been. He knocked hard, twice.

Footsteps echoed from inside, along with a couple of deep barks. The door swung open and Liam almost swallowed his tongue. Rachel wore skimpy gray cotton shorts and a T-shirt without a bra.

He had more serious things to think about than how her nipples strained against well-worn cotton and how her brown hair tumbled around her shoulders as if calling to his hands.

"Major?" She reached down, her hand falling to rest on her dog's head without her even looking to see that he'd slid into place beside her.

Liam cleared his throat and thoughts. "I'm sorry to bother you. I know sleep is scarce—"

"Understatement—"

"Right. Sorry. Honest to God, I am. But one of my team members, the one you found, he's gone missing, along with the woman and child he rescued."

"I'm not sure I understand." She blinked fast, her brown eyes still fuzzy with sleep and exhaustion.

"He went to visit her and the little boy at the hospital."

Liam braced a hand against the door frame. "They all three vanished. Franco was supposed to be back hours ago. He's an edgy worker in the field, but he is always, always there."

She stepped outside, her dog staying at her side as she closed the door on the house full of sleeping rescue workers. "No one saw them leave?"

"It's not like the facility had working surveillance cameras. The nurse doesn't actually remember them checking out, just thinks they did." He wondered why it was so easy to come to her, to bring his problems to her doorstep.

He might be halfway in love with this hot woman, but that didn't mean he intended to *need* her on some level deeper than the search. "Something's off. I can sense it. Maybe I'm overreacting, but my guy wouldn't let his team down. And since the last place anyone saw them was at the hospital, I was hoping your dog—"

"Disco." The dog nuzzled her hand.

"Since Disco found them before, we could set him on their scent again at the hospital. Maybe he can give us some clue as to which way they went. I know it's a lot to ask and your resources are needed out there. But so are Franco's, and if we can get you both out there again..."

"Time's wasting and I need to throw on some real clothes. You can have Disco and me for one hour. Period." She grabbed the knob behind her. "Do you have a ride or are we walking to the hospital?"

Joggling Joshua on her hip, Amelia struggled to keep her balance while Hugh scavenged as much as he could from the van before the vehicle blew up. Smoke billowed from the crumpled hood. The leaning palm tree's roots snaked up from the ground like tentacles from the underworld to claim the two criminals inside the van.

She kept her eyes off the front seat, where Oliver and Tandi's bodies lay. Tandi stared lifelessly. Oliver slumped unconscious, his hands now bound. Amelia squeezed her eyes shut, still woozy from smacking her head against the side of the van, not to mention being knocked unconscious earlier. The swirl of nausea told her she probably had a concussion, but complaining wouldn't achieve anything. They needed to move, to get back to civilization. She refused to slow them down.

Grunting impatiently, Joshua wriggled and fussed and she rocked faster, shush-shush-shushing him. It was obvious he just wanted down to run. But he didn't have shoes and there were rocks and prickly vines and God only knew how much wildlife on the ground. He was probably hungry too, and his diaper was soggy. No wonder he was cranky.

She wanted to cry and scream too. For days. While eating ice cream in a hot bubble bath. Then curling up to sleep beside Hugh while her body recharged from this nightmare.

But she didn't have that luxury.

Survival was paramount right now, right along with making sure she didn't fall on her face. She braced her feet farther apart to keep from toppling over and making things harder for Hugh. It was her fault he was in this mess. How many times would he have to come to her rescue? She might not be able to get out of this on her own, but she would be damned before she let him bear the full burden.

Hugh reached into the van.

"Please be careful, Hugh." The words fell from her mouth before she could stop them. "The smoke looks like it's getting worse."

"Got my eye on it." He hauled Oliver's unconscious body out and dumped him against the rotting log. "Let me know if he so much as twitches. I'm taking the weapons, anything that could be of use to us... or that he might use against us. We need them."

"*We* need *you* alive," she gasped, determined to be a help, but still scared out of her mind. Usually when she faced criminals, she had a bailiff or a couple of city cops with her, not to mention handcuffs or bars for the person who might want to use her as leverage in an escape.

Who else might try to find them now?

They were in the middle of nowhere in a lawless country, with no means of transportation and only however many water bottles they could carry. "Tell me what you need for me to do."

God, she hoped he had some tricks up his sleeve with that military training because she was way out of her element. She hadn't even been a Girl Scout.

Hugh's big body leaned deeper inside. "Just let me know if you see flames."

Flames? Oh God.

He pitched another knife on top of his growing arsenal. He jogged around to the back of the van, stuck his head inside, and pulled out a crate of bottled juice.

Hugh pried open the lid with his bare hands and a

hefty grunt. "We'll drink our fill now, then take as much juice and water as we can carry."

"I really think we should go. Now." She leaned to pluck out a bottle.

"The time is well invested pulling together as much as we can in survival gear," he said, his voice steely calm and cool, as if they hadn't almost died a few minutes ago. "If the van wasn't about to blow, I could set up a lot more."

"So we stay here and wait for someone to follow the smoke signal to us?" She twisted off the cap, took a sip to check the drink—pineapple juice—then tipped the bottle to Joshua's lips.

"Actually, that's more of a worry than a help." His head ducked back out. Blood stained his pants along a tear.

"Exactly who do you think will be looking for us?"

"They had time to call their boss—the 'Guardian' person—and that concerns me. But I'm armed. I'm ready." He faced her full-on, his features and body still warrior-set. "And I'll be damned if I'll let us be sitting ducks."

※

The early morning charged upward too fast, time slipping away. Liam didn't have much longer to make use of Rachel's expertise before they both went back for another grueling day searching for survivors in the rubble. He wanted to believe this was the right choice, snagging her resources, exhausting them both further, on the hope that he could locate Franco. Choices were damn near impossible when there were so many to save at times like this.

And God help Franco if they found him tucked away in some corner making out with his new girlfriend.

Rachel walked with Disco alongside her as they made fast tracks up the dusty road to the nearby school-turned-hospital. Rachel Flores had taken five minutes to put on her gear that she'd called her PPE: personal protective equipment. A safety helmet with a headlamp, glasses, gloves, steel-toed/steel-shanked boots, along with kneepads. Goggles dangled from the pocket of her dark blue pants.

The look worked for her, sexier than any froufrou pink lingerie and heels his third wife had collected as avidly as some collected stamps. There was something hot about the way Rachel charged ahead without hesitation rather than waiting for him to clear the way.

Still, he hitched his M4 more securely over his shoulder and kept his eyes trained for any threats. "I owe you for this."

"Damn straight, you do." Dust puffed from under her steps. "Don't think this gives you the right to put me on speed dial for all your personal emergencies. I'm taking time out of my sleep only to get you and your guy back out there on the job. We need you. Every one of those trapped individuals needs you. Now walk faster."

"I'll buy you a five-star meal when we get back to the States. Where is it you live?"

She eyed him incredulously. "Are you actually hitting on me?"

He held his hands up with overplayed innocence. "Just asking where you're from to narrow the restaurant choices."

"You know full well my FEMA urban search and rescue task force is from Virginia."

True enough, since the only USARs designated to work international missions with the air force were from California and Virginia. "I spend a fair amount of time in D.C. taking care of Pentagon BS. I could make good on that dinner."

She stopped dead in her tracks, her black Lab halting in step. "Is your friend actually missing? Because if you're wasting my time, I'm going to kick your ass with my steel-toed boots, then I'm going to go back to work helping people who actually need saving."

"Whoa, whoa, hang on a second." He reached for her arm, pausing when she cocked an eyebrow at him. "My guy is most definitely missing, since he left the hooch last night just after that last tremor. I forget sometimes that people don't know what an irreverent bastard I am. I crack jokes at funerals and hit on women during earthquakes. Makes coping easier."

"Fair enough." She gestured forward. "Lead on and let's find your missing airman."

"Thanks, and I promise not to ask you out to dinner again."

She clicked and her dog trotted alongside her. "That would be best. I hear the service isn't so great around here right now."

Without another word, she made tracks. He wasn't big on silence. Left too much time to think, especially at times like this. "What made you get into this line of work?"

She veered off the path with Disco to let a family of four walk past, backpacks overflowing. So many people on the move, the masses became almost invisible. "I could ask the same of you."

"You first." He reclaimed his spot beside her.

"Fine. You want my life story? Okay, but it's not bar pickup cutesy. My mother was a hoarder. She hoarded dogs." Her pointy jaw jutted. "She died when the animal crates fell on top of her, and since then, I've had a mission to rescue."

"Holy shit." Her words knocked the stuffing right out of him, a damn rare occurrence. "That's... uh..."

"The stuff reality shows are made of? Yep, it sure is." She clapped a hand on her chest. "And in my case, it's not true. I'm joking."

And there she went, with a surprise second punch.

"Oh, right." He stared at her, trying to figure her out, and if he couldn't figure her out, how come he was so into her? "And why did you feel the need to lead with a reality-show fib?"

"You said jokes are your way of coping with stress. I was just doing my part to help out."

At the fork in the cracked dirt road, she steered her dog left, the school coming into sight a hundred yards ahead, just past a topsy-turvy playground. A dozen or so staff moved in and out of the building, probably a shift change.

Liam jogged to catch up with Rachel, a different feel, since he was usually in the lead. His knees groaned a little more these days after his years jumping from planes as an Army Ranger, then cross-training to become an air force PJ. But he could still keep up with a challenge, whether locating a friend...

Or bantering with a sexy lady dog handler. In which case, he should be sure of one little detail. "Is there a Mr. Flores?"

"Only my father," she shot over her shoulder.

Good so far. "Ever been divorced?"

"Never married. Never had the time. I have my dogs for companionship." A dark brown strand slipped from under her helmet, catching in the wind. "My career keeps me on the road most of the time. Not many men are interested in a wife who's never around."

"Ever been in love?"

She pivoted to face him. "Ever been called nosy? Or rude?"

"More than once." He stopped in front of her, a few feet shy of the school's front steps.

He reached into his vest and pulled out the wadded-up T-shirt Hugh had left after his shower. "This is the door the army nurse—Lieutenant Gable—said Hugh would have left out of. And here's something he wore yesterday. It's filthy and reeks, but there's definitely plenty of Hugh Franco's sweat here for your dog to work with."

"We would call this the PLS—point last seen."

"Right, okay then." Swallowing hard, he passed over the dirty cotton.

Rachel swapped into professional mode in a snap—as if she hadn't already been all business. Disco's loping manner morphed to sleek attentiveness. Rachel unwound a lengthy leash, about thirty feet, attached to his harness, different from when he'd run freely on top of the piles of earthquake debris to locate survivors. She held the shirt out for the dog.

"Go find," she ordered. "Go find."

Disco buried his nose in the soiled shirt, sniff-sniff-sniffing, while Rachel let him take his time to get a solid read. Disco tipped his head into the airstream left and right, then shifted his attention downward, to the ground. He worked in circles outward, farther and farther away in some sort of doggy grid system Liam couldn't help but notice and admire.

He kept his silence, not sure what protocol she would prefer. And God, he hoped Disco could work some kind of SAR magic that located Hugh holed up somewhere taking a nap or enjoying a hefty breakfast with the woman and kid.

Except while Hugh Franco was one edgy bastard, he was always, always, one hundred percent in the mission.

Rachel followed her dog at work, watching his path with narrowed eyes. "Actually, I was engaged once," she said softly, catching Liam off guard. "Right after graduation from high school. He proposed just before he deployed overseas. He never came back."

"I'm sorry," Liam said automatically, insufficiently, but sincerely.

"Me, too." She looped the leash around and around her hand. "I had my chance, found my soul mate, and lost him. End of story."

"So you're determined to spend the rest of your life alone? Come on, no disrespect meant to your first love and all, but do you really believe in that soul mate crap?"

"I take it from your oh-so-sensitive answer that you're not a believer."

"Three failed marriages will leave a guy jaded about the lasting quality of love."

"Three?" She simply smiled. "Because you didn't find your soul mate."

"Touché." He followed her as Disco continued his grid search of the concrete. "Although that's damn presumptuous of you to assume I didn't fall as deeply as you did."

"I'm sorry. You're right. It's not my place to speak about your feelings… for all *three* women you loved more than life until—"

"Fine, your point is made." He tucked closer to her as the foot traffic picked around the playground, kids and adults looking at the swings as if unsure whether playing was okay again after such a tragedy. A couple went from one person to the next, flashing a photo and asking if anyone had seen their son. Like so many other couples here searching.

Liam tore his attention away from them and back to Rachel. "And since we're saying to hell with personal boundaries, do you really plan to spend the rest of your life single?"

"Do you really intend to risk more divorces?" she snapped back.

"My banking account can't take another split." And wasn't that the truth?

"So what do you say we have a raging affair?" she said matter-of-factly, without taking her eyes off her black Labrador.

The air crackled with her words.

"And if I fall head over ass in love with you?"

She looked over her shoulder slowly, her exotic dark eyes undressing him. "I'll already know you're a fickle-hearted man who's had three wives, so I won't believe your declaration of undying love."

Her proposition obviously wasn't serious, but still it lay out there between them. What would it be like to have an affair? With this woman? Exactly what he'd been hoping for since the second he'd laid eyes on her—except when he thought about sex, his mind traveled to the possibilities of what it felt like to be in love, plan for forever.

Although forever and love hadn't gone that well for him so far. There was also a fundamental difference here. Rachel wasn't like other women he'd been drawn to. She was making it clear she would never fall for him, never lay claim to his overused last name and paltry bank balance. Yet for some reason, what should be simple confused the shit out of him.

Disco barked sharply.

Liam looked up fast as Rachel announced, "He's locked in on the scent."

Chapter 9

FOR FIVE YEARS HE HADN'T HELD A KID.

Now Hugh had one strapped to his back like a papoose as he and Amelia walked toward civilization. Wildlife screeched and called on one side in the trees. Waves rolled and crashed against limestone on his other side. Rock iguanas bathed in the sunlight, brown and nearly three feet long.

He'd weighed all his options before choosing this slightly longer route following the beach. The van had veered so far off the beaten track before he overpowered Oliver, he'd decided it was better, not to mention safer, to follow the water. While he could find his way through the wooded area, if something happened to him, Amelia would almost certainly get lost. So, water route it would be for them.

Shrugging his shoulders, he adjusted the fit of the baby carrier he'd rigged from his survival vest, holding twenty pounds of kiddo that weighed much heavier on his soul. He stifled a curse that the kid would likely parrot back at him. Marissa had almost had a coronary when Tilly fell off her Big Wheel and said, "Shit." Of course, once her mom reprimanded her, Tilly had said the word again and again for nearly a week before losing interest.

His throat clogged.

He resisted the urge to thrust Joshua at Amelia. She

could barely stand up straight after their daylong hike through the jungle and now along the beach. Carrying the kid would slow her down even farther as she trudged through the sandy earth.

Intellectually, he knew this. That still didn't help the cold knot in his chest or memories of hiking trips with Tilly in a kid carrier on his back, her tiny fists holding on to his ears as she whispered, "Love you, Daddy." Her tight grip hurt like hell and was the sweetest thing he'd ever known.

He glanced back over his shoulder. Joshua babbled nonsensically, all gums and six tiny teeth, and so damn cute.

Hugh tripped over a root.

He regained his balance just shy of slamming into a coconut tree.

God, he couldn't do this. He couldn't go there again, even for a few hours of pretend parenting. And while Joshua already had a mom and dad, after watching Amelia, he could see clearly she was meant to be a mother. She'd obviously wanted that during her marriage to the rat bastard.

Not that this kid liked him much. His tiny body went stiff when Hugh reached to take him out of Amelia's arms. Now Joshua had relented enough to hold on to his shirt in fists still sticky from downing a banana. Joshua had to be tired. His head even bobbled every now and again, but the stinker held tough about not resting his head on Hugh's shoulder as the sound of crashing waves lulled him.

Amelia swatted her way past fronds poking out of the jungle. She jabbed and poked ahead, checking for the snakes he knew terrified her, but she just kept jab-jab-jabbing. He couldn't bring himself to mention that one could fall out of a tree on top of her.

She would edge closer to the water and get fried by the sun beating down on the beach.

Jab, jab. She walked ahead, branches snagging on her scrubs and shoelaces. "Are you sure I can't carry him for a while? You both look rather, uh, uncomfortable."

"If you get tired, you'll slow us down, and that's not good for the kid." He studied her fair complexion, already turning pink. He needed to start keeping an eye out for aloe plants.

"That Superman thing again." She laughed hoarsely. "You've got the most endurance, the fitness required, an extra twenty pounds wouldn't faze you. And you're right. I'm sounding like a wheezing asthmatic, which just proves your point."

"You should drink some water," he said, even knowing she would ignore him. Again.

A rustle sounded in the underbrush. Amelia tensed. A raccoon-like creature scampered past and she exhaled hard. "How far do you think it will take us to get back or at least find people?"

"I'm hoping before dark." He scanned the horizon, frustrated as hell that they still hadn't come across some signs of civilization. "But if we do have to stay out here in the wild, I have the training to build us adequate shelter."

"Does that training have any tips on how to fashion a diaper in the wild?"

"We'll make this work." Yeah, he already had a warm wet spot in the middle of his back, but he'd mucked through a helluva lot worse. "You're doing good, hanging tough."

Better than he would have expected, even though he'd already learned not to underestimate this woman. Still, she and the boy had been through too much.

Eyes watching the trail for wild boars, he spotted a pigeon plum hanging low. He tugged it free and polished it on his pants leg. The dark fruit offered a natural cure for diarrhea. The kid hadn't shown signs of any such problem, but that wasn't a risk Hugh was willing to take.

He started to pass the plum back to Joshua—then stopped. He cut the fruit in half, pried out the pit so the toddler wouldn't choke on it, then gave him both halves.

Old parenting skills returned in a snap, bringing too many memories rolling back. All the more motivation to haul his butt out of here as fast as possible.

Amelia gripped a walking stick she'd started using about two miles ago. "I'm not going to let you down. I will hold up my end of things."

"I believe you." And he really did.

"I've never failed at anything in my life, you know. I made straight As. I behaved in school, always did my homework." She stabbed the sand with the stick again and again. "The only time I ever got a detention was for reading a romance novel behind my history textbook in class. I already had an A in the class."

"Of course you did." A smile tugged through his frustration. The sound of Joshua's contented chewing even felt right, despite the fruit juice dribbling on his neck.

"I brushed my teeth four times a day no matter what— well, except for that earthquake incident and today. Do you happen to have toothpaste in that vest of yours?"

"I have gum." He reached into one of the pockets on his vest, glad he could do something to help this stubborn woman.

"I would kill for a piece of it."

"No need. It's yours for free." He tossed her the pack.

Leaping forward, she caught the gum in midair with two hands, struggling for a second not to drop if before holding it up victoriously. He thought it was probably best not to tell her she'd just hopped right over a pygmy boa constrictor.

She peeled off the wrapper and pulled out a piece. She tossed the pack back to him and unwrapped her stick. Popping the gum into her mouth, she chewed slowly, sensually, taking so much obvious pleasure from that bit of spearmint, he found his mind zipping uncomfortably back to the cleaning closet. He forced his attention back onto her words.

"My parents taught me that if I worked hard enough, anything was possible." She trailed her fingers over a bush, her fingers snagging on the bloom of a yellow elder, the national flower, which bloomed year-round.

"I sense an *until* coming."

"My marriage." She shot him a thumbs down. Joshua threw the pulpy remains of his plum into the bushes as if to punctuate Amelia's anger. "Big fat F. Failing grade. But you already know that."

"His fault, his failing grade, not yours."

She blew a small bubble with the gum, popping it. "I know that now. Still sucks though. I tried so hard to do everything right. I ran an organized house. Even my spice cabinet is in alphabetical order. I read relationship books, went to marriage retreats, shopped at Victoria's

Secret." She shook her head, twirling the stem of the yellow elder between two fingers. "And still the rat bastard cheated on me. He left me for a totally disorganized, lovely person who couldn't balance her checking account if you implanted a calculator into her palm."

He took the bloom from between her fingers and tucked it behind her ear. Memories of their time together at the hospital filled his mind, hell, even seemed to pack the space between them. "Your jerk of an ex didn't appreciate how lucky he was."

"That's nice of you to say." She cupped his hand against her cheek for a second before starting out again. "I can't even hate his new wife, because she's stuck with him."

"You should hate her," he said forcefully. "She screwed a married man, and the jackass had such a small, uh... ego, he couldn't handle being married to one of the strongest women I've ever met."

"Only one of?"

"By the end of this, I may be willing to give you top honors."

She laughed wryly. "Heaven knows, I work for grades."

"It's a wonder you don't have ulcers."

"Yet. Give me time." Her smile faded. "What I really hate is how those people—Oliver and Tandi—caught me unaware. I should have been smarter than that. I should have been on guard."

"How? How could you have seen that coming?" Thank God she'd caught them in time. The thought of the kid at the mercy of those two... Anger turned the sunset a deeper haze of red.

"It's my job as a lawyer to see through crooks. I put

puzzle pieces together in a flash all the time to get to the truth."

"You got two loud screams off without dying." The echo of those in his head still sucker punched him. "That's pretty impressive."

"But what if I missed something because I was distracted… from earlier?"

No doubt about it, the memories weren't just in his mind anymore. They were out in there in front of them, as tangible as the sand and waves. "From when you walked out on me before I could zip my pants?"

"If I'd stayed with Joshua"—her hand gravitated to the sleeping boy's head as it rested on Hugh's shoulder— "none of this would have happened. He would be safe."

He needed to keep her spirits up, as important as her energy on a trek like this. "People like those are determined. They would have found another opening when you went to the bathroom or fell asleep. You're human, you know."

"Easy for Superman to say." She picked her way over a fallen tree. "I'm sorry for how I handled things afterward, back at the school. Being with you wasn't what I expected."

"What did you expect?"

"Less."

He just smiled, ready to take this conversation down to a less serious level, to ease the stress lines on her face.

She smacked his shoulder. "That wasn't a size comment, you Cro-Magnon."

"Hey, just an attempt at some lightheartedness." Except he wasn't usually the one to crack jokes in a crisis. That was squadron funnyman Liam McCabe's forte. "It's been an intense time, with the earthquake, that time underground. We were both on edge and those aftershocks just sent us over. We needed an outlet and we found it. Together." He held her eyes with his. "I don't regret that."

Yet rather than being reassured, her faced scrunched with even more worry. "I just wonder what would have happened if I hadn't walked away. Or if I had made it back to the nursery. Or never left in the first place."

"Life is so full of what-ifs, you can drive yourself crazy." He knew all about regrets and self-recrimination. He should have realized he couldn't make this any lighter for her.

Just as he'd failed to lift her spirits, he'd also failed to get them back to civilization before dark. He couldn't ignore it any longer. He was going to have to spend the night in the jungle with Amelia…

And the baby.

Feeling helpless as hell, Aiden stood outside the tent shower and listened to his wife cry. And there wasn't a damn thing he could do to fix this for Lisabeth. He could only stand outside this crummy refugee-like bathhouse and make sure his wife was safe while others filed in and out of the shower stalls and latrines.

His hand rested on his 9 mm, now in a leather shoulder harness he'd been given by a local cop who'd insisted, after Aiden stitched up a gash in the guy's arm. The policeman said he hadn't wanted Aiden shooting his foot off with that weapon tucked in his waistband. The weight of leather and metal seared through his scrubs.

He eyed the shift and shuffle of shell-shocked humanity under the umbrella of halogen lights. Generators droned along with night beasts.

His wife cried softly on the other side of the tarp curtain.

They'd arrived at the temporary hospital at the school only to learn that both Amelia and Joshua had gone missing. No one seemed to know what had happened to them. They'd even sent out a search dog, only to have the dog lose the scent in the parking lot.

Their best bet? They'd gotten into a vehicle to leave. But with whom? To go where?

Even though he'd heard that the search and rescue dog handler had given up, he and Lisabeth still spent hours more questioning people at the hospital. They'd passed around the one photo of Joshua that had survived the earthquake, a picture Lisabeth had carried in her purse for the weeks prior to the adoption. Since she'd had her bag with her, it hadn't been lost in the hotel.

No one remembered seeing the boy after the middle of the night. But he'd been there with a blonde-haired woman who must have been Amelia.

They'd been so close. Just a couple of miles away this whole time, only to learn too damn late. He just had to hang onto that hope that they were out there, safe and searching as well.

Meanwhile, he didn't know how much more stress Lisabeth could take. There was a tension in her worse than anything he'd ever seen in his normally unflappable wife. He'd taken comfort from her serenity from the start of their relationship. She thought him such a calm man, but he just kept a steely band around his emotions because with the least fissure, all would overflow like acid on everything.

So how did he go about making this right for her when he had no experience to draw on in helping her? And wasn't that a piss-poor testament to what kind of husband he'd been?

Shit.

Nothing to do but dive in headfirst and try his best.

He parted the shower curtain and slid sideways inside, careful to block the opening with his body until he could seal the cubicle closed again.

Lisabeth gasped, lurching back and covering her nakedness with an arm around her breasts and a hand between her legs. Then she sagged with relief. "Aiden, God, you could have given me a little warning."

"I heard you crying." He thumbed away a tear leaking from the corner of her eye as the pooling water soaked his shoes.

She swallowed hard, touching his chest. "All right, then. Thank you for letting me know so I won't bother everyone else, but you could have just whispered a warning through the curtain. Have you gone crazy or what?"

"Just worried about you." He unholstered his gun and set it on a shelf along with his glasses before moving closer, the spray soaking his head.

Sniffling, she shifted uneasily, the shadows in the corner playing peekaboo with the sleek body he knew intimately well.

"You should go," she said. "You're getting your scrubs wet."

"At least they'll be cleaner." He braced his hands on the steel poles on either side of the curtain. "I'm not going anywhere."

"This isn't like you." Frowning, she traced one finger

down the leather of his shoulder harness on the shelf. "You're not exactly an impulsive man."

"Is that a problem? Like now?" He captured her hand in his and squeezed gently, trying to offer comfort. Trying to keep his eyes on her face and not on her nakedness. "I know you're upset and there's nothing I can do to fix this."

She smoothed his damp hair. "I love you as you are, always. You know that, right?"

"I do." He stepped closer, unable to resist the draw of her. His hands fell on her shoulders, warm and slick under his fingers. "Although I'm not always sure why."

Her chin quivered as she swayed forward. Her naked body pressed against him, a perfect fit as always. "I just need to hear that you love me too, no matter what."

Water beaded over her shoulders, trekking a sensuous path around and between her breasts.

Worry fragmented as his eyes took in her caramel, rich skin bathed in the glow penetrating through the mesh overhead. Droplets glistened, begging him to taste every inch of her. All the frustration of the past couple of days, of the weeks prior to this trip, gnawed at his gut, demanding an outlet. Somehow time and tension had stolen a month from them since they'd made love. And maybe it was crazy—maybe *he* was crazy—he needed to have his wife.

Aiden dipped his head, kissed her, gathered her nearer, his hands spanning her waist and lower. She melted against him with a soft sigh and he growled his approval into her mouth. His hands glided lower until he cupped her bottom, lifting her against him until she wrapped her legs around his waist.

He knew this wasn't wise, and it wasn't at all the way he allowed himself to behave. Losing control had never been an option for him. But right now he could feel his world spinning out of control and damned if he could do a thing other than hold on tight to the woman he loved. Because, God love her, she was holding on to him every bit as tightly. Always, always she'd been there for him. His fears the week before they'd come here must have been misdirected edginess from the adoption—

Shit.

He didn't want to think about the adoption or his missing son. He needed to ease the tension inside him before he snapped.

Lisabeth clung to his shoulders, kissing her way along his jaw, over his ear, until her face was buried in his neck. "I love you, Aiden, so much."

"I know, baby, I know." All he needed to do was inch down his pants and he would be inside her slick damp heat. She would be all around him. His wife. The honest-to-God love of his life, something he'd never expected to have...

The woman he'd vowed to protect.

His skin chilled and it had nothing to do with the water. His head fell to rest on her shoulder.

"Lisabeth, we can't. I don't have a condom"—his breath came out in ragged huffs—"and since all our luggage got lost, your pills are with it. We can't risk pregnancy, especially not now."

He twisted off the shower and yanked the fresh scrubs off a high shelf positioned out of reach of the shower's spray. Her chin quivered, which sucker punched him so hard he almost caved and hauled her back to him again.

Then her jaw jutted and she yanked the clothes from his hands. She jerked the top over her head, tugging the hem over her hips. "If you feel so strongly about this, why haven't you just gotten a vasectomy?"

Her question stunned him almost as much as the fierce anger in her hissed words. "I realize you're upset, but the last thing we need right now is to fight with each other."

"Why would you think we're going to argue?" She stepped into the pants, her hands jerky, angry. "We never quarrel. Ever."

She whipped aside the curtain and stormed out, leaving him standing in waterlogged clothes. He should be pissed off, but he was still so shocked by what she'd said he didn't move. Why hadn't he gotten a vasectomy?

And why hadn't she ever mentioned it before, unless she was secretly hoping he would change his mind on not having biological children?

"Dude?" an impatient voice cut through his thoughts.

A soldier covered in mud stood waiting, looking every bit as exhausted as Aiden felt.

"Sorry." Aiden picked up his gun and glasses.

"Yeah, well, as long as you left some warm water in there." He stepped back for Aiden to walk out, water squishing from his shoes. "Your lady went that way, toward the chow hall."

The soldier slid into the shower. Aiden looked at the food tent, then toward the bunks where he and Lisabeth had side-by-side cots in a warehouse full of rescue workers. He didn't even have to think twice about where he had to be right now to keep his sanity.

Aiden made tracks back toward the church, to the waiting patients.

—⁓—

Moonlight glinting off the rolling waves, Amelia rinsed her face and hands in the surf while Hugh constructed a lean-to for them to sleep under for the night. She'd offered to help, but he'd said he could work faster on his own if she would keep an eye on the kid.

Joshua was toddling in hyper circles in the sand, glad to be walking after a day constrained. Hugh had wrapped the child's feet in leaves from banana trees to protect his soles. His diaper had been soaked, so she'd washed it and his tiny T-shirt in the ocean and draped them over a stretch of limestone to dry. There was something so endearingly innocent about a naked baby splashing in a little tide pool.

The day with Hugh had been so surreal—the fight in the van, the trek through the jungle, and now setting up a site for them to sleep together like some family on a camping trip. Except they weren't a family. This wasn't her child. Although right now he looked so heartbreakingly happy and perfect, her chest hurt over the dreams she'd once stored up about having babies.

Her eyes tracked back to Hugh. He spread foliage on top, mostly more banana leaves. He'd called the structure a hide site, designed more for evading than comfort, in case Oliver's people decided to come after them.

Joshua toddled over to the small camp. Amelia pushed to her feet, her body creaking with exhaustion as she trudged across the sand. "Joshua? Come back here, sweetie."

While Hugh had carried the child all day, there was no missing how uncomfortable he was around the boy.

Joshua clapped his hands, babbling and pointing.

Hugh frowned, reaching into a small pile of fruit he'd gathered. "Are you hungry? Banana? Is that what you want, kid?"

"B'ana?" Joshua tipped his head to the side, salt water still glinting off his dark hair from his tide pool bath. "No, no."

He pointed to the mango.

"Yeah, right. Here." Hugh peeled it with a knife, carved a slice and passed it to Joshua, so obviously careful to keep his distance.

She dropped down to sit beside them wearily and reached for the mango and knife to finish feeding Joshua. Hugh reached into his pocket and pulled out a fistful of plant stems. "Aloe. Just break each stem open and squeeze the liquid on your face. It'll ease the burn. I've also got some bay geranium. It's good for itching skin and even makes a decent tea. Let me know if you need it."

"The aloe's great. Thanks." She snapped open the squishy stem and pinched the liquid onto her finger. She smeared it over Joshua's cheeks before turning her attention to her own face. "You're good at the whole shelter-building gig. After all we've been through, you've handled everything that's come our way. You're obviously in the right line of work. Was anyone else in your family in the military?"

"Not a one. I was a regular Middle America farm kid with dreams of traveling the world. I even got an appointment to the Air Force Academy..." His voice trailed off as he tossed aside a branch.

He'd been on the path to become an officer?

She passed another slice of mango to Joshua. "What happened?"

Hugh dropped to sit beside her, hands on his knees, watching the little guy eat, with eyes so full of... pain? "My girlfriend and I weren't as careful as we should have been. We got married and became the parents of a beautiful baby girl."

He said it so simply, so few words, but such a depth of emotion packed into each one. There could be no missing how very much he loved his family. And no married man with a love that deep had sex with another woman in a closet. Something had gone very wrong with his beloved family.

Waiting for him to talk seemed wisest, but her hands trembled as she offered the last of the fruit to Joshua. The little fella shook his head and crawled under the lean-to, testing out a stack of leaves in the corner. Amelia looked sideways quickly and realized Hugh was watching along with her.

"I had a daughter."

Oh God. Please let this just be a divorce story, not what she feared was coming. "Had?"

"For five years... Then... She... They..." He swallowed hard, looking down.

But she didn't need the words. She made her living reading the undercurrents in what people left unsaid. His wife and child had died somehow and the pain she saw in his eyes was beyond bearing.

She touched his foot lightly, uncertain how much comfort he would accept but unable to do nothing. How strange to know his body so intimately and his soul not at all.

Scraping a hand over his face, Hugh continued. "When my daughter was in preschool—about four years old—she woke us up one night in a panic because she'd forgotten to tell us she needed a rock for class."

Waves pulled at the shore just as the tension radiating from him pulled at her while she listened, just let him talk.

"I promised her we would get one in the morning, but she couldn't go back to sleep. So my wife and I went out to the backyard to see what we could find." He looked at her for the first time, his raw eyes reflecting the moonbeams. "Did I mention we lived in Alaska and it was December?"

She smiled because he seemed to need that from her, but her insides burned with an ache for where he was going in his mind. Her hand fell to rest on Joshua's back as he settled on the leaf bed, curling up with heavy eyes.

"My wife held the flashlight while I shoveled through the snow. I was determined my little girl would have the *best* rock in class. After tossing aside a half dozen 'inferior' stones, I found the perfect one—probably weighed about five pounds."

Her hands circled on the baby's back, the moment so quiet, and heavier than that five-pound rock.

"So the Christmas program rolled around. We walked in to find this table set up with a display of all the kids' art-project gifts for their parents." He cut his eyes at her, a smile tugging at his face so beyond perfect, it took her breath away. "They'd made pet rocks."

"Oh, my," she whispered, falling so hard into those eyes and that nostalgic grin from a world she'd never known.

"Yeah, the table was full of tiny painted cats and

dogs and cows. And right there in the middle was my girl's boulder, completely unrecognizable. It had glitter and feathers and blobs of paint. The label called it a pet gerbil."

He laughed, shaking his head and she laughed with him, even though God help her...

Hugh Franco broke her heart.

He stirred up the sand at his feet, scooping and dumping, scooping again. "She and my wife died in a plane crash." Sand drifted through his fingers. "Tilly... my daughter's name was Matilda, and my wife's name was Marissa."

She looked into his eyes and for once hated the instincts that allowed her to perceive so fully what lurked under the surface. She'd thought of Hugh as Superman, going all the way to the edge, risking his life again and again for others.

And now she realized that he pushed himself to the limit out of a grief-filled need to chase his family to the other side.

Chapter 10

THROWING THE JEEP INTO PARK BESIDE THE BURNED-out van, the Guardian leaped out from behind the wheel, engine idling in the crisp morning air. "What the hell?"

The utility vehicle was nothing more than a blackened hull against the palm tree, also charred. The pyre had offered a beacon to locate the missing van even when communications from Oliver and Tandi ended.

And speaking of Oliver and Tandi...

The Guardian sidestepped a log, work boots crunching along the foliage, and pressed a hand to the still-warm door frame and looked inside. A burned corpse was slumped in the front passenger seat, horridly disfigured. Unidentifiable. Nothing but melted flesh over bones remained.

The Guardian whispered a string of curses before walking around to the rear of the van. The back was empty, other than exploded glass from incinerated crates.

Damn it.

Informants had already clarified that there'd been a screwup at the hospital that resulted in the wrong child being taken. Something about the wrong file attached to the wrong basinet or playpen or whatever the hell they were using. The whole system was a hodgepodge mess, with patients dying, new arriving, faster than a makeshift, understaffed hospital could handle.

Excuses.

Punishments would be doled out later. Right now? Nothing mattered but ensuring the safety of the child they'd taken and protecting the identity of the organization.

A groan sounded from inside the bushes. A quick search through the leafy green underbrush showed… Oliver bound by his hands and feet, lying on his side. His face was bruised, his eyes both angry and fearful.

"What the hell is going on here?" A ridiculous question to ask, since the man was gagged with his own bandanna. Tearing off the hemp ropes and swiping away the rag from Oliver's mouth, the Guardian asked again, "What happened here? Where's the little boy? And the woman?"

When the van exploded, had Tandi or the extra woman they'd picked up died?

"Tandi… They…" Oliver swallowed and swiped his wrist across his mouth. "Tandi is dead. The others… got away."

Got away? This wasn't making sense. But the clearing was disturbed, undergrowth trampled from lots of foot traffic. And where were Oliver's weapons? "You and Tandi were both overpowered by a woman with a child?"

Oliver stood slowly, stretching after being bound for so long. Except his unease seemed to be rooted in something else, something more. His eyes darted around like two bees unable to settle on a flower. "She, uh, had a man with her."

Anger simmered through the confusion. "When you picked up the child, you kidnapped a woman and a *man*? And you didn't bother to tell me this when you and Tandi checked in."

He rubbed his neck. "The man got into the back of

the van as we were driving away." His words picked up speed. "We tried to control him with the gun, but he rushed the front of the van and…"

"You screwed up."

"He was military, trained; there are soldiers crawling everywhere around here." Oliver stepped closer, tipping his head confidentially while eyeing the wreckage site even though there clearly wasn't anyone alive to hear. "Perhaps this isn't the best time and we should put our runs on hold—"

The Guardian whipped out a gun and leveled it at his big, fat, incompetent head. "*You* don't decide who and when. We're needed now. Our troops are needed now. And I'm wondering if you even have the same goals anymore, if your motivation for taking the woman was… less than necessary."

Oliver started shaking, his lying eyes wide. "No, I would never—"

The gun pressed deeper. "Did you take the woman because you had to or because you wanted to? What did you intend to do with her?"

The stench of sweat, the smell of fear, radiated off Oliver's skin as his mouth worked soundlessly.

"Don't even bother answering. I can see it in your traitorous eyes."

The bastard.

The Guardian pulled the trigger.

—∾∾—

Hugh checked and rechecked his guns until he felt like his teammate Bubbles. Going through the motions in-stinctively helped restore order to his mind after a long night keeping watch to make sure no stray animals—or people—found their camp.

Although that was the easy part. It had been much tougher tamping down thoughts of the past he'd dredged up for God only knew what reason.

He'd all but opened a vein last night, pouring out more than he had to anyone. He still wasn't sure why he'd said as much to her anyway. There was something about her, had been from the second he looked into her cornflower blue eyes. But he didn't have it in him to go there again, especially not so soon.

Today, he needed to hold it together better as they approached "civilization" again. He lined up the weapons, his knife and Oliver's. His 9 mm and the two SIG Sauers from the van. He hoped like hell he wouldn't need to use them. But between the wild animals running loose in the jungle and the lawlessness running just as out of control, he couldn't be too careful.

With luck, by noon they would arrive at the outer city limits. Once there, he would notify someone with security forces to pick up Oliver and question him. To find out what the hell had happened back at the hospital.

And then he would get Amelia and Joshua the rest of the way to the security of town—and onto the first military cargo plane out of here.

He tucked his 9 mm back in the holster and one of the two extra guns in his vest. His knife was strapped to his leg. The others would go to Amelia. He trusted she would do what she needed to if necessary. If she'd had one or the other back at the hospital, he felt certain she would have used them to protect Joshua.

His eyes slid to the little boy on the beach. The first

rays of morning stretched over the seaside patch of sand. Joshua ran in figure eights through the sand, his diaper in place again, the tiny T-shirt on his body again. The palm tree and bird spelling out *Bahamas*. He'd almost worn out his leaf shoes already.

Amelia scraped her hair back and used a strip from the edge of her scrubs to tie it in a short ponytail at the base of her neck. They were grimy, sweaty, and essentially how he would expect after this impromptu nature hike without much in the way of gear. He was used to conditions like this. He'd been filthier on missions. Although Amelia… she'd been hanging tough but he didn't know how much more she could take before collapsing.

"Amelia," he called, waving her over. "We need to regroup before we head out."

Her head tipped to the side, she picked around seaweed and driftwood washed up on the shore. She stopped in front of him. "Yes?"

"I should have given these to you yesterday." He passed the SIG and the knife. He also scooped up the gun belt he'd taken off Oliver. "Do you know how to use them or do you need a quick how-to now?"

She took the weapons from him carefully. "I can handle them well enough, thank you."

"Good, then." He stroked her cheek, wanted to do more, but the time wasn't right.

The discussion about his wife and daughter was still too fresh. He willed her to see in his eyes his need to keep things level.

She leaned into his hand for a split second before backing away with a curt nod that bobbed her scruffy ponytail. "Let's get moving then."

Kneeling, she stretched out her arms for Joshua.

Hugh reached between them, a hand on her shoulder. "We already covered this yesterday. I'll carry him."

She looked up at him with those pure blue eyes, and he saw written sympathy for every word he'd said the night before. Even if he didn't mention it and she kept quiet, his baggage was still hanging out there between them. In fact, as silent as he'd stayed about it over the years, it was still there, biting him all the time. Pushing him. Leading him to take risks that put other people in danger if they had to haul his butt out.

He scooped up the kid and tucked him into the backpack sling. The little guy didn't protest as he had the day before, but he still wasn't giving in completely.

Amelia took up her walking stick and gestured for him to lead the way. "Talk to me about your—"

He tensed.

"—your job. The pararescue mission."

He snatched up the chance to talk about anything else as handily as she snagged two bananas left from their food stores of last night.

"We train for rescue missions—land, sea, mountain. There are only three hundred of us."

"Sounds like a movie title." Grinning, she tucked her walking stick under her arm and peeled a banana.

"You're poking fun?" He cocked an eyebrow. "You're supposed to be suitably impressed with my kick-ass profession."

"Like a groupie?" She pinched off a piece of the fruit and passed it to Joshua as she walked. "There are groupies, I assume."

"There are people impressed with the uniform, more so than the actual mission, the calling," he conceded.

"To rescue airmen and other service members. I think I read somewhere you motto is something like…"

"'That others may live.'"

"Heavy stuff. Honorable. And very lucky for people like me." She smiled her thanks again, before continuing, "Given that you're here, you're obviously called in during natural disasters."

"And smaller-scale civilian rescues on occasion." He studied her gait, wishing she had boots like his rather than the simple gym shoes she'd been given at the hospital. "We also work with NASA during water landings in case of emergencies. We work with SWAT and the FBI."

"You're in Florida now?"

"Florida, Japan, Alaska twice…" His mind traveled back through the years to that first assignment after training. His first tour in Alaska. With Marissa and Tilly.

"But you're in Florida now." Amelia snapped him to the present again with her crisp, no-nonsense voice.

"Technically, although we haven't spent much time there. We were in the Middle East until a couple of months ago." While most people looked forward to homecomings, he would have preferred to skip that part, all the happy family reunions.

"You must be ready for some downtime."

He looked ahead, steering her past a thick overgrowth of poison ivy. The kid did not need exposure to that. At least the dust was thinner here than in the city.

"I'm not much into vacations. Too boring for me. What about your job?" He wanted to hear, and how strange was that? They had this in reverse, sleeping together and then doing the bar-style pickup conversation, getting to know each other. "You have a high-pressure career of your own."

"Go ahead and get the lawyer jokes out of the way." She peeled the remaining banana for herself. "I believe I've heard them all, but you're welcome to give it your best shot." She bit the top off with a wicked smile.

Was she playing with him? "I wouldn't be so rude."

"Then I'll go ahead for you..." She danced ahead of him, walking backward along the sand. The landscape stretched ahead with trees and more trees hemming them in, closing off any view of the city still miles away. "There are only two lawyer jokes, you know."

"Really? Only *two* lawyer jokes?"

"That's right." She winked. "The rest are true."

Her words jolted a laugh out of him. Beyond not coddling him this morning, she'd managed to do what not many could at times like this. She made him smile. "You have a sense of humor about yourself. That's rare."

"Believe me, in this profession, you have to laugh or you would go crazy." She turned away, walking ahead with her stick in front of her again, stabbing at bushes. "People lie..."

She jabbed. "And they lie."

Again Amelia jabbed. "And they lie some more. Even upstanding people flinch at telling the complete truth. I can spot bullshit a mile coming."

"You still haven't told me why you became a lawyer."

"And I don't have to tell you." She glanced back with another of her glittering smiles, but there was ice in her blue eyes this time.

"Ah, lawyer skills." He couldn't resist jabbing too, with words. "You get me to spill my guts, then you don't say a thing."

"No one forced you to talk." Her whisper drifted over her shoulder, the edge carrying something else he recognized well.

Pain.

"You're right. You didn't." He lengthened his stride and walked alongside her, the soft sand giving under his boots. "My apologies."

"No"—she glanced up at him—"I'm sorry. We've gone past the holding-back stage, I think."

"Getting naked—or almost naked—together does take away certain boundaries." And just that fast the air crackled between them, the awkwardness that he'd caused last night finally—thank God, finally—easing.

"I was thinking more of the life-and-death thing, but whatever."

"Ah, that's right. The sex meant so much to you that you walked away before I could pull up my pants." That stung now even more than before.

Her hand fell on his arm, soft and cool against his sunburned skin. "That wasn't very nice of me. I'm sorry again." She reached past to tickle the chin of the kid squirming in the pack. "I don't do so well with relationships these days. The past has a way of dogging a person, you know."

That he did. He reached back to pat the wriggling kid's shoulder. "You would blame all men because your ex was a jerk?"

"Are you really sure you want to have this kind of conversation?" Her feet slowed, her smile fading. "I got the impression this morning that you want to keep things lighter…"

That he did.

He grasped the shift in conversation with both hands and settled on the first topic that came to mind. Easy enough, with the kid grabbing hold of his ears tightly. "Your parents must be excited about their first grandchild."

The air went thick, heavy with more than humidity. He ducked under a branch.

Her hand slid from her nephew and she stepped over a turtle lumbering across their path. "My mother doesn't speak to my brother and me anymore."

Surprise slowed his stride for a step. "And your father?"

"Is dead," she said unemotionally, smoothing a hand over her pulled-back hair as if to restore… composure?

"I'm so very sorry." He wasn't sure what to read into her flat tone, her stiff spine. Her ponytail barely moved she was so in control of her every movement. "You must miss him…"

"All the more because I'm not close to my mom? If only it could be that simple. There's no easy way to put this. My issues with men go back further than my ex-husband. My father was a convicted criminal… statutory rape was the charge… I have another far worse term for him." She scraped a hand over her pulled-back hair again. "He killed himself rather than go to prison."

Hugh tried to wrap his brain around what she'd said, definitely not where he'd been expecting this conversation to go. He searched for the right thing to say… and came up dry. Emotional stuff? Not his forte. He absently patted the toddler's leg to keep him content, to give Amelia the quiet to gather her thoughts.

"He was caught with my brother's girlfriend. She was fourteen, and she was not anywhere close to consenting." She swept ahead of her with her walking stick, drawing semicircles in the sand ahead of them. "Dear old dad was going to cut a deal with the prosecution. He would get out after five years. He and Mom would move to the Keys afterward and start a new life away from the scandal. Away from others who might come forward to accuse him."

"Your mother stayed with him?" Where had their children been in all of this? Defensiveness for the child Amelia had been seared through him.

"She vowed my brother and his girlfriend set him up, but I knew better." Her upper lip curled. "I was the witness."

The realization of how things unfolded struck him deep in his gut. He felt her pain, wanted to fix a wrong for her already over a decade old. "And your mother didn't believe you?"

"She explained that away, as well. Said I was upset over not being Daddy's little girl…" She rolled her eyes. "If he hadn't killed himself, she would be with him now, starting off with her morning mimosa."

"So you became the incorruptible lawyer." Her quest for justice fell into place. What career would she have chosen with a different kind of childhood, a different father?

"And my brother is a surgeon with a specialty in genetics. Spends his spare time traveling for programs like Doctors Without Borders and Operation Smile, fixing the smiles of kids with cleft palates. Fixing children's smiles… there's symbolism there if ever I saw it." She whacked a tree, sending a flock of birds flying.

He grabbed her shoulders, stopping her there under the sprawling branches. "You don't have to pay for what your father did. It's okay to live your life."

"You're one to preach about moving on with life," she snapped.

Her words struck home. Hard. He should have followed his first instinct and stayed away from deep conversation and soul-searching today. But he couldn't simply walk away from her. Maybe if he just... hugged her? He tugged her closer.

Her eyes went wide and he had to admit he was glad to have surprised her. Maybe that meant he was on the right track. She reached toward him...

Past him?

She shoved him aside with one hand and fell past him. Her push was surprisingly strong and he stumbled once before realizing she held a snake in her fist.

Shit.

She threw it away as he drew his gun and shot the head off.

The world went still. His ears rang, the gun in his hand pointed toward the headless snake, still thrashing. A scream split through the aftermath. The baby. Joshua grabbed and clawed at Hugh's shoulders. He reached around and pulled the boy out, holding him.

Amelia slumped down with her back against a tree, drawing in shaky breaths one after the other. She hugged her knees to her chest.

"Amelia"—he knelt beside her, holding Joshua—"I thought you were scared of snakes, but good God, woman. You didn't even flinch."

"I was afraid if I took the time to say something..."

She turned toward him, burying her face in his chest. "It was so close to Joshua. I didn't have a choice."

He kissed the top of her head and rubbed her arm. If they were alone he would have done more. His insides were shaking with relief. "You did well."

Her breath hitched one after the other, visibly pushing back hysteria. "Hugh, I need to know. Was it a poisonous snake?"

Hugh looked at the thin length—about five feet long. "A brown racer, a mature adult. They carry a minor poison, for small animals." He tucked Joshua closer. "A child would have been particularly vulnerable. Even some small adults, given its size."

"But Joshua's okay?" She skimmed her fingers along her nephew's cheek. The little boy hiccupped as his cries died down.

"He's fine." Hugh scanned his tiny arms and legs again to be sure. "Just scared. I don't see a mark on him."

"Good, good." A sigh of relief shuddered through her. "Hugh?"

"Yeah, Amelia?" He rested his chin on her head, willing his heart to slow.

"You were really great there, doing your Superman PJ rescuer." Her fingers toyed with his survival vest.

"You weren't so bad yourself."

"Yeah, well, I need you to be the medic PJ now." She looked up at him, the fear finally showing on her face as she held up her arm, her hand puffy and red. "The snake... It bit me."

Chapter 11

AMELIA'S HAND HURT. *REALLY* HURT.

It throbbed as if she'd been stung by a wasp a million times. She glanced down and—

She squeezed her eyes shut to block out the two puncture marks on top of her puffy, red hand. She'd been bit on the same hand that had been cut in the earthquake. She resisted the urge to make a fist. Something told her she needed to hold still, not circulate the venom around. Tough to do when she was shaking like a leaf in the aftermath. Or maybe that was another aftershock buzzing the ground under her feet.

Hugh clasped her trembling fingers in his. "Keep it below the level of your heart. Don't panic. Everything's going to be fine."

"Joshua? Where is he? If there are more snakes…" She shuddered. She wasn't feeling nearly as brave now as she had a few minutes ago.

"He's okay. Right here beside me and I don't see any sign of more snakes." His calm bass rumbled over her just as it had at the earthquake site. That voice was pure intoxication.

Sighing, she felt her pulse settle and her eyes fluttered open. Hugh tugged his T-shirt off—*gulp*, there went her heart rate again—and he started ripping it into strips.

"Put Joshua in the baby sling again anyway, please." Her hand throbbed and fear clogged her throat. "No matter what you say, I won't be able to stop hyperventilating until I know he's not going to get bitten by Sammy the Snake's brother or sister lurking around in there."

"All right, all right." He started plucking things from his survival vest… alcohol swabs, gauze, and some kind of ointment.

Then he shrugged into the vest again and the makeshift baby pack. He tucked his arms under Joshua's armpits and swung him around, settling him in place. The toddler locked his arms around Hugh's neck.

She kept her eyes averted from the throbbing snakebite. "What do we do now? Do you cut it open, draw out the poison?"

She eyed his knife and struggled not to wince. Whatever needed to be done. Right?

"Sucking out the venom is a myth from Wild West films."

Thank God. She sagged with relief.

He twisted open a bottle of water and poured it over the bite. The coolness momentarily soothed the heated sting. Hugh tore open antiseptic pads and cleaned around the puncture marks so gently she barely knew he touched her. She remembered well those same fingers stroking elsewhere, so controlled and tender… just before they'd both turned frantic and overheated.

How had she walked away from him? More importantly, why? But it was too late to think about that now.

"Hugh, you have to leave me here. I can't walk. I'll hold you back. Take Joshua and go get help."

"You're not going to die." He cradled her face in a broad palm, calluses rasping along her sunburned skin before he shifted his attention back to her hand.

"I don't want to slow you down." Her head spun. She was dizzy even sitting, for crying out loud. "Or what if I pass out?"

"Then I'll put your pretty ass"—he winked, actually winked, so it must not be that bad, unless this was another technique to keep her calm—"on a sled and drag you home. Now quit arguing." He pinched a string of antiseptic along her hand before placing gauze on top. "When did you become defeatist?"

"Excuse me for being a little upset." Her voice went squeaky with encroaching hysteria. "But I just got bitten by a very big, very scary snake."

"That's the Amelia I know and—" He stopped midsentence.

Her heart slammed against her ribs as fast as his gaze rocketed up to meet hers. His green eyes gleamed with an awareness she was beginning to recognize well, an awareness that echoed inside her. She wanted more time with him, normal time on a date or even just coffee...

Except that regular date or coffee would end with sex that was far beyond ordinary.

The reality of that, the need for more from a man who was still so lashed to his past, still painfully locked in love with his lost family... God, she really knew how to pick 'em.

He looked back down at her stinging wound. "The venom from this particular snake isn't strong enough to kill you or even make you sick. But I want to be sure you don't get an infection and that you don't suffer any tissue damage around the bite site. I'll clean it and bind the area. Then we'll have you checked over again when we get back to civilization. Hey, trust me. You're going to be okay. Do I look worried?"

Wow, he should bottle that calming voice, because it worked better than any tranquilizer. For the most part. Until she sneaked another look at her fingers puffing up. "Of course you're going to say that. And you never look afraid."

"But I also told you I wouldn't BS you."

She gave him a shaky smile. "Actually, you said for me not to start freaking out or you would have to BS me."

"If I was worried about that little bite, would I take time to do this?" He tucked a knuckle under her chin and skimmed his lips over hers.

Then kissed her again, holding. Closed-mouthed and totally appropriate, considering he was holding a kid and she had a snakebitten hand. But there was something special about the kiss, something even more intimate than their out-of-control tongue tangle in the closet at the hospital.

This wasn't about sex. It was about feelings and connecting, which somehow was a turn-on too. What a helluva time to realize she hadn't loved her ex-husband nearly as much as she'd thought, because even his best kisses had never touched her heart like this. The ground vibrated under her feet again and she knew this wasn't an aftershock, but Hugh's touch rocking her balance.

A new panic settled over her, humming in her ears, growing stronger and louder until she realized—

Hugh stepped away sharply. "Someone's coming."

His body tensed with a professional alertness she was learning to recognize all too well.

The sound of an engine carried on the ocean breeze. She searched the water and beach, following the sound down the stretch of sand. A speck appeared from around a bluff, a vehicle of some kind.

Hugh's hand slid down to his gun. "Take Joshua out of the pack and go into the woods until I see who it is."

Until they learned if they were being rescued— or attacked.

An infant girl cradled in his arms, Liam picked his way down the staggered levels of the collapsed apartment building. Structural engineers had said the place was made from piece-of-shit-quality materials. The slabs of concrete looked like a tilting stack of pancakes heating up in the midday sun. He tucked the tiny weight closer, safer.

"You're out now, baby girl," he whispered, her skin soft under all the grime.

He forced his body back on autopilot, training ramping into overdrive because he couldn't afford to think or he would go fucking nuts remembering what he'd seen down there.

The overall frenzy of noise from early on had dulled to a more despondent, low hum of hailing calls—people yelling into piles of rubble and listening for a response. Fewer and fewer came through anymore, just weak whimpers for the most part.

The stench of decaying remains thickened by the hour.

They couldn't give up the search for potential live victims. But the wins were such a mixed bag.

After Rachel's dog got the hit on a live find around what must have once been the third floor, the crews had started digging—a laboriously slow process with everything from jackhammers to pry bars. The voices answering were high-pitched. Kids. A baby girl and her five-year-old brother. Stuck below with the dead bodies of their parents and another brother.

The little girl was in his arms, while Bubbles carried the boy.

An army nurse waited at the base of the rubble with a papoose board and actual transportation. As he neared he recognized her from when he'd gone to the hospital housed in the school. "Lieutenant Gable?"

"Hello, Major. Did you ever find your friends?"

So much for asking her if she'd seen them. He squashed down another disappointment on an already-crappy day. He passed over his charge. "Six-month-old girl, parents died along with one of her brothers. The kid there is the only other survivor in the family."

Even saying it sliced him through with memories of seeing the dead mother's body curled around her other son. The father had shielded the two living kids at the expense of his life. His eyes met the tiny girl's heart-melting gaze that—thank God—could still focus. He forced himself to look away, to disengage.

Or at least try for now, because he knew the faces of this entire family would haunt his sleep later.

Lieutenant Gable took the bloodied infant gently. "I'll make note of that in her files. We'll do our best to keep the brother and sister close to each other."

He stepped away, his body fried from exhaustion as well as the heat. "Thanks."

Gable hesitated for a split instant. "Did you find your friends?" she asked again.

He shook his head. "Not yet."

"Sorry, sir. I'll let you know if I hear any more from them." She pivoted away with her patient toward a waiting transport van.

In the distance, a shout went up. "Dog on the pile."

The call carrying on the breeze made him think of Rachel. He glanced over quickly even though he already knew it wasn't her. Rachel was sitting off fifty yards away on a tarp, her arm wrapped around her dog, Disco, as she stared off zombielike, not even noticing the water truck stuck in a mob scene so intense the vehicle couldn't move farther.

Without another thought, he jogged toward Rachel, his jump-worn knees creaking with each step. The closer he got to her, the more he could see how zoned out she was. The Labrador's ears perked up, twitching in his direction. But Rachel didn't move.

He slowed, finally stopping alongside the edge of the tarp blanket on the ground. "Are you doing okay?"

Her eyes shifted up; she snorted, then looked down again silently.

"Of course you're not all right. No way to be here, see all of—" He gestured around them, shaking his head. "This is war-zone material."

"Got that right." She tugged her hat off and pitched it on the ground, thick brown ponytail unfurling down her back. "Did you find your friend?"

He winced. "Not yet."

She looked at him, sympathy in tired eyes. "I'm sorry. I should be comforting you rather than the other way around."

And he should be doing something, anything, except

he was out of ideas other than sitting with this woman and hydrating before cranking up for the next rescue.

He dropped down beside her, tarp crackling under him. "This isn't a game of whose life sucks most right now, especially when I look at everything folks here have lost. And the lives lost…"

He uncapped his water and drank… and drank…

Rachel's fingers worked along Disco's neck. "That's a very sensitive thing to say."

"You don't have to act so surprised. I can be a sensitive guy, when the situation calls for it." He gestured toward Disco. "Is there some rule again me petting your working dog?"

"He's off the clock right now." She half smiled. "Knock yourself out."

He passed Rachel the rest of his water bottle and held out a hand for the dog to sniff. "Disco? Hey fella, remember me? Just a friend of Rachel's, so don't go postal on me, pup." The dog nosed his fingers, so he scratched behind the Labrador's ear. "I gotta confess, I can't take credit for the sensitivity. My first and third exes were both into marital counseling. I may have ended up divorced, but I came away with a ton of insights."

"Why no therapist with wife number two?" She tipped back the bottle.

"Pictures changed my mind. Lots of pictures. Of her with a number of different guys." He'd been an idiot marrying on the rebound, not wanting to stay in his crappy-ass apartment alone. "One of those guys had a wife pissed off enough to hire a private eye. I got a complimentary photo album. Didn't see much point going to a therapist in light of their *Kama Sutra* pictorial."

"Ouch, that's, um…" She rolled the bottle between her palms.

"No worries about me." He leaned closer conspiratorially. "I didn't pick up any diseases from my ex."

"This isn't funny, and that wasn't what I was thinking." Her voice was tart, but her eyes were sweet.

He liked her. A lot. Like was more unsettling than love.

"Well, you can sure as hell know it's exactly what I was thinking. Cheating isn't just damn disrespectful. It's dangerous." Ex number two had blamed the infidelities on his long deployments, vowing she thought he'd stepped out too while away. She'd been wrong, and hell yeah, he was still bitter. "I may have been married three times, but when I'm with a woman, I am always, always monogamous."

"Okay, so no therapy with wife number two. Still, therapy obviously wasn't successful with number three either if you ended up divorced."

Some of the tension left her face as she settled into the conversation, so he kept going with it. They both needed the distraction, even if only for a few minutes, to take their mind off what they'd seen since arriving in this nightmare.

"The counselor for marriage number three was especially savvy. He figured out I choose relationships destined to fail… He just talked me through to that revelation a little too late."

"Hmmm…" She brushed the dirt off his shoulder. "And you feel the need to continue to affirm his diagnosis by picking me?"

"Sure"—he kept his tone light for her—"but it works better now since I don't make the mistake of proposing. And if I'm crazy enough to pop the question, the woman—you—would be forewarned."

"You're an odd man," she said with what actually sounded more like interest.

Good.

"That's a fairly benign insult compared to others I've been called. I think maybe you're starting to like me."

Her dark eyes heated, steaming along him. "My impression of you is organic, open to change."

"That's promising." He skimmed her hair back over her shoulder.

She didn't move or speak. So he dipped his head toward hers, waiting for her to object, but she still stared back at him steadily. He slanted his mouth over hers, taking in the softness slicked with some kind of lip balm. They were both exhausted and sweaty and there was no way this kiss could go farther out here in hell on earth. But for just a second, touching her made the roar in his mind recede.

"Sir?" someone called breathlessly, footsteps sounding. "You can't be over here."

Liam pulled away from Rachel fast, shooting to his feet, hand on his holstered 9 mm. A harried local cop who looked like he'd been given his badge yesterday chased a couple walking in his direction. A man and woman in surgical scrubs raced toward him.

He held up a hand. "This is a restricted area. Not to mention dangerous. Medical personnel are supposed to meet up over there in that tent. The policeman here will show you the way." He clasped Rachel's elbow. "We should get going."

He started to pivot away.

"Hugh Franco," the man said with an American accent.

Liam turned sharply, already tensed for another sucker punch. "Excuse me?"

The woman pushed past the other and grabbed his wrist urgently, her wide brown eyes steely with... fear? "I believe one of your men—Master Sergeant Hugh Franco—is with my son and my sister-in-law."

—◆◇◆—

Hugh studied the top-off Jeep driving closer.

Amelia hadn't been thrilled about going into the woods where she was sure the snake had a gang full of buddies nearby. He was more concerned with the possibility of a shady character driving that beach buggy across the sand, and that had been enough to persuade her to make sure Joshua was out of sight. This hell just didn't seem to end; in fact it got worse the longer he spent with Amelia, because the need to keep her safe was sliding past personal.

The vehicle sped closer, spitting sand out from behind the back wheels. With luck, it would be a cop. But he didn't count on luck.

The driver behind the Jeep's windshield was a blur, other than a hat and shades. He stayed close to the jungle in case he needed to duck for cover, and he wasn't taking his eyes off the driver's hands on the wheel.

He cocked his head to the side as he scoped out the situation. The face under an outback hat came into focus—a woman's face. She wore bulky work clothes and gloves that had made her less distinguishable from a distance. A strand of gray-blonde hair striped out from her hat.

The Jeep fishtailed to a stop.

Standing, the woman pulled off her sunglasses. "Would you mind taking your hand off the gun, young man? I'm here to help."

Except now he could see she had a 9 mm strapped to her waist, belting in her loose white shirt. Of course anyone who had a weapon would be wise to keep it close right now, with the country in such unrest.

And shit, was that another aftershock? He eyed the rolling ocean. He didn't even want to consider the possibility of a tsunami.

"Ma'am, I'll keep my hands off mine if you'll do the same."

"Fair enough." She jumped out onto the beach, her boots packing earth, green work pants tucked into the tops. "My name is Jocelyn Pearson-Stewart. I own a small sugarcane plantation nearby."

The woman didn't have a local accent, instead sounded like an American.

She smiled as if understanding the unspoken question. "I'm from Miami originally. It would be nice if you would speak. Just let me know if you need a ride or not, and then I can head home."

"How did you find me?" A movement out of the corner of his eyes flashed, and damn it, Amelia stepped out with Joshua. He wanted to tell her that just because this Jocelyn person appeared to be in her fifties didn't mean they should lower their guard.

"I heard your gunshot," the woman—Jocelyn something-or-another—said, her eyes skipping over his bare chest to the torn-up strips of shirt in Amelia's fist. "Is everything all right?"

"A snake went after her little boy." He wasn't sure why he'd called Joshua her son rather than nephew, but it seemed smart to go that route, to keep the connection tighter. "But he's fine. The snake's dead, and while she got bitten, there's a blessing in it all, since you heard the gunfire."

Hitching Joshua onto her hip, Amelia walked to Hugh's side, watching the woman in the Jeep with that lawyerly look of hers. "If you could take us to the capital, I can't tell you how much we would appreciate it."

Jocelyn shook her head slowly. "I'm sorry, but the roads in and out of the city have been closed. I'm afraid even your uniform, sir, won't gain us access, even if I did have enough fuel, which I don't. The aftershocks took out bridges, and the access ways that are left are being checked for structural integrity. But I can take you all back to my place."

What she said made sense, but that didn't mean it was true. It also didn't mean they had a lot of choices. He could walk the rest of the way with a kid and a woman who was *probably* going to be okay from a snakebite and hope that the bridges were open. Hope? He hadn't had a lot of luck with that.

"We would appreciate the hospitality and the use of a phone. I need to check in with my unit. Amelia has family that will be worried about her."

"Absolutely. Anything I have at my house, you're welcome to use."

Amelia looked at him, her eyes questioning. He nodded and gestured to the Jeep. He knew he could outdraw the woman if he had to. He smiled his thanks at Jocelyn as Amelia and Joshua settled into the front seat of the Jeep. Then he swung around into the back, standing. Ready.

Jocelyn rammed the Jeep into gear and pulled a three-point turn on the sand, just out of reach of the rolling waves. "And your names are?" She smiled at the baby. "Since you're going to be my guests and all."

"I'm Amelia. This is Joshua. Thank you for your help."

Jocelyn met his eyes in the rearview mirror. "And you, handsome marine?"

Marine? He almost rose to the bait to snap back—until he saw the twinkle in the woman's eyes. "I'm Hugh."

"Nice to meet you, Hugh." Laughing softly, the woman steered onto a narrow road back into the jungle.

He turned on his mental GPS as she drove away from the beach—away from the direction of Oliver and Tandi's crash site. The woman drove like a speed demon racing along the dirt road like it was the fucking autobahn as she talked with Amelia, shifted gear, and drank from her water bottle all at once.

The Jeep was a working vehicle and a real mess. Tools rattled in the box beside him. Papers were stuffed in the console. And a silver angel swayed from her rearview mirror.

"I would imagine it's been difficult for you out here alone with such a little child. How did you say you became lost out here?"

He tensed in response to the question, ready to jump in.

Amelia turned toward her without missing a beat. "I was out walking with my son when the earthquake hit. We got cut off from help. I wandered around lost. We probably would have died out there if he hadn't found us."

Her lie fell out of her mouth so easily he would have believed her if he hadn't known better. She'd seemed so trusting as she walked out of the jungle to his side. Of course now that he thought about it, that latest aftershock may have put her as on edge as he was. Although even on edge, she was keeping her wits enough to play it close to the vest — as he was.

The Jeep jostled over another dip in the dirt road, sugarcane fields on either side of them until they entered a clearing with a small homestead fenced off. Thick vines grew over most of the length, muted the harsh metal. Jocelyn reached down to her keys and thumbed a remote that opened the main gate. The graveled drive led up to a beige stucco house on stilts as protection from hurricane floods, even though they weren't on the beach. It wasn't a plantation home, but it sure wasn't a shack. Porches circled the entire place. Plenty of means to leave quickly if he needed to, not far to scale down.

Hugh scanned the outbuildings — a shed and a large barn that appeared to serve as a garage. A couple of RVs were parked alongside as well. It seemed some people had taken refuge at her place. Her family, maybe? Or some locals? But it certainly wasn't the jam-packed mayhem they'd left behind in the city. And everything here seemed intact.

He could treat Amelia's hand, give her and Joshua both a chance to clean up, eat, and sleep. They would all definitely be more comfortable here than in a jungle lean-to or a cottage halfway sliding off the edge of a bluff, assuming trouble didn't follow them to Jocelyn Pearson-Stewart's doorstep.

They might have a few more amenities here for the night. But he still wasn't letting Joshua or Amelia out of his sight.

Chapter 12

THE LATE-AFTERNOON BREEZE CURLED OVER AMELIA as she sat cross-legged on the porch floor, rolling a ball back and forth with Joshua. She could grow seriously addicted to staying out on this porch. Safe. Peaceful. And relatively clean, thanks to a quick sink rinse-off and change of clothes. Although God, she couldn't wait for a shower after they all ate dinner, while there was still daylight to stream through the open floor plan.

A generator was being used to power the fridge and freezer. Windows, windows, windows and French doors were open to reveal the living room, dining area, and kitchen. The place was made to capture breezes blowing through, perfect architecture for the Bahamas. Someone had spent some serious dough building this place. But it appeared that money had stopped long ago.

The kitchen would have been top-of-the-line twenty years ago. High-end appliances, slate floors, and counter-tops were pristine clean but showing signs of age with scratches and dulled yellow.

She'd worried at first that the woman—Jocelyn— might be affiliated with the Guardian, perhaps his wife. But Jocelyn said she was a widow living with her two nieces. Jocelyn's supply of baby gear had seemed strange, but she'd smoothly explained it away as leftover from frequent visits from her nephew's family in Miami.

If she was lying, she was doing it so damn well, even

Amelia couldn't read a hint of deception in the woman's calm hazel eyes. And this place certainly didn't appear to be the affluent compound of someone trafficking in babies and women.

She'd seen that this was a working farm—Jocelyn stepping outside to give fertilizing instructions to a worker on a tractor, staking the trunk of a fledgling tamarind tree in a pot off the back step, tending a spice garden on the kitchen sill. She'd witnessed the evidence of time and effort put into the sugarcane plantation, and Jocelyn clearly knew how to keep the cogs in the machine running smoothly.

They were safe. For now. Her hand was barely even throbbing anymore, and she could move her fingers again.

Joshua pushed the soccer ball toward her, sweet baby laughter rolling free just as fast. He was such an adorable child, six teeth gleaming as he smiled. His joy just reached out and filled her right up.

"Beautiful boy," Jocelyn Pearson-Stewart said from the open doorway. She'd ditched the hat on her gray-blonde hair. She was one of those women who aged with grace, comfortable in her own skin, free of implants or injections.

Amelia couldn't help but think if she'd met this woman in everyday life, she would have liked her, respected her. She wanted to do that now, but this experience had made her a much more cautious person.

"Thank you, Jocelyn, for taking us in. Truly." Amelia rolled the ball back to Joshua. "You've been so generous."

"It's nothing." She sank into a wide rattan chair, a palm fan in her hand. "In a crisis, we all do what has to be done."

"Once I'm back in the States"—she caught the ball as it rolled to her again—"I would like to reimburse you."

"Don't be ridiculous." Jocelyn fanned her face with slow swipes, but her eyes were sharp, alert. "I don't have any needs."

"All right." Pride was a tricky thing. "Do you have a favorite charity? I'll make a contribution to show my appreciation."

"That's very thoughtful." Jocelyn nodded regally, odd given she was wearing stained khakis and a loose peasant shirt, but somehow, the whole package fit. "Something to do with the homeless would be appreciated. That's first in our minds after a tragedy like this."

The horrible catastrophe a few miles away came roaring back to the forefront of her mind. "Joshua and I are very lucky to be alive."

"You've both been through a lot. I'll be happy to watch this little sweetheart while you sleep."

Amelia looked up fast, then forced a smile through the protective urges flooding her. "Thank you. That's generous, but I can't stand to be apart from him, especially after all we've been through. You understand."

"Of course." Jocelyn pushed to her feet. "I actually came out to let you know we'll be eating supper in about fifteen minutes. Nothing fancy, but it'll be a step above the mangoes and bananas you've probably been eating." She dropped a kiss on top of Joshua's head. "See you inside."

As the woman left, Amelia snagged the fan left behind on the chair and whipped up a breeze for herself. Jocelyn was doing everything right, being completely nice and gracious. Still, Amelia desperately wanted to take Joshua and run somewhere… anywhere else, but her reality was here and now, making the best decisions she could in between earthquakes and snakebites.

The ball bounced off her foot. Joshua giggled, pulling her attention back to him. Where it should be. Where she wanted it to be.

"Hey, there, cutie-pie." She waved the fan in front of his face until he laughed again, tugging the palm from her hands and whacking the ball.

Such a perfect moment. So simple, but pure. Normal, after far too much insanity.

Other than some scratches on his arms and one leg, there were no signs of the hell he'd been through. His arms waved with excitement and energy. His eyes were bright and alert. There was just… happiness. Happiness in spite of an earthquake and kidnapping. In spite of the fact that he'd been in an orphanage last week and his new parents could be dead.

Which left Joshua… where?

She rolled the ball back. With a soft baby chuckle, he flung himself over and into her arms. She hugged him close automatically. Then tighter. He wasn't going anywhere except with her.

And God forbid anyone try to get in her way.

~~~

Jocelyn Pearson-Stewart pulled a knife from the wooden block in her kitchen and whipped the edge across the sharpening stone. Again and again, flipping the blade to get both sides.

She had always trusted her inner circle completely — until she'd been forced to put a bullet through Oliver's head today. Killing Oliver tore at her soul. He was hired muscle, and disposable for the greater good of making sure her organization wouldn't be exposed. She'd been warned he might be a loose cannon, but he'd been efficient. She hated those moments when she was forced into positions that made her feel no better than her drug-dealing family.

Forcing a smile for her dinner guests, she turned to the tile-topped island and a pile of the last fresh vegetables. She set to work chopping a salad—lettuce, cabbage, carrots, celery, radishes. *Chop. Chop.* She monitored each of her "nieces"—not blood relations, since all of hers were about as trustworthy as rats in a cheese shop.

Her nieces—sergeants in her business—carried plates and a serving bowl full of canned spaghetti. Their surprise company sat at the long table, illuminated by the sunset.

Chop. Chop. Everything in her world looked nice, normal, and most importantly, under control.

After Jocelyn had heard the gunshot on the beach, she'd found the trio within minutes, saving her hours of driving around, searching for them, once she'd realized how hugely Oliver had screwed up. She'd taken her time to assess them just beyond the cover of trees and decide if she should kill the two adults outright or if somehow this could be salvaged with no more loss of life. Especially since they appeared to be innocents who were in the wrong place at the wrong time. She preferred not to kill unless absolutely necessary to protect her operation. She was in the business of saving lives, not taking them.

Time. *Chop. Chop.* She just needed time to see how

much they knew and if it could be traced back to her. So she'd called her compound to prepare. They'd been instructed to take the children—eleven of them—to the beach cabana. A skeleton crew was left at the main house, pretending to be her nieces, Courtney and Erin.

Number one rule for them to remember right now? Pretend they had no means of communication with the outside world and limited fuel until she figured out what to do with their unexpected company.

Thanks to her contact at the hospital, she'd learned Amelia was not the boy's mother, but rather an aunt who'd only known him for a few days. It was unclear whether his parents were alive or not. Now she would use this opportunity to decide how much Hugh and Amelia knew, then proceed from there.

She sped—*chop, chop, chop*—through the rest of the vegetables, tossed them in a bowl, and circled round the island toward the carved oak table. Placing the bowl in the middle, she eyed the child sitting on his aunt's lap as she fed him spoonfuls of cut-up spaghetti.

Jocelyn sat at the head of the table. "Sorry about the canned dinner, but our options are limited. We have fuel for the generator, but we're conserving."

Swiping Joshua's mouth with her good hand, Amelia said, "Just sitting at a table feels… unreal. Sardines and crackers would be gourmet."

Courtney grabbed the tongs and served herself salad. "Not a joke. That's up soon on the menu."

Erin gripped her water bottle in a white-knuckled fist. "How bad is it out there, Sergeant? We've heard reports on the radio."

"It's even worse," Hugh said simply, wearing a white

T-shirt with his camo pants. "The devastation is intense. The death toll has risen into the thousands."

Jocelyn forked spaghetti up slowly. "I would like to help, but it sounds dangerous. We have to be careful, three women out here alone. Although I'm thankful to have my nieces for company."

She reached to pat the hands of the two women on either side of her.

Courtney had been married to a well-connected husband who also had a quick temper and quicker right hook. He'd ruptured her spleen and bought his way out of prosecution seven years ago. The auburn-haired soccer mom had opted to leave Atlanta and relocate anonymously with her son to keep him safe. She had been with Jocelyn ever since.

And Erin? The former Oklahoma cheerleader was on the run from her high school sweetheart-turned-stalker. Nearly three years had passed since the underground network had brought her here.

Now they helped her with a deep loyalty since she'd rescued them from certain death. And they had a deep empathy with the other women and children she saved, understanding the way a hellish background could scare some people away from making the right decisions for their future. Courtney and Erin understood that frightened victims of abuse or neglect sometimes needed prompting to do the right things for themselves.

Something Jocelyn hadn't realized until long after she'd made the break from her oppressive background.

She'd married someone her parents approved of, someone in the family business. She'd turned a blind eye to what her drug-running family — what her drug-running *husband*—did to pay for her big house, pretty clothes, and nice vacations. All had seemed idyllic.

Until she'd confronted him about selling to junior high kids. That wasn't right, she'd told him, something she'd realized then from the perspective of a prospective parent. Her husband had beaten the crap out of her. She'd lost her baby girl, and the chance to have any more.

Her brother had killed her husband, but still she'd known she had to get away from the whole business. She'd spent the first thirty-four years of her life trying to make everyone happy, make everyone love her. She'd even married the pasty-faced blue blood everyone expected her to. The nineteen years following his death? She was living her life her way.

She'd left Miami for the vacation home in the Bahamas to take up residence, increase the sugarcane business. And when a friend had sought sanctuary at her house to hide with a child from an abusive husband, Jocelyn had found her way. She used her profits to help other women relocate. And she saved babies, since she hadn't been able to save her own. She funded international adoptions, ones not tied down by red tape, ones that placed children quickly so they didn't languish in already-underfunded, understaffed orphanages.

She used her money to help others. She wasn't like her family, damn it, not anymore.

At the opposite end of the table, Hugh pushed his empty plate aside. "You're right to be careful, to stay here. While we appreciate that you saved us, that was really risky, picking us up."

Hugh Franco was a tough one to read. He'd kept quiet

and observant. She'd only seen a flicker of emotion on his face once. When he'd walked by a guitar hung on the wall, he'd stroked the strings lightly, almost automatically, as if he didn't realize what he'd done.

"You're welcome and you're correct, Sergeant Franco. My husband would have worried about us out here too." Jocelyn twisted her gold wedding band on her finger, worn as a reminder of what *not* to do. "He died in a boating accident nineteen years ago. My life and work here fills my time now. Amelia, will you keep working, now that you have the baby? And what was it that you do?"

"I'm a lawyer." She spooned another bite into Joshua's Cupid's-bow mouth.

Interesting and possibly problematic. Especially considering she already had a solid family lined up for Joshua. She'd heard from Tandi that she'd located the perfect baby for a family that had two adoptions fall through and wanted to go a different route to reduce the emotional trauma of another adoption abruption. With their political connections, she had hopes of easing channels in the future. She'd already used her satellite phone to alert them.

She was torn. Joshua had a caring family now, even if she knew the overly cautious aunt Amelia chose to lie about her connection.

"Your parents must be proud of you. What kind of law do you practice?"

"I'm a county prosecutor." She answered simply, flexing her bandaged hand carefully.

"Good for you, hon." Jocelyn toasted her with a water bottle. "Stand up for what's right. You have to live with yourself at the end of the day. People think I'm all about the money and I have to confess, I appreciate the power this money gives me over my life. But it gives me the power to make choices."

Soldier man cleared his throat. "And speaking of power, when will you have access to more fuel and communication?"

Jocelyn toyed with her dinner knife, spinning it on the table. "I'll know more in the morning. All my vehicles are out delivering supplies, but they should return by the morning." Long enough for her to decide what to do about the two of them. "We can take you to your unit, Sergeant. And Amelia could stay here with the little one. He will be more comfortable here."

Hugh glanced up from his meal. "Or I can put Amelia right on a plane to the States."

"Ah, you're the protective kind. One of those men who takes *alpha* to a whole new level." She twirled her fork in the spaghetti. "But you haven't figured out how tough Amelia is yet, have you?"

He cocked an eyebrow at her, but stayed diplomatically quiet.

"Forgive me for being presumptuous. Let's eat and get some sleep. There's nothing more we can do until the truck returns in the morning." She lifted her water bottle. "Another toast, to having life restored to normal. Now let's clean up before it gets dark."

Once she got her guests settled for the night, she could slip out to check on her charges. The first three would be smuggled out of the country on a departing C-17 tonight as the children of three of her staff. That still left the eleven orphans in the guest house. At least a dozen more would be coming in later tonight in the trucks delivering "supplies," children ranging from newborn to eight years old. Their well-being rested on her getting them out of the country as quickly as possible so she could accommodate the others that would need her. She'd never dealt with placing such large numbers at once.

She'd never been needed more than now.

If these two surprise guests presented a risk to her operation, then she would be forced to deal with them, just as she'd been forced to deal with Oliver. Joshua would be safe either way.

But she could not allow *anyone* to stand in the way of getting these children to safety.

"Do you get the feeling we're staying at the Hotel California?"

Amelia's softly spoken question smoked through Hugh's focus as he checked out their quarters. He turned on his heel toward her. She sat on the bed with Joshua, mosquito netting draped on the thick four-poster.

She leaned forward, snapping her fingers. "Hugh? Don't you agree? Hotel California?"

The Eagles classic echoed around in his brain until his fingers tapped along the top of the rocking chair.

"Uh-huh," he said as he stared outside at the pitch-black nothingness.

No lights, which didn't mean no people, just no power, or others conserving their generators. Even if Amelia and Joshua weren't depleted, trekking back with them in pitch-black wasn't safe. Alone, he could find his way, but alone wasn't an option. He couldn't—he wouldn't—leave them behind here. So they would stay until the morning, resting and recouping, and then head out in the morning.

Could they trust Jocelyn Pearson-Stewart? Hell if he knew.

At least the woman hadn't questioned their request to share a room so he could stay near Amelia and Joshua. The room wasn't large, but it had a private bath and a nook with a crib. Jocelyn had given them everything they could need, including clothes and toiletries, all with perfect explanations for why she had extra on hand, nieces and nephews who wore the same size as him—and Amelia and Joshua.

His fingers strummed along a small chest of drawers with their clothes and a guitar resting on top. Interesting that Jocelyn had picked up on a single moment when he'd admired the guitar on the living-room wall.

She was watching them every bit as closely as he was assessing her and the house. That could be natural behavior for a woman who'd been on her own so long in a remote corner of this island. But what if she had a more ominous reason to be that vigilant?

The bedroom wasn't packed with other furniture, just the rocker and sofa. And of course, that big bed draped with thin mosquito netting.

Amelia cradled the drowsy kid in her arms. "Come on, kiddo, go to sleep, go to sleep so I can wash my hair three times." She cooed softly to the little guy. "And if you don't go to sleep I'm going to start singing, and you do *not* want to hear my voice."

She swung her feet off the mattress and started

walking the floor, patting the baby's back until his head settled on her shoulder. "Looking for anything in particular?"

"Just checking the lay of the land," he said.

He wasn't ready to talk, and right now, finally, there wasn't a rush. They had time. They had tonight, here, together, while she and the boy rested. And while he pulled together a plan for what to do next.

While he hated to lose the breeze, keeping the doors closed and locked was wisest. With her bandaged hand, Amelia cradled the back of Joshua's head as she carried him to the nursery nook Jocelyn had set up. She'd said she had a nephew who came over from Miami with his family to visit sometimes.

A plausible explanation.

And yet "Hotel California" kept playing through his brain.

Shit.

He slumped back against a bedpost, watching Amelia with the baby. She was good with the kid, a natural. Careful not to wake the sleeping little one, she lowered him onto the duck-patterned sheets.

Scratching over the tightness gathering in his chest, he watched the too-sweet mother and child image play out. Joshua squirmed for a couple of seconds before settling on his belly, his sleep deep and exhausted. Amelia rubbed soothing circles along his back even though he'd long ago given up fighting bedtime.

She traced a finger down his nose, then over his perfect shell ear. "On the plane trip here to the Bahamas," she said softly, "I was so envious of my brother and Lisabeth, and now I feel as if I've stolen their future somehow."

Her voice cracked on the last word, yanking him out of his own thoughts. He charged across the floor and pulled her back against his chest. She sniffled and he turned her toward him, gathering her in. Her shoulders shook as she buried her face in his neck. He backed out of the nursery nook, still holding her close. Keeping one arm locked around her, he reached to unhook the ropes holding the curtains back and let them slide together, sealing off Joshua's room for the night.

Looking up, she blinked fast, a tear sliding free. "Aren't you going to offer me platitudes about how my brother and his wife are still alive?"

"You wouldn't believe me and it wouldn't help." He squeezed her shoulders.

"That flight seems forever ago, a world away, like it happened to a whole different person. We've gone through so much together in such a short time." Her fingers moved restlessly over the nape of his neck. "This is all crazy. Sometimes I wonder if all this is even real."

He looked into her eyes and medic training kicked in, telling him Amelia was about to have a meltdown. He skimmed his hands up and down her back, searching for ways to soothe her, calm her, do anything he could to take the tears from her eyes. "It's all real and way too much for one person to deal with."

"No kidding."

"You need to decompress, unwind."

She choked on a laugh. "Are you propositioning me?"

"No... God, no." He stroked back her tangled hair, his mind finally settling on a way he could help her, something productive he could do during this downtime until morning. "Not that I wouldn't welcome the chance to be with you again, but it's clear you need something else from me right now."

"What would that be?"

His fingers forked through her silken blonde—dirty—locks. "I'm going to wash your hair."

Chapter 13

ANTICIPATION CURLING THROUGH HER, AMELIA looked from Hugh to the opaque curtain over the nursery nook, then back again. As he stood by the open bathroom door, his steady gaze met hers and she couldn't miss his intent. She also couldn't ignore the need inside her, the desire to be with him again.

Hugh raised an eyebrow along with a bottle of shampoo. "There's homemade shampoo, and soap with bay geranium and another with orange sage, all locally grown, I'm guessing. Your choice. What do you say?"

"You're offering to wash my hair?" She closed the last few steps between them and flattened her palms to his chest. Her fingers played along the soft cotton of his shirt.

"I live to serve."

She looked up at him through her eyelashes. "Perhaps I can take care of that myself."

"The nozzle on the shower is insanely low and I wouldn't want you to get a backache." He stroked along her scalp in a tempting, teasing preshow. "Thought I would do you a favor, since your hand is bandaged."

"Hmmm… I had such good medical treatment, my hand hardly hurts at all." She trailed her palms down his chest, over his abs, which were so ripped she could count through the six pack. "I could just sit in the tub and let all that amazing well water wash over me until I'm finally, finally clean."

"Yes, you could." He linked his fingers with hers and tugged. "Or you could sit in the tub while I clean every inch of you."

A shiver of possibility tingled through her. "What about Joshua?"

"The kid's asleep behind that curtain. Exhausted. Out for the count." He grazed his mouth over her ear, hot breath and even hotter proposition flowing. "We can leave the bathroom door open to listen for him."

He dispelled concerns with a few sensible words. Sounded perfect. His hands along the back of her neck felt even better than perfect, and exactly what she needed after the hell they'd endured together. Why wasn't she pitching off her clothes and racing for the tub?

Because she was finally feeling safe enough to think about the future. "Are you suggesting we pick up where we left off in the supply closet?"

"Whatever does or doesn't happen in there will be different than the first time. Right now is about us making decisions rather than just reacting." His forehead fell to rest on hers for two deep exhales before he continued, "I'm suggesting that I wash your hair, since you mentioned wanting it cleaned three times over."

Her eyes drifted closed as she savored the gentle pressure soothing away a headache she hadn't even realized was there. "You sure do know how to make a pitch."

"So what'll it be?"

She snuggled closer, hugging him low around his waist. "Orange sage and your magic fingers."

"And just so you know, this *will* be different than that time in the storage closet." He backed her into the retro pink washroom.

"How so?" She chewed her bottom lip as his next step danced her farther, the heat of his hard thigh pressing between her legs.

"This time will be slower."

Goose bumps prickled along her skin. "And?"

"It's not going to be as easy for you to make a speedy exit afterward."

His hands on her hips, he backed her the rest of the way. Her bare feet padded along the raspberry tile until her calves bumped against the old-fashioned claw tub. Moonlight streamed through the skylight in a romantic rosy glow.

Her chin tipped. "I hear you, and I don't have plans to go anywhere. Rather, I wouldn't go anywhere even if I wasn't completely dependent on Jocelyn's hospitality right now."

He dipped his head and she waited, anticipated his kiss, only to have his words caress her ear again. "Do you want me to help you undress?"

"I think I'll take care of my clothes."

"By all means, take your time. I'm not in any hurry." He leaned against the sink, crossing his feet at the ankles.

Grabbing the edge of her shirt, she tugged up, inch by inch. His heated gaze warmed her bared flesh.

Grinning, she toed off her shoes one at a time. He folded his arms over his chest, seemingly a disinterested observer. Except she could see how thickly, how *obviously* aroused he was. So much so, he would have to ditch his own clothes soon.

She shimmied off the pants and stood in just the white cotton underwear and bra. And how ironic that the passion she saw in his eyes far surpassed anything she'd seen with her husband, even when she'd spent a fortune at the lingerie store.

Argh! She cut that train of thought off short. Right now she didn't want to think about her ex-husband. The past needed to stay there for the moment.

She yanked off the bra and scraped down the panties, kicking them all into a heap. Hugh raised an eyebrow at her abruptness. She stepped into the old-fashioned tub, the spray from the low-set shower hitting her. Her stomach muscles contracted at the luxurious spray of water.

"It's warmer than I expected," she said, her nipples beading from the bliss. "Lukewarm, sure, but it's water, water, water, and more water..." She tipped her head back and let the stream hit her on the face.

"Your bandage is getting wet," he cautioned.

"Then you'll just have change it for me afterward." She glanced sideways at him, rivulets trickling down her neck. "Now hurry up and undress so you can warm me."

"Ooh-rah."

"Ooh-rah?"

"Military talk for *oh yeah.*"

Muscles rippling, he tugged his borrowed T-shirt over his head. It was such an everyday thing, taking off a shirt, but this was Hugh, bronzed and defined, with a tattoo across his left pec, some kind of musical scroll that made her curious.

Hugh stood in just khaki pants, low-slung on his hips. Only his pants. And that skylight let in just enough moonlight for her to see him.

The hair on the back of her neck prickled with awareness. His chest and feet were bare and damp from water misting out of the shower. Somehow it was the naked feet that made things feel more intimate. He wasn't just some ripped man of the month, eye candy with his shirt off. He was a man alone with her—a man she happened to have had sex with not too long ago. Back before they'd actually known anything about each other.

She extended her hand for him to join her, waggling her fingers. "Join me."

"Not yet." He shook his head. "I told you. I'm going to wash your hair."

His hands landed on her shoulders, gently easing her down to sit again. Moaning, she sank into the tub and clutched her legs, her forehead resting on her bent knees. Porcelain was cool against her bottom, then warm and warmer as the water gathered... Yeah. This was good.

He grabbed a plastic bottle with a homemade label— "Orange sage" written in calligraphy with a piece of fruit drawn in the corner, signed JPS, Jocelyn Pearson-Stewart. Would a wheeling-dealing criminal make her own soaps and shampoos? She relaxed a little deeper in the tub. The lukewarm beads caressed her like a liquid orgasm tingling over her dry, scraped skin.

Hugh sat on the edge and rubbed the shampoo over her hair, gathering up the ends to work it all into a lather. His fingertips pressed along her temples. He thrust his fingers through her hair and massaged her scalp.

He was thorough, God, he was thorough, with all three shampoos and rinses that tingled from the roots all the way to her toes. The scented suds cascaded down her body, washing away grime, exhaustion, and something else indefinable. Barriers, maybe? Or the will to hold herself together. And in this vulnerable turned-on moment, emotions slammed over her faster than a tidal wave.

A shaking started deep inside her. Was she losing it? After all they'd been through, now she had to unravel? She hadn't even realized her heel was stuck in the drain and the tub had started filling up. Her jaw trembled and she was pretty sure her legs wouldn't hold her. Much longer and she would start crying over, hell, everything.

She turned her head on her knees, letting the spray caress her face. "Really, you should join me."

"Yes, ma'am." Somberly, he shucked his pants and underwear at the same time.

What a time to realize she hadn't seen him completely naked before. The supply closet had been too dim, their encounter too hurried. But she looked him fully over now, taking in the raw strength of him. Not just bulging arms and muscular roped legs, but his ridged stomach, the breadth of his back declared his strength beyond anything she'd ever witnessed. She'd certainly seen all that strength in action, the power that couldn't be gained from just pumping iron in a weight room.

And the tattoos. Plural. While she'd noticed the music scrolled across his chest, she definitely hadn't noticed the green footprints inked on his calf. There was a story there, no doubt.

Except then he stepped into the water and her thoughts scattered. He sat behind her, bringing the water higher around them as his legs stretched out the length of the tub. His thick erection pressed against her back with a promise as large as everything else about the man.

He cupped her shoulders, guiding her to rest against his chest. "Relax…"

Really? *Really?* She was far from relaxed, with tension of another delicious kind seeping through her.

Then his hands slid forward to cup her breasts and she eased down into the water, giving him fuller access to keep caressing, soothing. The lingering soap on his hands made his touch slick against her nipples. The calluses along the pads of his finger rasped an added pleasure with each stroke, touch, plucking. His hands splayed wide, palming her in his broad, possessive hold.

Heat pooled between her legs, a sensation that had more to do with Hugh than the shower. And from the way he throbbed against her spine as she moved, he was enjoying this every bit as much as she was. Although, she could take things even higher by being a more active participant.

Swiping the washrag from the hook and the bottle of homemade liquid soap, she lathered a cloth, eyeing his muscled hairy legs on either side of her. She skimmed her fingers carefully around the angry red scratch on his calf where Oliver had cut him during their struggle in the van.

She dabbed along the angry red line. "Are you sure you're okay?"

"I'm a medic, remember?" He kissed and nipped down her neck and along her shoulder. "I can take care of myself. I'm also military, which means I get a crap ton of immunizations. Think tetanus times twenty."

Her hand slowed along his leg, the water chilling around her. "In case you're injured in the line of duty."

"Uh-huh," he mumbled against her neck.

"And have you been?"

He stroked down from her breasts to her stomach, inching lower still until his fingertips were under the soapy water. And then he reached lower still, dipping one hand between her legs. "Do you really want to talk about that right now?"

Her knees parted and it was her own slickness, her arousal, that smoothed his touch back and forth along her plumped, oversensitive flesh.

"Guess not." She shook her head against his chest, her breath hitching as his fingers dipped lower, lower... just low enough. "Oh... Definitely not."

"Good." His laugh vibrated against her, *through* her. "Me neither."

She tipped her face up toward him just in time to meet his kiss, opening, and what a time to realize there hadn't been the luxury of time for making out. They'd shared life-and-death moments, deep personal secrets, and even mind-blowing sex. But somewhere along the line they'd missed out on this...

Careful not to break the passionate connection, she angled around and onto her knees until she straddled his lap. Water sluiced over the sides again as she settled on top of him. Facing him, she explored him with her hands and the soap. The shower sprayed on her back, sprinkling around onto him and swishing away the suds. She kissed her way over clean manly flesh. And God, she loved the way his pecs twitched under her lips. So she flicked her tongue, tasting, savoring as she worked her way across until the texture changed with his musical tattoo.

Abruptly, he stood, turned the shower off, and scooped her up into his arms in a move so smooth she barely had time to loop her arms around his neck before they reached the bed. His arms bulged with unmistakable strength under her legs and along her back.

He lowered her on the wide mattress, the crocheted

spread enticingly abrasive against her bare skin. The moonlight streamed in through the windows, pouring down his naked body. Hugh stretched out over her, settling on top of her as he captured her mouth. And as much as she was enjoying the make-out session, she was ready for this to move forward.

Her fingernails dug into his flanks and she ached to have him inside her.

"Hurry…" She arched against him, wriggling her hips.

"We're not rushing it this time."

"Can we have fast"—she nipped his chin—"then slow?" She flicked her tongue over the same spot.

"Or slow… and even slower still." He shifted positions with athletic fluidity, lifting her as he slid underneath her.

His erection pressed against her, nudging the tight bundle of nerves that screamed for attention and relief. He rocked his hips, sliding along her but not in her, a sweet torment, so much so, she grabbed his shoulders in a white-knuckled grip to keep from melting over him, off him.

His hands spanned her waist, steadying. "I've got you. Just relax and go with it. Let everything fly loose from the past few days."

He sounded so in control, a part of her wanted to take the control away from him, make him as insanely on fire as he made her.

Faster and faster he guided her until a flush of anticipation prickled over her skin. Her breasts went tighter, her whole body gathering into a knot of need. She rocked more fully against him and reveled in the groan that slipped from between his gritted teeth.

That deeply growled sound of appreciation snapped the tension inside her. Her head flung back, her damp hair grazing her spine. Each brush stimulated and electrified her every heightened nerve, sending her closer and closer to completion. And he watched her as if reading her face, her body, as he stroked her while laving her breast with his tongue, tugging lightly with his teeth.

The bliss built… and built… until… release unfurled inside her. Pleasure shimmered over her nerve endings as if he touched every part of her at once. Her fingers dug into his shoulders, her trembling arms all that kept her from collapsing on top of him. He'd pleasured her to the roots of her hair and still she wanted more of him…

"Protection," she gasped. "We need protection. Or maybe I could—"

"Hold on." His hand left her breast to scoop his survival vest from the bedside table. "I've got this."

She remembered their conversation from the supply closet about a condom being kept in the survival vest, a more compact way to keep a water carrier. He pulled the packet and tossed aside the vest. Hugh sheathed himself before the last glimmer of ecstasy seeped from her. And then he was inside her, wringing fresh spasms of pleasure from her with each forceful thrust. She came again and again, and thank God for his bracing hold that kept her upright, taking him deeper, because she couldn't have stayed upright without him.

Biting her lip, she held back the need to shout. While the curtain shielding the cubby room gave them privacy, they still needed to stay silent or risk waking the sleeping little one… not to mention everyone else in the sprawling stucco home.

Finally, finally, the last spasm wrung through her, leaving her limp. Replete. Her fingers unfurled against his chest and she hadn't even realized she'd scored his skin.

Aftershocks shivered through her until she found herself clutching his shoulders tightly again. She wasn't the scratching, screaming sort—or rather she hadn't been before Hugh.

She slumped against his chest. His whispers flowed hotly against her ear as he thrust faster, his voice more urgent. His arms banded around her as he hissed his own release. Muscles bunched and gathered in his arms, tendons tight in his neck.

Once the last shimmer faded, she considered rolling off him, cuddling, but she couldn't will her body to move. The wind whispered in through the open window, cooling the perspiration on her skin. She drifted in and out of that hazy afterglow.

Her toes skimmed along the tiny green footprints inked on his calf. "What are all the little footprints?"

"It's a work thing." His voice vibrated against her, through her.

"Such as?" she asked, enjoying the normalcy of talking as they lingered in the afterglow.

"During Vietnam, pararescuemen were most often transported in a big-ass helicopter called the Jolly Green Giant," he explained while drawing lazy circles along her back. "Green footprints became our signature tat."

"Big-ass helicopter?" She chuckled. "Is that a technical term?"

"HH-3 and HH-53, actually. But big-ass chopper just paints a more vivid picture." Moonbeams through the windows illuminated his grin.

"I agree." Her fingers skipped along the scratches on his chest. Then from there to the other tattoo, which she suspected held an even deeper story—a staff of musical notes scrolled across his heart. "And this tattoo?"

His hands went still on her back.

"Hugh?"

"Yeah, uh…" He shifted from under her and pulled the sheet over them both. "It's, uh, a riff from my daughter's favorite song."

His answer knocked the wind out of her. She eyed each musical note, a lump settling in her throat. She sagged onto the pillow beside him. No matter how hard they tried, the past was a part of who they were now.

He stroked her wet hair behind her ear. "Aren't you going to ask me what the song is?"

Patting his chest, she shook her head. She couldn't probe that wound.

His hand closed over hers. "It's from a Jimmy Buffett song called 'Little Miss Magic.'"

"I've never heard it, but it sounds…" Sweet? Heartbreaking? "Special."

"Yeah…" He squeezed her fingers once gently, and moved them away to his shoulder.

"We should, uh, sleep." Her cheek rested against his shoulder, slick with water, sweat. The light welts of her scratches pressed against her face with a reminder of how easily she'd lost control. How quickly she became someone different with him, a man who was still deeply locked in grief for his dead family.

Amelia slept like the dead.

Hugh wished he could stare at her all night long, learn more about her. The way a person slept said a lot about them. She curled on her side, knees tucked tight and protectively. He wished she could be more relaxed, free in sleep, but her body told a different story. But then after all she'd been through, he shouldn't be surprised. He just wanted to stick around and learn more, be there when she uncurled with security again.

Her rebandaged hand was stretched out toward him.

He smoothed the overlong night shirt over her hip. He could just make out the word *Bahamas* printed across the front in twisted cartoon palm trees. The scrolled letters made him think of that night back at the hospital when he'd seen Joshua sleeping in her arms, wearing a similar tourist T-shirt.

His eyes slid from Amelia to Joshua.

Shoving to his feet, Hugh tugged on a pair of khakis and walked to the nursery nook. He scratched the old tattoo, just over the tightness around his heart. Stress. He knew the cause, but he hadn't figured out how to get past it.

He reached for the curtain three times before he found the guts to pull it back. Joshua sucked on his fist in his sleep, completely relaxed. As a child should be.

Before Hugh even registered the thought, he held the guitar Jocelyn had left behind. It felt right there. He played a riff and tuned it, the old Lyon & Healy a bit worn around the edges, but with a little tuning, the notes took on a full, warm tone.

His fingers plucked along the strings, not Tilly's tune, but another Buffett song... slow... "Son of a Sailor"... and yeah, he wasn't a sailor and this boy wasn't his son. But the music leveled him out, easing the knot in his chest.

"You're good with him," Amelia said softly from the bed.

His fingers slowed, then stopped. He looked over at Amelia. She sat hugging her knees, her chin resting on her hands.

"Instinct, I guess." He rested the guitar on the ground and spun it. The polished rosewood glinted in the moonlight.

She slid from the bed, her bare feet barely making a sound as she crossed to the nook. She rested her arms on the rail of the white crib. "A kid is a pint-sized package of possibility. Stare at a baby and you start thinking about what he or she will look like down the road, what they'll do with their lives."

"What do you envision when you look at him?"

Amelia sketched a finger over his fine, dark eyebrows. "With his face all scrunched up like that, I can envision him with little round glasses and a calculator."

"Sure, I can see that."

She kissed her fingers, stroked Joshua's forehead, before turning back to Hugh. "I liked what you were playing for him."

"I wouldn't want to wake up the kid."

"He didn't seem disturbed when you played before, or with us talking now."

He stepped away from the nursery nook, swinging the guitar back up to play softly, notes that went through his head when he thought of Amelia. He settled on the edge of the bed.

She sat beside him, her legs tucked up underneath her. "That's lovely, but I don't recognize it."

"Just some chords that went together for the moment." He played on while talking. "My mom was determined to bring up well-rounded sons. So my brother and I didn't just play sports, we took music lessons too. My younger brother picked piano and I chose guitar because I thought guitar would be easier. Wow, was I wrong. She signed me up with a classical instructor." He plucked through a few bars of Bach. "And it was forever before he would let me near the pieces I wanted to play."

"And you wanted to play?"

"Clapton. Hendrix." *Ah, Hendrix.* The songs he would play for Amelia if they had days and days together. His fingers found a classic blues riff, morphing into a Muddy Waters tune. "Hindsight, it was smart of my teacher, since it forced me to practice my fingers raw to get to what I wanted."

"What sports did you play?"

"Football and track, field events. Lots of sitting around after the shot put and discus. I played. The girls gathered around. And then I really practiced, especially for the girl next door."

His fingers moved easily over the fretboard, the changes and notes coming naturally from the training and practice, much like what happened when he was out in the field, on a mission.

She paused, frowned for moment before her blue eyes went wise and wide with realization. She slumped back against a bedpost. "You married the girl with the kitten."

His eyes slid back to Joshua in the crib and nodded once. "I did. And we stared at Tilly's face when she slept, and yes, we talked about what we thought that precious angel-faced baby would do with her life."

Amelia watched him with those piercing eyes, her lawyer eyes that saw so much.

"Tilly colored on walls and defended her rights in the playground sandbox. She was tiny though, born two months prematurely. She spent three weeks in the NICU."

He set the guitar aside, the fear of that time filling him up again even in memories. "I prepared myself to lose her during that time. But once she made it through?" He shook his head. "I let my guard down. I got complacent, let myself dream of the day she would start first grade, ride a bike, get her license... And while I know it's unreasonable to expect I could have saved her, I took her for granted, and that's what I find the hardest to live with."

She rested her hands on his knees and stayed silent, thank God, she stayed silent. There weren't words that could make this any better. Although the pain didn't continue to grow. Her touch didn't make it go away, but at least it didn't increase.

He thought that maybe he could actually explain how they died, something he always left to other people to explain. Staying silent, staying busy had been how he survived for five years.

But right now in the silence with Amelia, he found himself saying "I told you before that my wife and daughter—Marissa and Tilly—died in an airplane crash. A fluke, couldn't even pin it on mechanical error or pilot error. A wind shear forced the airplane down shortly after takeoff. There was no chance for recovery. The jet broke apart."

Looking in her eyes became too much, so he glanced away and stroked the neck of the soundless guitar.

Her hand rested on top of his. "I'm so very sorry. I can't even begin to imagine how painful that must have been, must still be for you."

And she needed to hear the rest. He needed to say it, finally. "It happened when Tilly was in kindergarten, the Christmas after the pet-rock preschool incident. They were going to spend a month with her mother since I was deployed for the holiday. We didn't really have the money for the tickets, but I surprised her anyway. Put the whole thing on a credit card because I felt so damn guilty about being away too much."

"You can't possibly feel responsible." She clasped his hands, dipping her head and forcing him to meet her eyes. "You couldn't have predicted that."

He tapped his temple. "Up here, I know that." He tapped his chest. "Down here has a tough time comprehending. If I'd gotten out of the air force and taken some regular nine-to-five job, she wouldn't have needed to go to her parents. She wouldn't have been so lonely and stressed-out. I wouldn't have missed over half of my daughter's too-short life."

She squeezed his hands harder… Except he realized he was the one holding so tightly. She hadn't winced even when he must have been close to breaking her fingers.

He let go abruptly. The reason for all this pouring out of his guts came to him. He needed to make her realize. "Amelia, I may be good with the kid, but I can't go there again."

Standing, he walked to the French doors, needing to keep his back to her, needing a second to pull his shit together. He needed to get back to the rescue site, back to work. He was technically AWOL by now. But that worried him less than the fact he was needed and not there.

The time in this place had been needed. But now they'd taken care of finding what they needed for Joshua. Amelia would have the night to sleep. In the morning, if there wasn't a vehicle available, they would have to leave.

Leaving them behind… He couldn't do that. Not with the past still dogging his ass.

He stared out into the darkness, with only the moon and a handful of stars. There was no city in the distance, no traffic, not even outbuildings. Only the buzz of bugs, the low hum of the generator, and the whistle of the wind rustling the trees. The branches swayed, moving, parting… revealing…

A light shone in the distance. A light that couldn't be incidental, since it required power, an extra generator. Moreover, the light came from a house on the property. A property Jocelyn Pearson-Stewart had said was empty except for them.

Chapter 14

"I NEED TO DO A WALKABOUT."

Amelia jolted upright in bed, wondering if Hugh had lost his ever-loving mind. "You're leaving?"

"Just scouting," he said, turning away from the French doors. "It may be nothing, but there's a suspicious light out there. If Jocelyn's hiding something, or if she's become a target because she helped us out, then I need to know. Oliver has no doubt managed to untie himself by now and is out there somewhere. We don't know why he targeted Joshua, but I need to be damn sure Oliver doesn't come near either of you again."

He crossed the room in five long steps and checked the lock on the door leading out to the hall. He tugged on his shirt and boots. Their weapons were lined up on the dresser, two guns and a pair of knives. He took one of each for himself. The fact that Jocelyn hadn't asked for them had to be a good sign. Right?

Maybe he was overreacting. It wasn't as if the woman had slipped tranquilizers or poison in the canned spaghetti. But even if their host posed no threat, that didn't mean Joshua was safe.

Her stomach jolted with nerves. "Um, do you think you could make that 'walkabout' really quick? Because I don't have a good feeling about this."

"Very fast. I promise." He dropped a quick kiss on her head, even though from his eyes she could see he'd already slipped away from her. "No one will know I've left. Keep the door locked and the gun close. If you have any problems or concerns, shoot once or scream your head off, and I will be back before you can blink. I swear."

Gnawing her bottom lip, she crossed the nursery nook and peeked behind the curtain, just to reassure herself Joshua was okay. His back rose and fell with each steady breath.

She let the curtain fall back into place and turned to Hugh. "You're certain about going? I can't help but think of those teenage horror movies where we all shouted, 'Don't go in the basement!'"

He paused halfway through putting on his survival vest and grinned. "So which is it we're living in here? Horror movie or 'Hotel California'?"

"Both?"

His smile faded. "This is my job. It's what I'm trained to do, and believe me, I wouldn't leave unless I thought it was absolutely necessary."

"All right then." She picked at the bandage on her hand and tried not to think about the human snakes with a much deadlier bite. "Pass me the damn pistol."

Hugh scooped up the other 9 mm, Oliver's, and placed it into her hands. "Just in case."

"Just in case," she repeated, her fingers closing around the cool steel.

"You are... *amazing*." He cupped the back of her neck, her hair a tangled damp mess around her face. But she looked in his green eyes and saw Hugh. Here and totally with her for this moment before he left.

He kissed her, another of those intense kisses that

was about more than passion. The kind that made her think about what life might be like after they left this nightmare behind. Then his touch slid away.

He opened the balcony doors, stared into the distance for an instant before he stepped out onto the porch and simply disappeared from sight.

His stealthiness gave her a moment's pause. Although she reminded herself that was a good thing. If she didn't see him while looking, then others wouldn't either. Still, butterflies kicked around inside her stomach. Fear. How much longer until she could feel safe again?

A rustling noise from across the room shook her out of her useless self-pity. Joshua shuffled and kicked in his sleep. She had to think of him first.

She yanked on her underwear quickly and pulled the Bahamas T-shirt back over her head. She strapped the gun belt around her waist and slipped into the borrowed khaki pants. If something happened, she needed to be ready to move. The boots Jocelyn had offered were much more practical than the battered and soggy tennis shoes she'd been given at the hospital a couple of days ago.

A cry from the crib carried her across the room. As she tugged aside the curtain, she found Joshua tugging himself up to stand. "B'ana? B'ana?"

He reached for her even as she stretched out her arms for him. A diaper change and song and cuddle later, he still hadn't gone back to sleep. He continued to chant, "B'ana, b'ana."

No doubt, the child was hungry. She tugged her T-shirt over her belt and hitched Joshua onto her other hip. After all he'd been through he would have catching up to do filling his tummy again and why, why, why hadn't she thought to bring snacks from the kitchen?

The thought of leaving the safety of their locked room scared the spit out of her. She did not want to qualify for the too-stupid-to-live starring role in one of those slasher films. She jostled Joshua faster, patting his back and making *shh*, *shh*, *shh* sounds. God forbid he wake up others in the house and have one of them see Hugh running around the compound.

Okay, so the decision not to go downstairs wasn't as clear-cut as she'd thought. She eyed the door, then the yard. Was that Hugh darting behind a tree?

Joshua's bottom lip jutted out with only a second's warning before he started crying again, harder this time, louder. If he kept this up, the whole house would be awake.

Keeping Joshua happy and quiet would be the best way to help buy Hugh more time and safety — which was in the best interests of all three of them.

"Okay, okay, sweetie. We'll go find a banana." And now that she thought about it further, she might as well use this opportunity to store up extra food in case they did need to leave when Hugh got back.

And she definitely needed to make this fast so she could be sure to return before him.

With each step down the worn wood staircase, she pushed back those thoughts of high school horror flicks. Picking her way through the dark didn't exactly help steady her heart rate.

Whispers from the kitchen slithered down the corridor. She hugged Joshua closer and walked softly on. Peering into the kitchen, she found Jocelyn's nieces,

Erin and Courtney, standing at the island with their heads close together as they talked. Courtney's long strawberry blonde hair contrasted with Erin's sleek brown bob. They didn't look much like sisters, about twenty years apart in age. Or were they cousins? Jocelyn hadn't been clear about the relationship between her nieces.

Both still wore the same jeans and T-shirts they'd had on at dinner time, which seemed strange this late at night. But then they could have gotten dressed again as she had, not wanting to wander around in a nightshirt with strangers around.

Their voices weren't loud enough for her to understand what they said. Their quiet could be chalked up to good manners, trying not to disturb others.

Amelia stepped deeper into the kitchen, fears for Hugh making the air too thick to breathe. "Where's Jocelyn?"

They jolted apart sharply. With guilt?

Courtney picked up a bottle of juice off the counter, her ponytail swinging, she moved so quickly. "She's asleep. What do you need?"

Easy enough to answer truthfully. "The baby's having trouble sleeping. I just need to find something for him to eat. Jocelyn wouldn't happen to have any baby food left over from that nephew's kid?"

Erin opened the cupboard doors. "Afraid not. But we have plenty of canned goods. SpaghettiOs? There's some applesauce. Crackers. Help yourself. Aunt Jocelyn has an open-pantry policy."

Courtney extended her arms. "Let me hold the little guy while you look."

"Um, thanks," Amelia clutched him closer, and God

love the little imp, he locked his arms around her neck. "I have to confess I'm clingy with him after all we've been through."

Erin pulled out a jar of applesauce and a pack of crackers. "All you've been through?"

"Right after his adoption"—she thought back to what she'd told Jocelyn when she'd claimed Joshua was hers—"Joshua and I got lost in the earthquake chaos."

Erin tore open the crackers and passed one to Joshua. "You both obviously got out unscathed."

"Thanks to Hugh," Amelia said simply, watching as Courtney played with Joshua's toes until he giggled. "You're really good with him."

Courtney looked up, smiling. "I have a son. He's twenty now, living on his own."

"You must miss him." She picked up the pack of crackers casually to take with her when she walked out of the room. Soon. But first, if she could gather a little more information about the people here and keep them occupied while Hugh was outside...

"I keep busy with work," Courtney said, sipping her juice.

Amelia took an unopened bottle from the counter and tucked it under her arm. "What do you do, Courtney?"

She blinked nervously. "I teach preschool."

In the middle of nowhere? Amelia's eyes flashed to Erin, who quickly busied herself with looking into a cabinet. Something felt off. Wrong. And she wasn't about to let on about the weird vibe she was getting here.

"No wonder you're so good with children." Amelia's inner alarms were clanging away even as she flattered her hostess's niece. These two women were hiding something, and the chances of them revealing it were very slim. She needed to get Joshua back upstairs as quickly as possible.

"I'll just take the crackers upstairs."

Erin passed a bottle to Joshua. "Hey, there's also plenty of juice. Why don't you take another upstairs with you in case he gets fussy again?"

"Thanks, you've all been more than generous." Amelia backed out of the kitchen and raced up the stairs.

Once safely back in her room, she looked around quickly and found it still empty. She reminded herself of Hugh's certainty. He'd managed to keep them alive so far.

She set the juice on the table along with the crackers and lowered Joshua to the floor. Once he was steady on his feet, she rose... and looked at the bottles again. What was it about them that niggled at her? She traced the label...

And as if a bomb had gone off in her brain, she remembered those crates in the back of the van. Surely plenty of people had crates of it stocked in their pantry, especially on a remote island where supplies had to be shipped in and groceries were limited. It had to be coincidental that brand was exactly the same that had been stacked in their kidnappers' van.

Chewing her lip, she watched Joshua playing on the rug in his new borrowed clothes. Another "coincidence" snapping into place. Her T-shirt here with its touristy lettering looked so very close to the one Joshua had been given in the hospital. Again, it had to be a fluke, all these connections between here and the hospital where they'd been kidnapped.

And if it wasn't just a quirk?

Her eyes shot to the balcony doors. Hugh couldn't return fast enough.

If she kept her eyes closed, Lisabeth could almost convince herself she and her husband were in a car, at home, cuddling romantically by the seashore.

In reality, they were still on an earthquake-ravaged island in the Bahamas. Given the shortage of private places to sleep, they had opted to bunk outside the hospital in the back of a church van that no longer ran, thanks to the telephone pole that had landed across the hood. Aiden had pulled out the seat and spread two bedrolls in the back. The windows were tinted. It felt like their own private nirvana.

She rested her head on her husband's shoulder, exhausted, but hungry to hang onto the peaceful moment. God only knew what tomorrow would hold. The smell from the pine air freshener dangling off the rearview mingled with the clean bleach scent of the bedrolls brought in by a humanitarian group today for the volunteer doctors.

Aiden stroked along her arm. "I'm sorry Major McCabe didn't have more reassurance for us."

She'd been so hopeful the air force officer might point them directly to Joshua and Amelia after one of the nurses at the hospital later remembered him visiting. They hadn't found out anything during their first visit to the other hospital, due to all the rotating staff. But information had worked its way back to them later.

There was some comfort in that, even if it didn't

bring all she'd hoped for. "I'm relieved to know Joshua and Amelia have someone so well trained in survival looking out for them."

He turned her head ever so slightly until she had to look him in the eyes. "You do understand they must have been taken? They may not even be al—"

"Shhh…" She placed her hand over his mouth. "There's no need to say it. I'm not delusional. I realize the state of things. But I also know that they made it through the earthquake and that for the first time in days, I have real hope. Let yourself have that too."

He kissed her fingertips. "For you."

His mouth against her skin felt so good and familiar in a world gone insane, she ached for more. Sliding her hand around, she urged him closer until her lips met his.

The bedroll rustled in the dark interior as he shifted to be closer, carefully cradling her face in his palms, deepening the contact.

Deepening the moment.

She needed this, needed her husband. She gripped his surgical scrubs tighter, pulling him to her. Or rather, she tried to, but he held back.

"Aiden, it's dark. We're alone. I need you."

"I need you too," he said, kissing her gently.

So gently she wanted to tug his hair and scream in frustration.

"I won't break, you know."

"What's wrong with wanting to be tender with my wife?"

"Aiden, you're an amazing lover, generous, and you have the most talented surgeon's touch." She kissed each of his long fingers to punctuate her words. "You know I'm a satisfied woman. I just want to make sure you're as happy… As completely happy as I am."

"What makes you think I'm not?"

She squeezed his hands harder, her fingernails digging in half moons. "You are not your father. And you don't have to make up for what he did every single day of your life."

He rolled away from her onto his back. "It's not that simple."

A part of her wanted to kick herself for bringing this up now. Without a doubt, there wasn't a faster way to douse the romance than to mention his father, the man who'd raped his son's fourteen-year-old girlfriend. "You need to find some kind of peace with what happened with your dad. Don't let it steal your joy at finally becoming a parent yourself."

The need to see this settled within him grew more urgent than ever. Aiden was already stressed to the max with the adoption. But hearing she was pregnant as well? She didn't even want to think about his reaction.

And there was no doubt about it. Aiden, her brilliant husband who traveled to the most dangerous parts of the world to help others, was terrified of becoming a father. He'd always told her it was because he had no role model of his own and he refused to shortchange a kid by being a crappy parent. She'd thought she was okay with that. She'd been sure their devotion to helping others would fill her life, and how could they continue with that life's work if they had children to consider?

Except over time, she'd changed her mind. Not about their work. But about being a mother. Aiden had agreed because he loved her. She'd convinced herself

the man she'd seen shed tears over the pain of a tragi-
cally deformed infant in Somalia could surely be a tender, caring father.

She'd held onto that hope, until she'd seen the unmistakable tension in him when he'd held Joshua for
the first time. She felt that same tension radiating from
him now. In that moment, she'd realized things weren't
going to get better. Wishing wasn't going to make this
magically all right. They were so isolated from one another now, despite being twined together in the dark, she
had nothing to lose by telling him the truth.

Rolling to her back, she stared at the stars into the
near pitch-darkness and said, "I'm pregnant."

The inside of the car went so still she could hear her
own heartbeat mix with the distant sounds outside, rescue
vehicles and generators, the occasional shout. But nothing
was as loud as the silence hammering between them.

Aiden still didn't speak, so she went ahead and filled
the void. "Birth control fails sometimes, even for mature
adults who are medical professionals."

"How far along are you?" he asked in a voice so
controlled, she wondered if words could shatter like ice.

"Only a couple of months. With the excitement and
preparations for Joshua, I missed the signs, then chalked it
up to stress. Deluding myself, I guess. But I'm sure now."

A soft *pop*, *pop*, *pop* echoed in the vehicle and she
realized his knuckles were cracking as he opened and
closed his fists.

"Lisabeth, you do realize the adoption counselor ad-
vised giving Joshua time to bond with us before adding
other children?"

She rolled onto her side again, resting a hand on his

heart that—oh God—was beating so damn fast in spite of his calm voice. "Believe me, Aiden, I know and I want Joshua to have the very best we can give him."

"There are very real reasons why they advise against having a baby so close to the adoption." His eyes slid toward her, even if his body wouldn't. "So many abandoned kids or children from troubled backgrounds have bonding issues."

She held his gaze and refused to let him look away. "Do you think it would be better for Joshua to spend another six months in an orphanage in a country devastated by an earthquake? That's if I could even bring myself to give him up, which I *can't*." Her fingers dug into his chest as she gripped more than his shirt. "He's already *mine*, damn it. He is my son every bit as much as this child I'm carrying. To me, there's no difference."

"I wish it were that simple for me."

A chilling possibility iced through her brain. He couldn't possibly be thinking…

"Are you actually suggesting I have an abortion?"

He stayed conspicuously silent.

Her whole world fractured. Her whole understanding of Aiden, of her marriage, twisted like an image in a funhouse mirror. Distorting unrecognizably and making her so dizzy, the ground trembled beneath her more fiercely than it had when the earthquake came.

"Oh, God"—she reached for the door, fumbling with the lock—"I think I'm going to be sick."

Reaching past, he whipped open the handle with one hand and scraped back her hair with the other. She vomited onto the cracked parking lot, heaving until her stomach emptied out and her eyes filled with tears.

Finally, once her gut settled and the world steadied, she straightened, her wrist pressed to her mouth. Aiden silently passed her a water bottle. Her hands shaking, she dug through her duffel and pulled out a cheap plastic toothbrush. Their whole world right now was contained in a bag at their feet. Rinsing and spitting out the door, she wished her mess of a life could be as easily cleaned.

She twisted the cap back on the bottle. "I know that you didn't want to have children because of your father, but I really thought you'd come to peace with that when we decided to adopt."

Adoption had seemed like such a perfect answer, as they'd seen so many children who needed homes—as her own longing for a child grew so big she couldn't contain it anymore without it exploding. And now it appeared to have exploded her marriage.

"Aiden, I'm going to have this baby, even if it means losing you."

She heard him swallow so hard, she worried he might need to open the door fast too.

"Amelia will help us if there are any legal aspects to my already being pregnant." If Amelia and Joshua were even alive, and just the thought of that choked her with panic. She forced steady breaths. "We—or I—will reach out to every resource possible in order to be a good mother to both of these children."

"Children," his voice cracked.

And something cracked inside her at that simple show of emotion from him. She held his face until he looked at her, really looked, and she was sure he could see the sincerity in her eyes. "I understand you have fears—And shhh! Don't go all macho guy on me because I dared say you're afraid of something. I understand you're a geneticist. I realize you have concerns about the kind of... person your father was. But Aiden, just as you're not your dad, neither is this baby."

"But who he is... who he was... It still messed me up inside." He thumped his chest. "I'm not... right. What I said about bonding, about kids with messed-up pasts, I wasn't talking about Joshua." His voice went raspy with emotion. "I was talking about *me*."

Shock radiated all the way to her toes. All this time she'd thought he was afraid to have children for fear they would turn out like his dad, and instead, he was worried he wouldn't be a good enough father? Incomprehensible to her. "Good God, Aiden, you're the most noble man on the planet. You're so damn perfect, it's tough to be married to you sometimes."

He laughed, a harsh and strangled sound. "Thanks for the compliment, but I'm not buying that and neither would the folks on my staff who call me the cold fish."

"Because they don't know you the way I do."

"Do you? Do you really know me?"

Something in his voice warned her he wasn't being flippant. "What am I missing here, Aiden?"

He toyed with a lock of her hair, twining the curl around his finger. "We've never really talked about my father, you and I. Amelia was the one to tell you."

"Because you wanted it that way." She would have welcomed the chance to have him open up to her. She would gladly carry part of the burden for him, although now her throat was closing up from fear of what he would say.

"The night before my father was going to accept the

plea bargain, I confronted him. Not because I doubted he was guilty, but because I just needed some kind of... hell... I don't know what I needed. There wasn't any way to erase having a pedophile for a father."

She rested her head on his shoulder and let him talk, taking each word in and listening to his heart. The nurse in her registered all the signs of extreme stress while the wife in her hurt right along with him.

"He told me what he'd done, not out of guilt but as if he could explain himself, justify it... God..." He ground his teeth audibly.

She didn't dare move or speak for fear any interruption would stop him from saying things he'd bottled up for decades, even holding back from her.

"He said he would rather be dead than go to jail," Aiden continued, his voice returning to the unemotional tones she knew he used to stay in control during his most heartrending cases. "I told him to do it, then. Save his family more pain. Save the state some money. And I gave him a gun."

She must have gasped, because he finally looked at her. His magnificent blue eyes glimmered in the dark with unshed tears. And in those tears she could see the image of the boy he was then, only a teenager himself, disillusioned and betrayed by his father in such a horrible way.

"I went to the gun cabinet, loaded the shotgun, and placed it in front of him on the coffee table. Without saying another word to my father, I walked away. As soon as I closed the door behind me, he pulled the trigger."

She'd known his father killed himself. Amelia had told her about the suicide, about how their father had raped at least four young teenage girls. But no one had said a word about this.

Because no one had known. Until now. And she'd better get talking fast, because if she knew her husband at all, he was about five seconds from shutting down, and she feared if he did, there might not be another window into him again.

Lisabeth slid on top of him and grabbed his face in both hands, urgently this time, firmly. "Listen to me, Aiden Bailey. You were a kid then. And even if you'd been older, you are not responsible for your father's actions. You may be scarred by the things that happened in your past, but you're a good man, a tender man."

"I knew what I was doing. I knew what he would do."

"What he chose to do. And damn him for being a selfish bastard by sharing his suicide wish with his child. What kind of monster does that? If he was crying out for help, there were dozens of other people that made much better sense."

Aiden's brow furrowed and she realized she'd made some traction with that last argument, so she pushed ahead. "I don't even claim to know all the answers or have perfect insights for what you went through with your father. But I do know that you're too good a man to walk away from your own children when they need you. Your children need you. And we'll do whatever it takes to build a strong, healthy family together."

Aiden stayed silent, as she expected. But she couldn't deny she'd hoped for something different, something more from him this time. The stakes were so much higher now, more than ever for the baby inside her and for their child she prayed was still alive. She wanted to

hold him, to comfort him, but past experience told her
that he would shut down, pull away, and block her out.

His jaw went tight, tendons flexing so blatantly in his
neck she could see them even in the dim moonlight. His
eyes squeezed closed, a tear sliding free from each. And
then her reserved husband did the last thing she would
have expected at such an emotional moment.

He reached for her.

Chapter 15

AIDEN PULLED HIS WIFE CLOSE, NEEDING TO ANCHOR himself, needing her. His arms banded around her. Tightly. Tucking her to him as they lay in the back of a crappy van in the middle of an earthquake disaster zone. She held on just as strong, her face buried in his shirt, which was growing damp from her tears.

Coming to the Bahamas, adopting Joshua, already had him in shaky ground—figuratively and literally. And now this latest revelation about a baby on the way as well had knocked his feet out from under him entirely.

For so long, she'd stood quietly by him even though she knew about his father. He'd asked Amelia to tell Lisabeth, since he'd found it easier to keep himself together by never speaking of it.

But no one knew about the night with his father and the shotgun. Until now. He'd carried that around inside him not out of fear, but because he'd thought it would be selfish of him to unload that pain onto someone else in hopes of making himself feel better.

And as he held his wife close, he wrestled with guilt, pain, relief, then more guilt. What kind of ass answered pregnancy news with horror stories from the past? A bout of tenderness shot through him for his wife and what she'd gone through on her own, worrying about how he would handle the news. And God forgive him for even letting her think for a second he would want her to get rid of the baby.

"I'm sorry for how I acted, for what I said and didn't say—"

"Aiden? You don't need to apologize to me." She stroked away his damned tears.

Shit. "Yes, I do. I love you and you deserve a helluva lot better from me."

He scrubbed a wrist over his face and pulled himself together. Or tried to. He didn't have jack shit emotionally to give Lisabeth right now, especially not some touchy-feely reassuring words. He didn't trust himself to speak, since God only knew what else would come pouring out of his mouth against his will now the lid was off. So he held her closer, sprinkled kisses across her forehead, over her eyes, until he brushed her mouth.

She gasped softly. "Are you sure this is what you want right—?"

"Shhh…" He silenced her with another kiss. Undoubtedly, she would have other questions she wanted to ask, and he owed her more than he'd given tonight. "I'm talked out for now. Later, okay? Anything you want to talk about, just later."

"All right," she whispered, her lips moving against his.

Again he kissed her, so damn thankful she understood. Her fingers slid from his arms around to his shoulders, her mouth parting—the kiss, the connection changing. He shoved aside any hesitation. The best realization of all was that now that she was already pregnant, no need to be careful. That freedom sent him into overdrive. He couldn't deny the need to claim her after the things he'd said that drove a wedge between them.

One kittenish sigh from her was the only encouragement he needed to roll to his side, pull her more firmly against him. Passion flamed inside him, sparking in the air until he was almost certain he could see the static energy snapping through the van. She draped her slim, long leg over his, locking him to her. He hadn't been planning on making love when he'd scrounged up this place for them to sleep, away from the crowded tents full of cots. He'd been more concerned with finding a way to ease the dark circles under Lisabeth's exhausted eyes.

But now that she moved against him, tugging at his shirt, he couldn't think of anything except having her. Here. Now. Watching her come again and again, giving them both at least a temporary escape.

The moonlight outside was muted by the tinted windows, but let in enough light for him to see the shadowy writhing of his wife's beautiful body. The spiral curl she could never quite keep out of her eyes. The long elegant neck that made her look like a foreign princess.

And thanks to those darkened windows, the place was private. The doors were locked, and the night was cool enough to be comfortable. The scent of bleach from the fabric bedrolls eased the thick air that made standing outside damn near unbearable.

His hand nowhere near surgeon steady, he tunneled inside her shirt, loose surgical scrubs, until he found the soft curve of her breast. And then touching her wasn't enough anymore. He had to see her. Taste her.

He swept off her top and palmed her breasts with a satisfied growl—cut off as she hooked her finger along the waistband of his pants, the tip of her finger brushing the head of his throbbing hard-on. But he wasn't off balance long. He teased her nipples with his thumb and forefinger. The tightening, her moans, the restless thrash of her head against the bedroll, urged him on as he lowered his face to take the pebbly crest into his mouth.

He knew every inch of her well, but now noticed the changes pregnancy had already begun to bring. The increased fullness—and sensitivity—of her breasts.

Her body moved against him with a sleek familiarity that never failed to turn him inside out. And she was even more stunning now than when he'd met her. A lithe exotic beauty, she'd glided into his life during fall semester, senior year in college. He couldn't even remember which class, because the second he'd seen her, his mind had short-circuited until he was oblivious to anything else around him.

He did remember exactly what she'd worn—gray workout tights and a pink tank top. She'd told him later how she'd overslept that day and come straight to class in the clothes she'd worn pulling an all-nighter study session. But God, the way she'd carried off the most casual clothes with a regal grace... He'd wanted that serenity in his life, wrapped all around him, like now.

And she seemed every bit as eager for this stolen night together, a chance to block out the world and forget everything except each other. He slid down her scrubs, and as she kicked them free of her ankles, he yanked aside his own pants. He lived to lose himself inside her. And there was no way in hell he would risk losing her.

His hands shook all over again. To think how close he'd come to doing just that, to screwing up the life they'd built together. He stroked reverently along her side, over her hip, savoring the warm caramel sheen of her skin.

A purr rising from the back of her throat, she clasped him, stroked the length of him with her thumb gliding over the tip, spreading the dampness for a slicker glide again and again. Arching her hips closer, the soft curls between her legs teased along his erection, invited him to take this further.

Still lying side by side, he pressed inside her, slowly, careful of her pregnancy. And as much as she said she didn't need to be treated like spun glass, he was careful. Treated her with reverence.

She was perfection to him.

The satin heat of her flesh clamped around him as he thrust, drawing him in over and over, closer to her, both physically and in other ways. Something had shifted between them tonight. She'd reached inside of him with her words and her love, touching parts of him that had been walled off for years.

Her leg draped over him, she dug her heel into his ass, locking them tighter together as their hips rocked, as he angled in just the way he knew made her breath hitch. She bit her bottom lip, her head thrown back, enticing him to nip, lick, kiss his way up to her ear. He cupped the back of her head, his fingers combing into her hair as he guided her toward him.

He burned to see her eyes as he moved inside her, wanted her to see how crazy with desire she made him. No walls tonight. No holding back.

Her lashes fluttered open, her brown eyes turning that sensual shade of golden just for him. He didn't know why she'd stayed with him, why she still held strong to him, but she did. The way she loved him humbled him and lifted him at the same time. In her elegant, serene way, she demanded he give all—in life and in bed.

Like now.

And as he watched her expression, the love he saw there rocketed through him, knocking him over the edge and into a shattering release. And damn it all, he wouldn't go there alone, refused to finish without her, because nothing in his life meant a thing without Lisabeth.

He pumped through his release, driving her, urging her to—Her blissful cry flowed over his ears, her arms and legs spasming around him as she found her release. He took her mouth and her sighs, whispering her name as she cried out his until the last ripple shuddered through him.

Lisabeth rolled to her back, her arm flung over her face as she panted. Her body shivered in a way he knew meant even the brush of air was almost too much for her skin in the aftermath of a powerful orgasm.

Words… he needed to find some, preferably coherent ones to say how much she meant to him. But his brain wouldn't engage. His senses were still immersed in the scent of their mingled sweat, the feel of her skin against his, the musical tone of his name from her lips.

He was a man completely in love with a wife he wasn't sure he deserved. And there weren't words enough to express that.

He slipped his hands over her stomach, still flat, but where she carried his baby. Their baby. Although just the thought scared the hell out of him, the reality settled a little more firmly in his brain. It would take him time to adjust thoughts and feelings he'd held for decades.

But for Lisabeth, for both of their children, he was determined to make it work. He just prayed he would still have that chance to prove himself with Joshua.

Hugh counted at least eleven children inside the beach cottage.

Crouched about fifty yards away, he'd been watching the sleeping children and the four awake adults in the well-lit hut for the past ten minutes. The two-room concrete structure was packed to the gills. Given how close in age they all were and how different they looked, he was certain they weren't siblings in some bizarre TV reality show. He briefly considered the Good Samaritan angle, but why not have some of them stay in the main house, where it was roomier?

Why hide them? Why not mention it to him or to Amelia? And why pretend not to know what's going on beyond the gates, when every damn one of those guards carried a two-way radio that appeared to be in full working order?

After what had happened to Joshua at the hospital and what he'd heard in the van, he knew he was looking at some kind of illegal adoption ring. And apparently he'd found the heart of it right here, on Jocelyn's land.

Once he'd slipped out of the house, he'd done a recon run around the property and spotted security cameras beyond what a simple sugarcane plantation should need. He wasn't sure if they were operational after the power outages, but just to be sure he avoided them anyway. At least he hoped he'd steered clear of them all.

The three armed guards, however, had been in full

working order with firepower to spare. He'd evaded them easily enough alone. Doing so later with Amelia and Joshua? That would be tricky, to say the least.

He'd located two trucks, another van similar to Oliver's, and an additional Jeep. He'd also located lines of gas cans, all full.

Stealing a ride would be easy. Getting Amelia and Joshua into that ride and out of the fenced-in compound without being spotted would be a bit more complicated. He couldn't afford to waste another second. Just thinking of how they were alone in that house threatened to steal his focus.

Backing away without a sound, he picked his way through the compound. The darkness was his friend as he moved from building to building, tree to tree, avoiding the cameras—not to mention the three guards Jocelyn had failed to mention.

As much as he burned to race into the main house and haul Amelia and Joshua out, he couldn't afford to rush. He couldn't risk detection, leaving them vulnerable here. One small corner of the house was hidden from camera angles by an overgrown tree someone had failed to trim. The one vulnerable vantage point to breach the property. He'd left from that side and now it was his way back in.

Gripping a ridge on the corner post, he hefted himself. Muscles strained as he pulled himself up, up, up higher still until he swung his legs up to…

Got it.

The toe of his boot hooked on the ledge of the second floor. He inched his finger along until he grabbed a porch rail and vaulted over. He landed in a cat's crouch. Waiting. Not moving until he was sure no one stirred.

Then step by step, he made his way back to doors leading into his room with Amelia. Through the open curtain he could see her moving around the room, jostling Joshua on her hip. And she appeared to be alone. The nursery-nook curtain was open, as was the bathroom door. No one hiding.

He breathed a sigh of relief and eased the door open.

"Amelia," he called softly, just to be sure she didn't freak and shoot him.

"Hugh," she whispered.

"We have to leave," he said at the same time as Amelia held up a bottle of juice.

"Have you seen this? Look at the label." She spoke fast, her hand shaking. "It's the same kind that was in the van. And the T-shirts—Wait." She stopped short. "You already know we have to leave?"

"Gather everything you can carry, food, baby supplies, anything," he said, glad she and the kid were already dressed. "There's a second house on this property, full of babies in cribs, and given what happened with Oliver—It's time to go. Now."

She yanked a pillowcase off and began stuffing it full of crackers, bottled juice, diapers, anything she could lay her hands on. "And how are we going to get out of here?"

Hugh tucked the spare knife into his gun belt and took Joshua from her arms. "We're going to steal a Jeep and ram the gate."

Chapter 16

SCALING DOWN A PORCH COLUMN WAS A HELLUVA LOT tougher than it looked. But then Amelia had never claimed to be superhero material. She preferred to fight her battles in the courtroom, with her words as her weapons.

All those litigation skills weren't going to do her much good right now as she struggled to find a toehold on her way down from the second-story balcony, which was actually more like a third story, if she counted the fact that the house was built on stilts. Hugh had his hands full with Joshua. Asking for his help would be—

Hugh planted a palm on her butt. How he'd managed to scale partway up again with a baby in his vest and a hand free to help her, she didn't know. But the broad steady support gave her just the help she needed to regain her grip and footing.

His deep bass voice drifted up to her softly. "Slow and easy. Slow and easy."

Then his hand was gone and she was on her own again. She could—she *would*—do this. An inch at a time, she shimmied the rest of the way down until the earth was close enough for her to let go.

Ooof. The ground was harder than she'd expected. Her bottom would be bruised for sure, but at least she was in one piece.

Hugh extended a hand and she was on her feet again. She clasped his fingers for a reassuring second before nodding. With her eyes, she let him know. *Ready as I'll ever be.*

He carried Joshua in the front of his vest now, not as easy to maneuver, but he'd said he would have more latitude in keeping Joshua quiet if need be. Although God help them if Joshua decided to cry or scream. It wasn't as if they could explain things to the little one in a way he could understand.

Skirting around trees and darting from cover to cover felt damn creepy. No lights. No sense of direction. And no way to see what she might be stepping on next.

Shuddering, she kept as close to Hugh's back as possible, trusting that wherever he put his feet would be safe. Night creatures scuttled through the undergrowth. The trees rustled overhead, the wind whistling until she could have sworn it all came together to play some kind of tune through the branches.

And then she realized Hugh was humming ever so softly to Joshua. She couldn't recognize the song, it was so low, nearly imperceptible, but obviously enough to keep Joshua content for the moment, thank God.

Hugh had told her it was only a quarter mile to where they needed to go, but the distance felt like an eternity, when there were armed guards posted. Not to mention the security cameras. Hugh had said he hadn't been able to determine if they were running off generator power or not. But it was best to assume the cameras were operational.

Eyes locked on Hugh's broad back, she followed and listened, taking some reassurance of her own from the soft crooning of his voice. Until it stopped. His body tensed into a block of stock-still ice. She froze in her tracks as well.

Footsteps sounded, snapping sticks and scrunching leaves. She stayed immobile, as Hugh did, even though the urge to run pulsed so heavily through her veins, her vision blurred. *Keep eyes averted*, she reminded herself. No matter how much she wanted to look around and see where the threat was coming from, she was better off not looking at the person. There was truth to the notion that someone could feel a person's eyes on them.

The footsteps halted.

Her heart sped up so fast and loud, she could have sworn it echoed in the trees, and oh God, what if Joshua cried now? She forced herself to breathe steadily, in and out, to keep from fainting.

The guard started walking again, the crunch of footsteps growing fainter, farther away, then gone altogether. She grabbed Hugh's vest to keep from sinking weak-kneed to the ground. He reached back to pat her hand before easing forward, humming again.

Three trees later, the barn came into view, with a couple of vehicles parking alongside, including Jocelyn's. It even had the angel dangling from the rearview mirror.

Hugh dipped his head toward her. "The vans in the barn look to be in better shape, but I'm concerned there may be alarms. I think we should hedge our bets and take one of these."

"Jocelyn's?" she whispered.

"Yeah, my thought too. At least we know it works."

And the fact that Jocelyn had chosen it when there were clearly sleeker options available doused her with a fresh slap of clammy fear. Why would she hide her assets and mislead them about her ability to travel freely?

Hugh passed over Joshua. "Take the kid and duck

down between the barn and the Jeep while I fill it up with one of the gas cans."

Tucking Joshua close, she crouched out of sight while she listened for Hugh—and didn't hear him. God, the man had ghostly footsteps. She drank in the comfort of his training in big heaping gulps of air.

The scent of gasoline drifted by and she realized he must already be filling the tank. Soon, they would be racing away. Stealing a car. Deliberately ramming a gate. Then driving off on a hope and a prayer that they wouldn't run into more trouble before they reached a civilization that was currently far from civilized.

But at least she wasn't stuck underneath a hotel building anymore.

Hysteria built and she fought back the urge to laugh. Giggles bubbled up inside her until her eyes burned with tears. It had to be from the fuel's fumes, because she refused to break down. She would hold up her end until she dropped. No quitting.

Hugh materialized beside her, so silent she hadn't heard him approach. "You and Joshua sit in back. Buckle both of you in, then drape yourself over him to keep both of you down and out of the line of fire. Especially when we ram the gate. It's not the perfect scenario for securing him, but it's the best we can do without an infant seat."

"Too bad her 'nephew' didn't leave one of those lying around where we could see it." Because from what Hugh had told her he'd discovered in that cottage, there had to be plenty of kiddy gear stashed all over this place to accommodate their baby-smuggling ring.

As a lawyer, she shuddered to think of the horror

those children could land into, their identities taken off
the grid and thrust into a world where no one was ac-
countable for their well-being. Child prostitution and
slave traffickers preyed on even well-meaning organizations that flew under the radar. The legal system and
channels weren't perfect, but they were a damn sight
better than anything going on here. What a realization that such horror could be happening here, in this
oceanside hideaway scented with frangipani and night-
blooming jasmine.

She snapped the seat belt over Joshua's lap, tightening the strap over his frighteningly vulnerable body.
Then buckled herself in as well, securing the pillowcase full of baby supplies under the seat in front of her.
While she understood Hugh's reasoning and knew that
the force of ramming the gate could wrench Joshua from
her arms, she still ached to hold him.

The Jeep tilted as Hugh settled behind the wheel. He
cranked the engine… and it caught. First try. Jocelyn's
place might not be brand-spanking-new looking, but
apparently she kept her machinery in good mechanical
condition. The engine hummed as smoothly as Hugh's
voice had.

Easing the vehicle forward, he drove slowly at first,
no revving or grinding gears or spitting rocks. He increased the speed at a steady pace so the noise almost
seemed to blend with the jungle night sounds.

He steered clear of the main house as long as possible, but even from her low vantage point, Amelia could
see that eventually they would have to drive within sight
of Jocelyn's home. Going straight to the beach wasn't
an option, as Hugh had told her the entire place was

fenced in. The front gate was the weakest vantage point for breaking out.

A car backfired in the distance. Then again.

Hugh cursed and nailed the gas.

Not a car backfiring, she realized. Someone was shooting at them. The windshield shattered. An inch farther to the left and the bullet would have hit Hugh.

She locked her arms tighter around Joshua. He squealed in protest, but keeping him quiet was pretty much a moot point now. Or would that be mute? God, there she went getting hysterical again.

"Brace yourself," Hugh said. "We're going through the gate."

"Can you give me a three count?"

"One. Two—"

Bang!

The Jeep jolted on impact, slamming her side back against the seat. She held her breath for a suspended second as he revved the gas and she wondered if they would make it—

Through.

Hugh ducked as parts of the shattered gate flew over the Jeep. They'd made it through. They had wheels and a tank full of gas.

"You two okay back there?"

"We're fine. We're completely okay? You?"

"I'm good," he answered, his words clipped. "Stay down though."

Her elation faded as she heard the sound of sirens, alarms from the compound. How soon before some of those other cars came after them, driven by people who knew the lay of the land better?

The Jeep jostled over the rough terrain, branches smacking the roll bars as they sped through the jungle. She had no idea how long he drove like a bat out of hell, but she kept herself draped over Joshua as he whimpered, protecting him, talking softly to him, even singing in her awful off-key voice. She thought she heard another car in the distance, the sound seeming louder. Maybe?

"Hugh—" she shouted.

"Roger," he barked back. "I got 'em in the rear-view mirror."

"What're we going to do?" Fear crushed her chest as she stared into Joshua's eyes. What impossible decisions a parent had to make to protect a child. This had to be a special hell for Hugh, after losing his wife and daughter. How could his big generous heart cope if anything were to happen to them now, despite his superhuman efforts?

"They're in vans. I'm heading toward the beach. It's more open, more exposed, but they won't have the same traction we will."

She stared at the back of his vulnerable head and thought about the gunfire earlier. "If you're sure."

"I'm sure it's our best odds."

"Okay, then." Like they really had a choice at this point.

He half stood in his seat, twisting to fire his gun at whoever followed them. Damn it, she could do that part.

"Give me the gun," she yelled. "I'll shoot. You drive." She would be in a better position for coverage and he would be a much safer driver.

He passed the gun over the seat. Thank God he saw the wisdom of her judgment and hadn't wasted time arguing. She eased up in the seat, aimed the gun at the van's radiator, and squeezed off a shot. The gun's recoil knocked her against Hugh's seat.

"You okay?" he shouted.

"Just fine." And better prepared now.

Pop. Pop. She squeezed off two more shots that made her ears ring. The first van spun out as the engine spewed smoke. A second van roared around, taking the lead as the other stopped altogether.

Hugh steered around a tree. "Good job evening up the odds. Need you to hunker back down, though, and hold on tight. This next part's gonna be rough."

Like the rest wasn't? She passed the gun back to Hugh.

Amelia ducked behind the seat again, staring at her feet bouncing on the floor from the rough ride. She locked her arms and gave Joshua a kiss on his forehead.

The Jeep raced out of the jungle, going airborne for an instant before landing in the muddy sand. Her teeth slammed together. Blood filled her mouth and she realized she'd bitten her tongue. Joshua started crying in earnest, his fearful wails tearing at her heart. She checked him over with her hands as best she could and he didn't appear hurt. Just terrified.

"I'm right there with you, sweetie," she whispered in his ear. "Hang in there."

Rear tires fishtailed, spewing sand as the Jeep worked to catch traction. Just when she'd begun to fear they were going to bog down... the four-wheel drive launched forward smoothly, flying across the sand like a sailboat over smooth waters.

She looked up at Hugh again in the rearview mirror, her mouth so dry she could barely form words. "Update? Please?"

Smiling, he winked back at her. "Other van's stuck in the sand. How's the kiddo?"

"Vocal." She eased up and checked every inch, kissing each precious finger and toe to be sure. "Pissed off, but completely unscathed."

"Nice work. In about ten miles we should be home free."

"Home free," she repeated, some of the relief seeping away since they were headed right back to the middle of a lawless city devastated by an earthquake.

Holding an IV bag, Liam raced alongside the litter carrying their latest rescue toward the open cargo plane of the C-17 preparing for takeoff on the crappy small runway—basically a long strip of dirt.

"Hold, hold," Liam shouted, as he jogged beside the victim he'd just freed from under a collapsed college building. "We've got one more. Critical. Head trauma and double amputee. Gotta get him out."

A three-ship of cargo planes roared overhead. Aircraft had been flying in and out at a regular clip, transporting humanitarian relief from the U.S., Canada, Brazil, Italy, and Cuba, and the list of countries grew by the day. More than twenty so far. Ports were beginning to fill with boats and ships as well. Some supplies, especially early on, were parachuted in.

The loadmaster in the C-17 raised a thumbs-up and waived them forward. "Haul ass, sir. We've gotta clear out."

There wasn't much parking space alongside the already-short runway, so as soon as supplies, troops, and relief workers were unloaded, the cargo hold was filled with departing injured and they were quickly airborne again. The C-17 was the world's premier cargo craft for delivering troops and supplies anywhere, anytime, able to land on dirt runways as short as thirty-five hundred feet and as narrow as ninety feet.

Communication was improving with more reliable cell phone reception, satellite phones, and radios. And still he hadn't heard anything more about Hugh Franco, the woman, and the child. Meeting the woman's family—Dr. Aiden Bailey and his wife, Lisabeth—hadn't brought any new information on the whereabouts of the missing trio. The Baileys had looked at him with such damn hopeful eyes, as if he could deliver their loved ones back to them. It had been hard as hell to tell them he knew nothing more than they did. Just that Hugh, Amelia, and the baby, Joshua, had last been seen together at the field hospital set up in a school.

Never had keeping his focus sharp been more difficult than now. One foot in front of the other, he kept charging ahead because he couldn't afford to deal with the emotional fallout until afterward.

His combat boots clanked along the load ramp as they passed over the patient. Turning, he almost slammed into a vaguely familiar military nurse handing off an infant to a refugee in the plane.

"Excuse me, ma'am," he said, angling past, checking her name tag, then remembering.

"No problem, sir," answered Lieutenant Gable, the nurse from the school/hospital.

Another reminder of how he'd screwed up in not keeping a closer eye on Franco. He'd known the guy was more on edge than ever and hadn't pulled him out of the field. Liam had weighed the risk to Franco against all the lives in danger here… and had chosen wrong.

After nearly twenty years of service, maybe it was time for him to call it quits. Liam had enlisted in the army at eighteen, become an Airborne Ranger medic, gotten his college degree, then switched service branches to become a PJ. Maybe his body was just past the point of being able to do this kind of work. Shit, it sucked getting old, and why the hell did nearing forty have to be considered old?

He tipped his head skyward, where life was crisper, cleaner, with only the clear blue, some puffy clouds and airplanes. He could almost feel the rush of plummeting out of the craft, arms wide as he hugged the air in free fall.

Too old?

Fuck that.

Stepping away from the C-17 as the load ramp raised, he scrubbed a hand over his bleary eyes, his hand coming back full of grime and sweat. He needed to haul ass over to the hooch to shower and sleep. But he was still too restless from the lack of information, too wired from the last rescue mission. He grabbed two water bottles from a relief station, drinking one in a long continuous swallow and then pouring the other over his head.

Since he knew from experience that sleep wasn't going to come his way anytime soon, he let his feet carry him past his quarters to the cottage next door. Seeking out Rachel Flores was becoming more and more of a habit over the past days. They were pretty much on the same shift…

An excuse.

He hadn't met a woman in a long time who intrigued him as much as she did. Who saw right through his bullshit. And who could stand toe-to-toe with him when life sucked ass at the worst level possible.

He knocked on the door, his knuckles raw and scabbed over even after wearing protective gloves on the job this week. Maybe he should go back to his place and clean up first—and maybe he should leave her alone to sleep.

Just as he started to turn, the door opened. He recognized one of the other dog handlers from her task-force team, a guy wearing a T-shirt with a fire department logo.

Before Liam could speak, the guy had already turned around to yell, "Rachel, it's your air force buddy."

So he'd become that obvious hanging around here, had he?

The fire department dude backed out of sight, making way for Rachel. She hovered in the doorway, wearing a fresh pair of khakis and a white tank top that fit her so damn well. She had two hairpins in the corner of her mouth, as she was in the process of pinning her long dark hair into a loose bundle on top of her head.

"Wanna take a walk?" he asked, already caring too much about her answer. "I know this great little joint that's giving away free orange juice in the half-pint cartons. It's pretty exclusive. I don't want to brag or anything, but I'm pretty sure I can get us in."

She studied him through narrowed eyes, assessing and obviously picking up on how much the crappy day weighed on him, because she nodded.

"Sure." She plucked the two bobby pins out of her

mouth and stuck them into her gathered-up hair. "Disco needs to crash for a while before we can go back out in the field."

Liam eased back as Rachel stepped alongside him. They couldn't walk far safely, but the two-block area where they were staying had become fairly secure even if the wind still carried the mourning voices of survivors calling out for lost family members.

He cupped her elbow and steered her around a parked backhoe. "Have you had lunch yet?"

While her stride was long and confident, she took two steps for every one of his. Her personality packed such a punch, he hadn't realized how short she was until now. Probably not more than five foot three.

"Is it lunchtime already? I've lost track of my days and nights." She looked up at him with serious brown eyes. "I'm sorry that couple didn't have more information about your friends. They seemed relieved to know the woman and baby were with a trained serviceman."

But for them to disappear? Someone had to have taken them or mugged them or God only knew what else, and Liam's gut churned at the endless possibilities—none of them good.

Even someone as highly trained as Hugh could only fight off so many people at once. To think they could have been killed for a canteen of fresh water? A pair of boots? He'd seen that and far worse, when individuals became desperate.

"If that couple wants to feel better because Hugh has some specialty skills, then I'm sure not going to burst their hopeful bubble. Life will do that soon enough."

"Sadly, you're all too correct."

They walked together in a strange kind of companionable silence, given the world around them. The landscape had changed somewhat. Less dust. More volunteers erected temporary housing, hammers and saws echoing while dump trucks hauled away debris from fallen structures. Engineers worked on better water and sewage removal. Red Cross workers were everywhere.

The only thing that remained the same? The appalling scent of decaying bodies still drifting out of the remaining rubble.

What a strange feeling to hang out with a woman who actually understood his job, who had experienced a good bit of the same kinds of hell he'd seen. So, she would probably understand his need to leave it behind for a few minutes before they had to plunge themselves into the thick of it all over again.

"So, ready for our hot date?"

"Date? Is that what we're doing here? I think not."

"Didn't anyone tell you that you want to sleep with me? I thought you already knew."

She choked on a laugh. "Wow, that was corny. Really corny."

"I thought you could use a smile."

"You're right, and thanks."

"Happy to oblige, again and again." He slid an arm around her shoulders. "So stop, drop, and roll, baby, because you're so hot you're on fire."

The scent of her freshly washed hair as she walked beside him chased away the rest of the world.

She groaned, but still kept on chuckling. "You're bad."

"No way. I'm entering the priesthood tomorrow. Wanna join me for one last sin?"

Her laughter turned to giggles until she hiccupped. "Okay, okay, enough already."

"I figure if I make you smile enough you'll sleep with me."

She swatted his stomach. "You're so sensitive it's a wonder all those women divorced you."

Ouch. That one stung a little. But he liked the way she didn't pull punches. And no, he wasn't known for his sensitivity. But he was known for his ability to make a person smile in the middle of a crisis.

He stopped at the Red Cross supply station, holding up two fingers for the worker dispensing boxed lunches, complete with the little half-pint cartons of orange juice. Liam took the two stacked meals and looked at the crumbled street around them. The chaos of a few days ago had shifted into a steady grind of tackling a cleanup that would easily take years.

There weren't exactly a lot of places to hang out by the beach and eat, so he steered her back toward their cottages. One of the porches would be as good a place as any to park it for now.

"Rachel, to be honest, I don't get the vibe from you that you're looking for sensitive."

"Hmmm… True enough, I guess. Comes from the way I was brought up. Around my house there was lots of love but no coddling. My mother was an ACO— animal control officer. Like those shows you see on the animal channel."

"Was? What does she do now?" He fell into the ease of their conversation much as they fell into sync walking side by side.

"Nothing. She's dead now." She looked at him

quickly, then away. "She was breaking up a dog-fighting ring. The owner didn't take kindly to having thousands of dollars' worth of assets seized."

Holy crap. "He didn't turn his dogs on—"

"No! Heaven, no." She sighed heavily, rubbing her bare arms. "The man was the killer animal—not the canines. The bastard came after my mother with an aluminum baseball bat and cracked her skull. She never regained consciousness."

She went silent with the kind of thick quiet that couldn't be broken with a smart-ass comment, the kind of pause that was best to wait out while she put her thoughts together on what she wanted to say next.

"I got my love of animals from my mom, but I can't do what she did." Rachel kicked a chunk of concrete ahead with the toe of her boot. "All of those people who hurt animals? I would go after them with a baseball bat myself."

The fire in her voice made it clear she would have done just that, for the dogs and for her mother. Rachel Flores was the kind of woman who brought everything to the table in life. No wonder he'd missed the fact she was a foot shorter than him. Her personality, her force of will, was off the charts.

"God, woman, I think I love you."

She snorted, rolled her eyes, and pretty much did everything to punt him in the ego except laugh at the size of his Johnson. "Okay, that line was your funniest one yet."

"You don't think I'm serious." He looked forward to proving it.

"Not for a minute." She shook her head and the

topknot went a little loose and lopsided. "You can't really be trying that high school move to get in my pants? 'I love you, baby, really, I do.'"

"Who says I was trying to get into your pants? Okay, wait. I did say that. Getting you to sleep with me is way high up on my list of personal goals, but I can wait. Something tells me you'll be more than worth the extra time and effort."

She clapped a hand to her chest with the melodrama of a seasoned soap star. "You're willing to wait to have sex with me? I'm devastated. I may never recover from the crushing disappointment that I won't get to have you as my naked love slave tonight after work. Because heaven knows, there's nothing more romantic than an earthquake zone."

He stopped in front of the cottage where her team was staying. "You know you're only making me love you more when you get all feisty like that. Oh, and in case you were wondering, when I fall in love, I most definitely want to have sex. Love? Big-time aphrodisiac in my book."

He'd stunned her silent. She was watching him with those sexy smoky eyes of hers as if trying to figure out how much of his bullshit to believe.

"The love thing, though? You should probably take it with a grain of salt, since I've been married three times and I was just responding to your sparkling wit." Liam sat on the steps, boxed meals resting on his knee as he patted the spot next to him for her to sit. "Would you like the rice and beans? Or the rice and beans?"

"Uh, guess I'll have the beans and rice." She sank slowly to sit beside him, taking the supper from his hand

and flipping open the lid. "Seriously, I don't want you to get any ideas about us as a couple."

"Are we sitting on the same step?" He pinched open the carton of juice. "Because I thought we kissed the other day, and I distinctly remember there being tongue involved."

"You're right." She grinned. "And you're actually funny. I mean it. But I'm not in the market for a relationship. I already told you why. And yes, I do date. I'm not a nun, but I just got out of a really messy breakup—"

"Sweetheart, I'm the king of messy breakups. Just read my divorce decrees. All three of them." He toyed with a loose strand of her hair, sliding it behind her ear. "You made it clear you're not interested in more."

"I'm afraid that's the way it's got to be," she answered, her voice going a little husky.

"Fair enough. I can honor that." He pulled his hand away, stroking her shoulder along the way. "You're smart to know I'm a bad risk at the white-picket-fence gig."

She swayed into his touch, only a little but enough, her tongue dampening her top lip. "Uh-huh."

His fingers trailed down the length of her arm, but his eyes never left hers. "However, if you want a man who will try his damnedest to give you a mind-blowing orgasm, then I'm your guy."

Blinking once, slowly, she swallowed hard and backed away, scooting over a couple of inches on the step. "How could I turn down such a *romantic* offer?"

Chuckling, he reached into the boxed meal for the wrapped plastic cutlery. "Now I'm the one who's crushed."

"Somehow I think you'll survive. You've had quite a bit of practice after all," she said dryly.

"Your sympathy for my heartbreak is overwhelming."

"If you want warm and fuzzy consolation, go talk to someone like that grandmotherly looking lady over there." She pointed to a woman with silvery blonde hair, a baby on her hip as she talked to one of the relief workers.

Liam tore open the prepacked beans and rice, dipping in his spork. Three bites later, he said, "Hey, thanks."

She paused midbite. "For what?"

"For taking my mind off the shit going on around here." He looked down into the mix of beans and rice, stirring slowly. "I needed that today."

"You're welcome." She waited until he looked up and then she smiled, really smiled. No teasing. Just honest compassion. "There's so much pain to go around here, it feels good to be able to help."

And it did help, her voice, her smile, just looking in her deep brown eyes. So he kept right on doing that for as long as she would stare back in their intriguingly comfortable silence. A realization sunk in that for all their sexual banter, regardless of how incredibly attracted he was to her, he needed to keep this relationship on a smart level. He was developing a friendship with this woman, something he'd never had before. Sure enough, if he let sex or love into the mix, he would screw the whole thing up. He always had and had come to accept he always would.

A sharp movement out of the corner of his eye tugged at his attention and he looked away. A security-force guy wearing another country's uniform charged up the stairs to the next cottage—where he and his team were bunking—and pounded on the door.

Setting aside his boxed meal, Liam stood, his brow furrowing. "Can I help you?"

The security cop turned toward him. "Major William McCabe," he said with a thick accent to match his Brazilian uniform. "I am looking for Major William McCabe."

"That would be me." He started down the steps, his gut twisting as all the concerns he'd managed to put aside for a half hour came rushing back. "I'm Major William—Liam—McCabe."

"*Graças a Deus*, thank God, a security force on the beach picked up three people—a man, a woman, and a child." The young serviceman met him on the buckled road between the two buildings.

Liam forced his steps to stay steady as he listened and hoped.

"They said they are looking for you, sir. You are missing one of your soldiers? No? Sargento Franco?" The Brazilian cop held up his satellite phone and continued, "He said it's urgent he speak with you."

Chapter 17

SATELLITE PHONE IN HAND, HUGH STOOD IN A TENT used to house security forces. A mixture of local police and military cops from more countries than he could count stood guard beyond, as far as the eye could see. Tasked with keeping looters from flocking to the epicenter of the earthquake damage, they'd been wary when Hugh had driven up with Amelia and Joshua.

After some fast talking, he'd convinced them to let him contact his commanding officer, even to give him a moment's privacy to relay what he'd seen. Hopefully McCabe could instigate some kind of troop force to raid Jocelyn Pearson-Stewart's property before the children were moved.

Hugh gripped the phone tighter, wishing like hell he'd been able to lay his hands on one of these two days ago. How different things would have been if Oliver hadn't tossed his comm gear out of the van. Although then they wouldn't have uncovered Jocelyn's operation.

"Major McCabe speaking." Liam McCabe's familiar voice traveled over the airwaves.

Hugh grabbed the edge of the back of a chair for support, sweat popping on his brow from more than just the muggy day. "God, am I glad to hear your voice, sir."

"Same here, Franco." A hefty exhalation echoed through the earpiece. "Now cut the 'sir' crap and just tell me where the hell you've been."

His gaze tracked to Amelia and Joshua sitting on a blanket, playing with a pair of handcuffs. She jingled them in front of the kid like some kind of toy, their half-eaten MRE forgotten beside them.

"Amelia Bailey and her nephew were kidnapped from the hospital, the one set up in the school." After he'd let himself get distracted from the danger and had sex with her in the closet. He ground his teeth, editing the story heavily. "I, uh, ended up being taken along for the ride."

That hellish moment slammed through him, that instant when he'd seen Amelia slung over Oliver's shoulder and hadn't known if she was alive or dead.

"Sir, it's a long story and I am more than glad to share every detail in debrief." Every detail except the part about sex in the supply closet. "But we have more pressing concerns first. While we were in the jungle, we stumbled upon what appears to be a black-market baby-smuggling operation."

He could almost hear McCabe sitting up straighter. "Wanna run that by me again?"

"It's some kind of under-the-radar child-trafficking ring. I can lead security forces directly to the location where they're holding at least eleven children. Although now that we escaped, they're likely to relocate soon. We have to act fast before they move them. And I need you to convince these folks that I'm legit."

"Can do. And hey, I'm glad you're all right. I would have missed having your sorry ass around."

"Love you too, sir."

"Get back here safely—Oh, and hell, wait a second. Your friend probably doesn't know. Her brother and sister-in-law are alive and well. They've been working in one of the local field hospitals when they weren't tearing up the place looking for her and the kid."

"She'll be relieved to hear." And he could be sure she was safe in her brother's care while the matter with Jocelyn was being handled.

"Okay, then, hand over the phone to whoever's in command there and let's get the ball rolling."

"Roger that." Hugh passed the receiver back to the Brazilian sergeant. "Major McCabe needs to speak with your commanding officer, stat."

Given the Brazilian guy's wide eyes, it appeared he'd been listening anyway because he didn't waste a second shouting out for a *capitão* the next tent over.

Hugh figured he had about three minutes with Amelia. And still he couldn't deny himself a second to soak in the sight of her, safe and whole amidst a veritable army of volunteers. No one would touch her. Or Joshua. The adrenaline letdown must have kicked in a double dose because his knees damn near gave out at the sight. He hunkered down beside her and the kid.

She looked up. "You spoke to someone in your unit?"

"My commanding officer is verifying my identity now. I'll be heading out with some of the cops here to go to Jocelyn's." He cupped the back of her neck. "I also found out that your brother and his wife are alive and uninjured."

"Thank God." She sagged against him, gasping, damn near hyperventilating. She blinked fast. "I can't believe it, but oh my God…"

He hauled her close to his side, barely able to believe they'd gotten out alive. "One of the cops here will escort you two back to them and we'll get you on the first plane out of here."

"And you?"

"I'm still on the job." His thumb stroked the side of her neck. Even though he didn't want to leave her, it was probably just as well he was going back into the field, since his emotions threatened to bleed right out if he didn't tighten up posthaste. "We'll talk, though. Soon. I promise."

She cradled his face in her hands. "Be careful. Promise?"

For five years he'd been anything but careful. He wasn't sure he even knew how anymore. But looking at Amelia and the little boy sitting next to her teething on a pair of handcuffs, Hugh actually cared whether he came out of this alive.

And having a woman hold his heart in her hands again scared him a helluva lot more than the hazardous mission ahead.

Jocelyn drove her other Jeep along a back road through the jungle. It wasn't her best four-wheel-drive vehicle. That military man and his girlfriend had stolen her personal transportation and escaped. Rage, frustration, and impending doom shuddered through her as tangibly as the latest aftershock shaking coconuts from the trees.

She didn't have much time left. Once that air force guy made his way to someone with a working cell phone, her whole compound would be exposed.

The Jeep jostled over roots and buckled earth. The remote road was known to few. But then she'd thought her homestead was secure as well.

She didn't know how he'd found out, but then she wouldn't have expected him to be able to steal her Jeep and escape with a woman and child in tow, no less. Why the hell hadn't she killed Hugh and Amelia when she had the chance? But she'd genuinely thought she had them safely locked down. Maybe she was getting soft in her old age. She'd hoped she could find a way to spare their lives. If they didn't know anything about her operation, she could let them go free. They were innocent people trapped by Oliver's mistake. God, she tried so hard to be better than her family, to prove she didn't take lives unnecessarily.

Her fists went white-knuckled around the steering wheel. She'd overestimated herself and her people. And the mistake was going to cost her everything.

Nineteen years of work, over in a day.

It wasn't as if she had millions of dollars tucked away in some Cayman account to help her slip away and start fresh. Every penny she'd made through those adoptions had gone right back into the operation. Helping abused spouses create new identities. Funding the forces necessary to take those babies in need and house them until homes could be found.

Branches whipped at the windshield as she tore along the narrow road her people had carved out of the woods. She'd been so certain this was her time, the moment she'd been created for. Where her whole operation could be the salvation for dozens, hundreds even, of those orphaned in this natural disaster. She would be their guardian angel.

Instead, this had ended her.

Already she could hear sirens in the distance. Police vehicles coming to raid her home. To arrest her warriors. To take all the children.

She couldn't let those sirens, the destruction of her operation, be the end. She had to save at least one more child. According to her contact, there was a U.S. cargo plane heading out today with space enough to slip one child in with falsified paperwork. And she had that one baby girl strapped into a car seat in back.

Now Jocelyn just needed to make it to the rendezvous point, to hook up with her guardian warrior from the United States—the military nurse who'd been instrumental in helping her smuggle out four other babies since the earthquake hit.

The sirens grew fainter as she put more distance between herself and the plantation. Only a few more miles until she could meet up with Lieutenant Gable. Together, they would save this last child.

And then? Jocelyn didn't care if she lived or died now that her mission of mercy had been brutally ripped from her. Without her children—her whole purpose for being—she was nothing but a bankrupt expatriate with nowhere to turn.

Perhaps a little of her mobster family's blood coursed through her veins after all. Because with nothing left to lose, now she lived only to make sure those responsible for exposing the Guardian paid the ultimate price for what they'd destroyed.

Lisabeth's whole body shook so badly her teeth chattered. She could hardly believe that finally, finally, the fear and grief would end. She would have her baby Joshua in her arms again.

Thank God for Aiden's supportive arm around her

waist as they waited in the small mobile command post
set up near the runway where air force planes took off
and landed at regular intervals. The command center
consisted of a tent and a bunch of computers and other
tech equipment on pallets, hooked up to a huge military
generator. Even nearly a week after the earthquake, this
place still looked like a bombed-out war zone, but at
least communications were improving.

They'd been told by Major McCabe that they would
be leaving on one of the night's flights out. Returning
home would feel like culture shock—but so very
welcome. As she stared at the destruction, her heart
squeezed with grief for those who didn't have the chance
to simply leave.

"Dr. Bailey? Mrs. Bailey? Could you step outside for
a moment, please?" The woman in uniform looked so
official. So serious.

Had something gone wrong? Why couldn't the
woman have just smiled? Lisabeth's head went dizzy
and she stumbled.

Aiden grabbed her elbow. "I'm here, Lisabeth.
Whatever happens, I'm always going to be here for you..."

She wanted to stand right here in this spot, in the
place where she still had a living son named Joshua.
In a time where her sister-in-law still might call at any
second, her dearest friend as well as family.

Aiden slipped his arm around her waist and guided
her forward. And how strange was that? She was always
the one who faced life head-on, while he lost himself in
work or moody silences. But something had shifted between them when they'd made love in the van last night.
Something amazing and beautiful. It seemed wrong that

they found this closer connection only to have to use it to support each other through grief.

She followed the uniformed guard from their tent into a smaller one set up next to it. He pushed the flap back and she saw—

Her knees gave out, but luckily Aiden's arm was still banded around her waist, even if he had gone pale.

Whole body trembling, she reached out to the precious, beautiful pair in front of her. "Joshua? Amelia? Oh my God, you're both here, alive, okay."

Her sister-in-law smiled, jostling the baby on her hip. Amelia was scraped and scruffy, wearing stained khakis and a loose shirt belted with a gun holster. She looked nothing like the poised attorney who wore power suits and pearls. A million questions raced through Lisabeth's mind as she wondered what had happened to Amelia since the earthquake.

But all that could wait.

She let her eyes settle on her child. Her baby boy, born in her heart if not from her body. He smiled with all six teeth showing, jingling a pair of handcuffs in his fist.

And somehow, even though she couldn't remember moving, they were all hugging, she and Amelia, with the baby between them and Aiden's big strong arms around all of them. Their words jumbled together.

"Where were you—?"

"—and how did you escape?"

"The hospital said—"

"—thought you were dead."

They stayed in the massive, amazing huddle for... she had no idea how long. The relief was so huge, so incredible, she felt like the collective hug held them all upright. Then the precious little guy between them started squirming in protest.

Laughing and crying at the same time, she pulled back enough to see him again. She kissed his forehead, stroked his hair, and studied every finger and toe as if he'd been newly born.

Dimly, she heard her husband talking beside her.

"Amelia, I don't know how to thank you. We've only heard a little of what you've been through, but my God, what you've done to keep him safe through the earth-quake and kidnapping... I'm just so glad you're both alive and in one piece."

"I can't take all the credit," Amelia said. "He's a strong little boy with a fighting spirit beyond anything anyone could imagine. And even so, without Hugh— you'll meet him soon—without the help of Hugh Franco, we never would have made it."

Lisabeth saw a flash of something in Amelia's eyes, as blue as Aiden's. A flash of emotion deeper than her words suggested.

Aiden skimmed a hand over Joshua's head. "I'm glad he could be there for you both. I look forward to thank-ing him in person. Is he around here?"

"I'm afraid not," Amelia said, worry dripping from her words. "He's out on a mission right now. I don't know all the details. Just that he's leading authorities to the place where we were held."

The reality of all they had been through, of what her sister-in-law must have endured to keep Joshua safe, was almost too much to take in. Lisabeth let the tears keep streaking down her face. She didn't even bother drying them, because there were plenty more that had been bottled up.

"Joshua." She sighed her child's name, which she'd chosen especially for him during the weeks she'd looked at his photo and dreamed of when she could bring him home. She slid her hands under his arms and—

He arched away. His tiny fists clamped onto Amelia's shirt and clung to her.

Her throat clogged with more tears. Had he already forgotten her? They'd had so little time together, only a couple of days as the paperwork was being finalized. She and Aiden had been planning to spend this week in the familiar locale to acclimate him to the new relationship before heading home. Had he acclimated himself to his aunt instead?

Amelia patted his back. "We'll take it slow. We don't have to go all or nothing today. I'm here as long as you all need me." A hint of panic slipped into Amelia's tone.

Pure panic slid through Lisabeth. Had her sister-in-law bonded with him?

Lisabeth looked up quickly at Aiden. Their peace, his acceptance of his role as a father, was still so fresh. Would he use this as an excuse to back out? His eyes were inscrutable behind the glasses as he studied his sister and the baby.

Who knew what he was thinking right now? Who knew what he would do?

Amelia pulled a wobbly smile. "When we were on the run, Joshua liked bananas and he especially enjoyed it when Hugh sang to him."

Nodding once, Aiden scooped Joshua out of

Amelia's arms so confidently and quickly, the baby blinked in surprise.

Then his bottom lip started trembling and Aiden said quickly, "Would you like a banana? I'm sure there's got to be a banana around this place somewhere."

"'Nana? 'Nana, 'nana, 'nana..." Joshua chanted. His lip steadied for a minute, even if his little brow was still creased into deep furrows.

His wide dark eyes went to Amelia, who stood off to the side, her bandaged hand covering her mouth, unshed tears welling.

"Hey," Aiden continued, "if you want a song, you'll have to get that from this beautiful lady here, your mom." He hitched Joshua on his hip like a seasoned parent. "Because I'm pretty much tone-deaf like my sister." All that time spent with other children—his patients— over the years had obviously taught him more than a few tricks in handling a frightened, wary child.

Amelia smiled, her eyes watering as she turned to Lisabeth. "He's really good with Joshua, don't you think?"

Too choked up to speak, Lisabeth nodded tearily.

Aiden kept up a steady stream of conversation with their son, who was so mesmerized he dropped the hand-cuffs and reached for Aiden's glasses. Seeing their two heads together, Aiden's so fair and Joshua's so dark, touched Lisabeth's heart.

There was something more here than a doctor comforting a patient. She'd seen that often enough to know this went deeper. The image of them together clicked into place in her mind.

Father and son.

Parent and child.

And in that moment, Lisabeth fell in love with her husband all over again.

Chapter 18

HUGH RODE IN THE PASSENGER SEAT OF THE MILITARY Humvee, the last in the line of four vehicles that had raided Jocelyn Pearson-Stewart's property. The caravan churned up a cloud of dust as they made their way back to the military compound near the airfield.

The victory had been swift, but incomplete.

Jocelyn had escaped before they arrived. In fact, the whole compound had been deserted. However they'd managed to apprehend some refugees from the property. They'd hauled in Jocelyn's "nieces"—Courtney and Erin—although it was clear now that they weren't actually relatives. The two women and a number of other guards had been driving away in a caravan of vehicles with ten children.

Ten. Not eleven.

He hooked his arm out the open window while the Humvee driver coordinated his route with the truck ahead. Hugh barely registered what they were saying, his thoughts scattered as hell even as he kept his eyes on the dusty city in the distance. Had he miscounted the number of kids? He didn't think so, but it was possible. His surveillance of the beach cottage had been late at night from a distance. He could have counted one baby twice.

But if he hadn't?

That meant Jocelyn was out there somewhere with a

vulnerable child at a time when lawlessness was rampant. There simply weren't enough security forces available to search for her. They'd been lucky to shut down the home base of the smuggling operation.

He just hated loose ends. Hated that there was a chance justice might never be served for heaven only knew how many children had been shuttled through her illegal organization.

Now he needed to find Amelia and let her know what happened. And yeah, *he* needed to see her. To reassure himself that she and Joshua were safely with their family.

It had been scary as hell having her and the kid vulnerable on his watch. Yet it hadn't flipped him out the way it would have a couple of years ago. He would never be whole, but then again, maybe he wasn't walking the same tightrope he used to—a razor's edge between himself and danger.

And he had Amelia to thank for that. She'd reminded him that he mattered and his efforts mattered. Whereas before, he'd been throwing himself into hellish situations as much to tempt fate as to save people. He wouldn't rest easy until they were on an airplane to the States.

And then?

Would he contact her in the "real" world? Ask her out in a regular kind of way? It wasn't as if she lived on the other side of the universe. Only a few hours apart.

The ground shook under his feet. Exhaustion or another aftershock? Just the Jeep stuttering along a rippled stretch of land leading to the airstrip. He was supposed to meet McCabe here—which was code for the major figuring out if he could trust Hugh back in the field.

The line of vehicles stopped one after the other. The

temporary base that had been set up shortly after the earthquake had grown since he'd seen it last—more tents, portable hangars, more parked aircraft, and definitely more personnel. The suspects and children would be held here until local authorities sorted through the kidnapping mess.

At least this place was on the outskirts of the devastation, a tent city of sorts constructed on open land. Uprooted trees and buckled earth were the only signs of the recent earthquake.

He vaulted out of the Humvee, scanning for McCabe—but looking for Amelia. She and Joshua had been brought here to reunite with her brother and sister-in-law.

Amelia was *here*.

His pulse ramped at just the thought of seeing her. God, he was turning into a sap. He was even pumped about seeing the kid—

Except the child would be with his parents now. As life should be. Still, his feet slowed and he wasn't sure why. He should be relieved to have Amelia to himself, to talk to her, to figure out where they would take things next.

The ground vibrated under his feet. Aftershock or airplane taking off? He scanned the dirt runway, already moving to the most open space, away from anything that could collapse on top of him. And where the hell was Amelia?

Shit.

It had to be an aftershock. He hoped. Because the alternative sucked.

The ground steadied. He waited. Still steady.

Exhaling, he shrugged a kink out of his neck just as McCabe stepped from around a tent. The major stalled in his tracks. He grabbed the tent pole, paling.

Hugh strode toward him. "You okay, sir?"

"Yeah…" He straightened slowly, his camos crusty and his eyes red rimmed, no doubt from round-the-clock shifts. "Just damn glad to see you alive."

McCabe hauled him in for a hug, thumping him between the shoulder blades, and Hugh had to admit he was choked up too.

"There were times it was touch-and-go." He pulled away, but wasn't in any hurry to be under shelter. The wide-open spaces looked better and safer all the time. "This place has turned into such a lawless mess since the quake."

"And every time the earth starts shaking again—like a few seconds ago—people go a little batty."

"Understandable." Hugh thought back to that time underground with Amelia, how she'd held it together in spite of how often it had seemed the building would collapse the rest of the way on top of her.

"Last report puts the count at seventeen aftershocks since the original earthquake, with more undoubtedly to come." Squinting into the sun, McCabe stared out toward the ocean. "At least they canceled the tsunami warning."

"There was one?"

McCabe looked over his shoulder at him, grinning. "Sometimes being out of touch can be a blessing, my friend."

"That it can." Hugh stepped alongside him and they stood together quietly. Hugh took in the still earth, the flow of business moving at a steady clip. Not dragging, but not too hurried either.

McCabe finally turned to him again. "Take twelve hours, check in with a doc, and then you're going to report in for duty."

"I can report up now."

"No offense, but you're not known for understanding human limitations. Take twelve hours. I've got half our guys out there now." McCabe was a lighthearted dude—except when he wasn't. And right now, he was wearing the no-bullshit expression. "You can join the rest when we rotate."

"Yes, sir." He knew an order when he heard one.

McCabe clapped him on the back once more before starting toward his Humvee. He called over his shoulder. "Just in case you were wondering, the lady you saved ran into that storage tent about ten minutes ago. She looked pretty upset."

Hugh snapped to attention, his focus zipping over to the supply tent, drab gray and so densely packed with pallets he couldn't see inside. He thought about her inside alone, and given the family reunion she'd just had, he could too easily figure out what must have happened. She'd passed over her nephew to his parents.

A baby she'd grown attached to this week. How could she not, after all they'd been through? She'd been ready to die for that child. Had fought to stay alive for him after the earthquake, making sure Hugh never forgot the boy was there, insisting he was alive when anyone else would have given up. Joshua owed her his life.

And again she'd given him a chance at a bright future in handing him over to his parents.

Hell, even thinking about not seeing the kid's six-toothed smile brought a lump to Hugh's throat. It wasn't as if he'd expected to keep Joshua. But the way Amelia had been chipping through emotional walls, getting him to dig around in his past, brought everything roaring painfully to the surface.

Shining through it all? Amelia, with her grit and her strength.

He didn't even have to think of what to do next.

His feet were already moving fast to find her.

Amelia sat with her back against a huge wooden crate of supplies resting on top of a pallet. The far corner of the tent was dark and private, the perfect place for sobbing her ungrateful heart out.

Hugging her knees, she rocked, her face pressed into her legs to muffle her cries. She should be thankful to be alive, to have come through everything with Joshua alive. Major McCabe had even given her a personal update to let her know the raid on Jocelyn's place had been a success. Not even a shot fired. Hugh was fine.

And her heart was shattering over relinquishing a child that had never even been hers in the first place.

The sound of footsteps startled her. She reached for her gun—only to realize she didn't have it anymore. It had been taken from her when they returned. She shot to her feet, nerves stirring in her stomach. How could she have forgotten already what a dangerous place this was?

"Amelia?"

The sound of Hugh's deep bass rumbled through the tent, and she sagged against the crate with relief. She just barely caught herself from sliding down to the ground again. Only pride kept her upright.

"Over here," she called, scrubbing her wrist under her nose. Her eyes were probably swollen and her nose red, but Hugh had definitely seen her looking worse.

She heard his steps come closer as he walked through the maze of crates and pallets, finally reaching her shadowy, private corner.

Leaning a shoulder against the wooden crate, he studied her so long she resisted the urge to swipe her nose again.

"Are you okay?" he asked.

"Not really," she answered honestly. "But I will be."

He stroked her ponytail until it draped over her shoulder and somehow that light pressure was like a soothing massage to her achy head.

"Amelia, I am so sorry."

"For what?" She didn't move, just enjoyed the feel of his fingers lifting lock after lock, stroking, lightly tugging.

"I know that had to have been tough for you, passing Joshua over to his parents."

God, she felt selfish. Hugh would never see his daughter again and here she was, weeping like someone had died. "It's not like I won't ever get to visit him. He's my nephew."

"True enough." His fingers thrust deeper through the strands, against her scalp, freeing the confining ponytail and rubbing as he'd done when he'd washed her hair. "You were a mama bear for him these past few days."

The warmth of his hand, the breadth of his chest, and insightfulness of his words calmed her as much as his touch.

"I had no choice, Hugh. He needed me."

"You were—you *are*—amazing." His forehead fell to rest against hers.

Her hands fell to rest on his chest, his heartbeat thumping against her palm. "I'm just so glad those other children are safe now, thanks to you."

He'd returned to that Hotel Californiaesque hell knowingly, to help save those children. As she thought of what could have happened to him, the tears started flowing all over again.

"Oh God, Amelia, honey, it's going to be okay now." He pulled her against his chest, arms locking her in tight. "Everybody's all right."

"I know." Although he would be staying here and she was leaving. What if something happened to him? Now, or on another mission? Life-and-death situations felt so much more real to her now. "I'm losing it here. I know that, but I can't seem to stop the tears."

"It's the adrenaline letdown." He shushed against her hair. "You don't have to be strong anymore. Everything you held in before is coming up now."

"Everything is just so"—she hiccupped—"so very quiet."

"It'll feel that way for a while."

She rubbed her cheek against the warm cotton of his shirt, breathing in the musky scent of him, so familiar now. "Do you go through this after every mission?"

He paused for a second before admitting, "This one was definitely more… intense."

It had to have been a nightmare for him, holding a baby that wasn't his own, but whom he felt responsible for nevertheless. Hugh had been so good with Joshua. He'd rescued them both in so many ways.

"Was it tough for you, too, letting go of Joshua?" Of course it had to be. She felt selfish for her tears and taking comfort from him after all he had been through keeping them safe.

"He's where he's supposed to be."

She tipped her face up to his. "I don't mean to sound snarky here, but do those kinds of platitudes actually work for you when you're upset?"

He laughed dryly. "Not really."

"They're not doing it for me either." She smiled back.

And how strange was that, to finally find comfort in their shared sadness? And of course the way he held her went a long way toward easing the knot of grief in her chest.

And as the pressure eased, she became more aware of the world around her, the crisp scent of the wooden crates. Her ears filled with the roar and vibration of airplanes taking off and landing, the cacophony of engines so loud it blocked most other noises. Most of all, she noticed their total privacy, which gave her a moment to view Hugh in all his protector glory. So strong, with such capable hands.

Another kind of tension altogether coiled inside her. Her fingers clenched in his T-shirt and she felt his heart speed up under her fist. A flush spread out over her skin, a burning tingle that only increased as she felt him harden against her stomach.

And just as quickly as the tears had come upon her, passion flooded through her, her emotions already volatile, ready to ignite.

She nipped his collarbone lightly, then harder. "How about we stop talking?"

"I think that's the way to go," he growled against her ear.

"It must be the supply tent. What is there about storage facilities that bring out the animal in me lately?" She tore at the buttons on his pants.

"Could be the deprivation of basic life staples in the earthquake has made you crave the surroundings of a well-stocked pantry. It could be a lifelong turn-on." He inched down her zipper.

Their laughter filled the sliver of space between them as he skimmed off her pants and she freed his erection.

"Condom?" she gasped, her body shouting in protest that this might have to end before it started. "Do you have one? Where's your vest?"

"I've been carrying around condoms since our time in that supply closet."

Confusion nipped at the edges of her desire. "You didn't mention it before, after the shower."

"My vest was closer."

Perhaps he hadn't wanted to let her know. They'd both been holding back something then that she hadn't even quite grasped. But not now.

Just thinking of the idea that he'd wanted her ever since, even though she'd tried to be so cool and practical about the attraction, sent sparks of anticipation showering through her. He had *wanted* her. And knowing she held that kind of sway over this complex man who'd become her personal superhero… that felt pretty incredible right now.

"But Hugh, I walked away from you."

"And I was damn sure not going to let you go so easily." He backed her more fully against the tall wooden crate.

Body to body they stood—even in this moment of total abandon he stayed between her and the world.

His broad shoulder blocked even a view of the canvas tent wall.

But then the rest of the universe basically faded when he touched her. All she could think about was the way he cupped her breasts, bringing each pebbled peak to his mouth as he feasted on one, then the other, going back again until she thought she would scream out from the pleasure pulling tighter at the core of her. Much more of this and she could damn well fly apart before he'd even thrust inside.

She wanted, needed for him to feel the same fire, licking at his skin with the same heat and intensity of his tongue against her nipple.

She dipped her hands into his pants, palming his butt, fingernails digging in just a hint before she raked around his hips farther still. She took him in her grasp, testing the weight and length of him in both hands. She stroked and explored the rigid length until he throbbed even harder in her grip. With efficient, swift hands, she rolled a condom over him.

Groaning, he slid his mouth up her neck and took her lips as firmly as she sensed he was about to take her. He hooked a hand behind her knee and brought her leg around, opening her to receive…

Him.

Her head fell back against the crate as he plunged inside her. Deeply. He withdrew in a slow, slow glide, then filled her again and again. His hips met hers, fitting as they rocked together. Her back flattened to the wooden panel in a sweet pressure and release that wasn't gentle but never crossed the line into painful. They danced close to the edge, though, mouths meeting, bodies grinding.

It wasn't about anonymous sex in a supply closet or romantically scented soaps; this was about a raw coming together. A hunger to be closer, a fear that there wouldn't be another chance, and a driving need for there to be more and more and more opportunities to lose themselves in this crazy connection.

Sweat trickled down her back just as it dotted his upper lip. She panted, breathless, but couldn't bring herself to let this end. So much was undecided between them, unspoken, and when they stepped outside of this tent they would have to say good-bye, him staying and her leaving. She would leave, not knowing if this insanely intense bond would hold up in the real world. Could he bring himself to commit to another relationship after all he'd lost?

The thought of never feeling this again, of never having him in her life in this way, made her ache to scream in frustration. Made her burn to hold on to this moment, hold on to *him* all the harder.

He drove into her again and again, the angle, the friction sending electric tingles from between her legs, showering higher. As the bliss tore through her, she bit his shoulder to keep from crying out, her mouth and her nails marking him in an outward way just as he'd marked her heart.

Fighting back the need to finish, she squeezed her eyes closed, her fists gripping and unfurling against his shoulders. He whispered along her neck, and she felt the words more than heard them. Perceived his own ravenous need to make this last, to milk every ounce of ecstasy until the sensation sharpened, gathering not just in the tight bundle of nerves but also inside her, converging, exploding.

She came apart in his arms, her body writhing against his, and thank God, he held onto her, covered her mouth with his. Wave after wave rippled over her, longer and more drawn out until the force of it left her limp and replete in his arms.

In some distant part of her brain, she realized his face was in her neck now as his arms convulsed around her, his hoarse groan of completion sending a fresh tingle along her oversensitive skin.

She held onto him, or maybe they just held onto each other and let the crate behind her support them. As the sweat dried on her body, she knew time was passing. *Their* time together was passing. Physically and emotionally she was completely hollowed out. Unable to form thoughts, walk another step.

Withstand another loss.

Losing Joshua today had almost been more than she could take. She wasn't sure how she could stand to let go of Hugh when the time came to step on that plane and leave him behind.

Chapter 19

HIS RELEASE STILL SHUDDERING THROUGH HIM, HUGH held onto Amelia, or maybe she held him up. He wasn't sure, as the aftermath of their explosive sex left him on shaky ground. So he dragged in breath after ragged breath, still buried inside Amelia while resting his forehead against the splintery crate.

Right now, he would give just about anything for a bed where they could both lie quietly while he got his head together regarding what had just happened. Because the olive green canopy and the dirt floor just weren't cutting it. He and Amelia had been through a lot, slept together, been through even more, but still, something different had happened here. A connection had formed. He'd lost his heart to a woman before, and he knew what sex with love was like.

It was different from sex just for sex's sake, different on some kind of transcendent plane that he couldn't explain, but God, he recognized it well. He'd felt that distinction while making love to Amelia.

He fit her against his shoulder, her silky hair trailing down his arm. Her scent, her softness, it was all imprinted on him and in him now.

There was no replacing Marissa in his heart. No one could be a substitute for her. Just as no one could be a substitution for Amelia. She was her own person, amazing and unique in her own way. There was no hiding from the truth any longer. He had done the one thing he'd vowed never to do again.

He'd fallen in love.

Now he had to figure out what the hell to do about that. Telling her in a drab military tent with their pants around their ankles seemed like a bad idea. And damn it all, he still needed to get his head together on this. He should be happy, the path simple and clear.

Instead, he was scared deep in his gut. Which was saying a lot for a guy who didn't think twice about parachuting into a minefield.

A rustling at the front of the tent yanked him out of his freaked-out self-indulgence. "Shit," he whispered, easing from her body and already feeling the loss. "Someone's coming inside."

He yanked her shirt into place as she pulled up her khakis. He made fast work of his own pants, then smoothed her hair back, finger-combing the silky strands quickly.

Kissing her hard and fast, he palmed the small of her back and steered her past the maze of crates. At the front, canvas flap open, he came face-to-face with one of the military nurses from… He couldn't quite place where, but his brain wasn't firing on all cylinders right now.

The sun was setting, security lights flickering off and on as sensors wrestled with the transition between day and night settings. A C-17 sat next in line to load up and head out. He even caught sight of his teammates Brick and Cuervo talking with a med tech as a couple of patients were loaded up.

Amelia stopped in her tracks just past the tent,

gnawing on her kissed-plump bottom lip. "Can we hang out here for a second longer? I'm not ready to face my family just yet."

"Do you want something to eat? Somewhere to, uh, freshen up?" There weren't a helluva lot of options and little or no privacy now that they were out of the storage tent.

"I don't have much time, actually." She looked around the bustling temporary airfield. "I'm supposed to get on that plane with them and go back to the States. Aiden and Lisabeth are meeting me here in about fifteen minutes with Joshua." Pain smoked through her eyes. "I needed a few minutes to collect myself, so I told them I was going to get an update on you."

Leaving? Her announcement knocked the wind out of him. Sure he wanted her out of danger, but he'd expected to have a little more warning on saying good-bye, a chance to figure out how he wanted to handle things after they both returned.

"But you're going tonight. That's good. Really good." So why did acid still churn in his gut? "I want you out of this godforsaken wasteland, the sooner the better."

And it would be hard as hell to watch her leave, even accepting it was for the best. He also knew how tough it would be for her to acclimate to regular life after the trauma she'd experienced. He wished he could be there to help her make that transition.

"Well then we have a problem"—she scratched her chin absently, her eyebrows furrowing together as if her lawyer brain was putting together something big— "because I don't want to go. I need to stay and help, even if it's just giving out those little half-pint cartons of orange juice to thirsty children."

Her face smoothed, and she jabbed him in the chest with one finger to make her point. "By some quirk of fate, I survived unscathed, and now I want to give back by helping those who haven't been as lucky."

He tipped his head, certain he couldn't have heard her correctly. "Listen, I understand where you're coming from. It's tough to walk away from people in need, but there aren't many chances to get out of here." And he was damn well going to make sure she was on that plane. "Right now, it's just your adrenaline talking."

She laughed lightly, but her sky blue eyes still weren't smiling. "Don't you think you're carrying the he-man stuff a little too far?"

Hands hitched on his gun belt, he measured his words to keep from snapping. Because right now what he really thought, what he really felt, was that he'd dodged enough of a bullet having her remain safe so far. Any more would be tempting fate. He'd done well in not thinking about Marissa or his daughter, but he knew damn well his own adrenaline letdown was due and it was going to be a helluva night trying to process everything that had happened.

He needed to be assertive about her next move. "If you stay, you will be in the way of rescue workers who need to do their jobs."

"You're trying to get rid of me." Hands falling on his chest, she brushed cotton wrinkles flat.

He clasped her fingers, stopping her. "I'm trying to keep you safe. Keep you alive." Frustration roiled inside him, searing along already-raw nerves. He needed her safe, damn it. He grasped her shoulders and willed her to understand how important it was for her to get on that plane.

"I love you, Amelia. Okay?" The words were damn near ripped out of him. He hadn't had the time to sort through what it all meant, but in weighing the cost, he hoped it would help the cause. "I've been through the hell of losing someone I loved once and I can't go through that hell again. I can't take having you here where something could happen to you."

She went still, her eyes stunned and giving him no hint of what she was thinking or feeling. "You love me?"

"Yeah, I think I do. Wait," he held up a hand, needing to get this right. There was no quibbling to give himself an out. There was no going back for him now. "I know I do."

"Oh, Hugh," she said with a hint of regret, her eyes turning sad. She bracketed his face in both her hands, even though they stood in the middle of a busy airfield. "What you're saying is beautiful, don't get me wrong. But I'm not so sure you're thinking clearly now. I believe this past week with Joshua and me has stirred up the pain of losing your wife and child."

No shit.

He bristled, her rejection stinging, especially after what they'd just shared. Or what he'd thought they shared. Damn it all, he was certain she'd felt it too. "I know that you and Marissa are not the same. In fact, you're nothing alike." He tugged her by the arm, pulling her out of the path of troops marching past, and stopping under a half-uprooted tree. "If you don't love me, then say so. Don't try to make up some bullshit excuse about me not knowing my own mind."

"Can you deny that you've been thinking of her?

Everything that's gone on has to have been tangled up in your feelings for what happened then."

"Okay, I get it," he said bitterly. "You're the one who's tangled up in the past. Just because your ex was a jackass who couldn't tell one woman from the other doesn't mean I'm a clueless bastard too."

She shook her head. "I'm over him, and you know it."

"And I believe you about as much as you seem to believe me." He stepped back, feet planted, shoulders braced. "It's time for you to get on that plane."

"That's it? One minute you're in love with me and the next you tell me to get out of your life?"

"This isn't about saying good-bye forever. It's about you staying somew—" He ground his teeth as a trio of Red Cross workers passed, carrying stacked boxes of meals. "This isn't the time or the place for an argument."

"Yeah, well, I disagree. If I've learned anything over the past week, it's that we can't take a minute for granted. I want to be here, to help, and yes, to be with you." Her scraped chin jutted, her sunburned cheeks peeling, and still she was magnificent. "I've also learned I'm a lot stronger than I realized. I'm not just a fighter in the courtroom, and then a wimp when it comes to facing the rest of the world."

"I could have told you that." Although her stubborn strength was a pain at the moment.

"Then why are you the only one who gets to be a crusader here? Why do I have to be shuffled aside to a safe little corner? Hell, it's not like I'm going to be crawling under collapsed buildings the way you are. What if I were to ask you to take on a safer role?"

"That's ridiculous. This is my job. My calling."

"Well, while this may not be my job, believe me when I say I do feel called to be a part of the cleanup efforts here, to do something for the place that gave my family Joshua—"

Her voice cracked, and she looked away fast.

Realization seeped into his brain. "You don't want to get on the plane with them. Do you?"

And as much as he knew it was going to hurt her, he said the words he hoped—he prayed—would make her get on that plane anyway. "I've heard there are no more planes carrying civilians out for God only knows how long, because they're locking down the island until Jocelyn can be found. We're almost certain she has one child with her and there could be more."

He didn't want her to miss that last plane, and he didn't want her to be here if he failed in a mission that had become everything to him. Desperation pounded through him. "I thought you said you weren't a coward? Well, get on that plane and face your brother and his family."

Her head snapped back toward him, her eyes blazing. "That was cruel and manipulative."

"I'm just doing what has to be done to make sure you don't end up dead."

Pressing the bridge of her nose, she squeezed her eyes closed, her jaw trembling for a vulnerable minute, before she looked at him again. Pain and anger blended in her eyes, jelling into disillusionment. "You know, Hugh, maybe we're both right here, in a sad way, not the good kind of way. Perhaps you and I are stuck in the past. You, so afraid of losing someone, it paralyzes you. And me, so afraid of being betrayed until I just can't trust what I'm hearing." She held up her hands. "So you win, Hugh. I'll go. For what it's worth, I think I could have really loved you too."

She pivoted away, her head high as she marched toward the C-17. The setting sun bathed her tequila-colored hues, giving her a golden sheen. Relief damn near made him dizzy. His head and his heart were too wrecked to consider the consequences, but he had to believe he'd done the right thing even if it tore him apart inside.

"Dude?" a familiar voice called from just behind him, Jose "Cuervo" Jones. "You okay?"

Cuervo studied him with perceptive eyes, everyone's buddy, always checking up on folks with their freaky weird sense of when people were about to crash. Wade "Brick" Rocha stood beside him, one of the Red Cross meal boxes in his hands and open. He shoveled down the protein bar in two bites. Must have been a long mission with no time to eat.

So was he okay? "Yeah"—no—"just tying up loose ends before I get back to work." Was that all he had left for the rest of his life?

"Uh-huh." Wade nodded, pulling out a sandwich. "Women don't like it much when you issue them military orders."

Jose leaned in. "Not that we were eavesdropping. You were mighty vocal there at the end."

Hugh scrubbed a hand over his head. "So I'm just supposed to let her hang out here in an earthquake zone when there's a perfectly good seat waiting for her?"

Raising his hands, Jose backed up. "I'm not the one to ask, dude. I'm still single."

Hugh's gaze skated back to Amelia, meeting up with

her family. She had her brave face on, smiling even as Aiden and Lisabeth Bailey hovered over their kid with that new-parent awe he remembered well.

And yeah, Amelia was right in saying he was scared of the thought of committing again. Putting his heart in another child's tiny hands? Damn. But what scared him most? Never having the chance to stand in a trio like that with Amelia—her, him, and *their* kid.

He pinched the bridge of his nose, kicking himself over his own thickheadedness. He clapped both of his buddies on the back. "I'll catch you later at the hooch. I've got something to take care of first."

Jogging toward the cargo plane, he kept his eyes locked on Amelia even as he wove around human traffic, litters being loaded, other refugees making their way up the load ramp. He even saw the nurse from the hospital—her name finally came to him: Lieutenant Gable—reaching for a baby in a woman's outstretched arms.

He frowned, something niggling at the back of his mind. He looked closer, his feet carrying him across the packed earth. The woman a few feet away behind Amelia looked like any number of other relief workers in khakis and a cotton shirt, waist cinched with a gun belt. Like a dozen others here, she wore a hat to shade her face from the sun.

The wind rolled in from the ocean and picked up the brim of her hat enough for him to see—

Horror iced the blood in his veins as he recognized Jocelyn Pearson-Stewart standing only two feet away from Amelia.

Standing with her family, waiting to board, Amelia kept a smile plastered on her face even though she ached to scream out in frustration. For heaven's sake, she made her living with words and persuasive arguments. How could she have let the conversation with Hugh go off the rails so abysmally? She knew full well why.

Because when he'd told her he loved her, she'd panicked. She'd picked a fight with him to avoid facing what the two of them shared back in the supply tent. To delay dealing with the love growing inside her so very fast.

She'd known they were heading in that direction, but she'd expected to have time to settle into the notion. Not to dive headfirst into the scary world of relationships again with a guy she'd barely known for a few days.

But oh my, what memorable days they had been.

Her eyes drifted back to where he'd been standing. Except he wasn't there any longer. His broad shoulders were parting the crowd as he ran toward her. Her heart sped up. Her smile became real and heartfelt as she waved at him.

He waved back, shouting something that got lost in the roar of jet engines warming up and planes overhead. And he wasn't smiling. In fact, he looked intensely serious. His arm shot out and he grabbed the arm of one of the security cops, hauling the man with him as Hugh continued to say something…

The wind rolling in off the ocean carried the hum of words. From the crowd? From Hugh. She could have sworn she heard the name…

"Jocelyn…"

Suddenly Hugh's waving took on a whole different meaning and she looked behind her just as a gun jammed into her side. She stared straight into the fanatical eyes of Jocelyn Pearson-Stewart.

The woman shouted, "Everyone move back. Do not come near or I'll shoot her. I swear it."

Hugh and the security cop stopped in their tracks, the crowd fanning out in retreat. Amelia looked frantically around, making sure Joshua was nowhere near this monster. And thank God, Aiden had tucked his family behind him, already backing them away, his eyes apologizing to Amelia for not being able to help her.

She hoped he could see in her expression that she understood. He was doing what had to be done to guard his child. What should be done for any child, truly, which made her wonder why the military nurse holding that baby wasn't moving away.

Hugh kept his hands high, in sight, unthreatening. "Jocelyn, you're not going to get away. Let's end this standoff now before someone gets hurt, like that baby over there. Can you really allow yourself to be responsible for even one more innocent life put at risk?"

The woman dug the gun deeper into Amelia's side. "I am saving the children. Don't you understand?"

And in the span of those few words, Amelia knew what she had to do. She'd heard that same tone in more criminal voices than she could count. Criminals with a zealous agenda. They all possessed a desperate compulsion to share their propaganda. If she could give Jocelyn that opportunity, she might just buy enough time for one of these guards to end this nightmare.

Amelia looked straight at Jocelyn without flinching and asked, "What do I need to understand? Tell me."

Like a moth drawn to the flame, Jocelyn turned her

attention to Amelia. "Without me, do you comprehend the lives they would have led?" Her skeletal fingers were surprisingly strong, banded around Amelia's arm as she kept her close to her side. "Who knows how long they would have stayed in orphanages? I compacted that time for them. I was their guardian, their *savior*."

As appalled as she was by the woman's God complex, she had to keep her talking. "Do you realize how you've endangered them, circumventing the rules? You gave a platform to criminals like Oliver."

"*I* took care of Oliver, just as I can take care of anyone who tries to pervert my mission."

From the corner of her eye, Amelia tried to check her peripheral vision but so far hadn't seen anyone move. Why the hell wouldn't that nurse with the baby step away and give cops freer rein to move in? "You killed Oliver?"

"I shot him. He deserved to die. You people don't understand what you have done in stopping me." She swung the gun in a wide circle at the dozen or so people remaining. "Those children would be nothing without *me*."

Amelia's heart lurched as the wide arc swept past Hugh's broad chest. His eyes met hers and held. She could see the steely determination glinting even from far away. She knew he would stop at nothing to be a crusader. What might he sacrifice now? Just the thought of how far he would go terrified her with images of his lifeless body sprawled on the ground.

Fear made her sway—and distracted her. She needed to pull Jocelyn's focus back to her before she shot someone else. "It's not about you and how fast you shuttle the most kids around. It's about them and ensuring their safety. And believe me, speaking as someone who spent some time with Oliver and Tandi, safety was not uppermost in their minds."

Something flickered in Jocelyn's face, something like… guilt?

Amelia pressed. "Do you really believe that was the first time Oliver pulled something like that? He was going to sell me as some kind of sex slave. God only knows what he did to children you thought had simply gone missing or weren't picked up."

Jocelyn reeked with the scent of a cornered animal. Amelia knew her nose for fanatical criminals, her sense of how to work a defendant, had paid off. She'd hit Jocelyn where she was most vulnerable.

Time to push hard and finish it, to make Jocelyn deliver the damning words that would resonate with any jury. "The only way to save them now is for you to tell us what you did, so we can try to find them. Otherwise you're every bit the criminal—the *monster*—Oliver was."

An agonizing acceptance slid over Jocelyn's face, and Amelia realized she'd won. The woman wouldn't have to be taken out by some risky sniper shot. This could end peacefully. Amelia held out her hand, the one with the snakebite bandage. "Please, just give me your gun."

The woman who'd single-handedly led an entire baby-smuggling ring sighed heavily, her face aging another ten years in the defeated moment. "You're right. I did become like Oliver, dirty as hell, just like my good-for-nothing family."

Jocelyn lifted the gun—and placed the barrel into her own mouth.

Chapter 20

Eyes locked on Amelia, Hugh vaulted toward the C-17 load ramp. He heard his fellow PJs in step alongside him but he didn't waste a second checking. He knew they would back him up as they sprinted toward the madwoman with a gun. Jocelyn might have it pointed at herself, but with Amelia still in her grip and snipers trying to get a clear shot...

He wasn't stopping until he had Amelia far away from the line of fire.

His heart was in his throat, his pulse hammering harder as he stretched his body to the max. What if the bullet ricocheted, hitting bone? What if Jocelyn reflexively pulled away from the shot at the bitter end, common in suicide shooters. That last minute twitch could have sent a bullet into Amelia.

Into *his* woman.

Denial howled through him, and maybe even from his mouth. His teammates could take down Jocelyn. But Hugh had Amelia. He refused to be too late. He hadn't been there to help Marissa, but damn it, he was here, now. He couldn't fail her.

He dove toward Amelia, went airborne, and hooked an arm around her middle. A shot echoed. From where? Jocelyn's gun. Blood spewed on her. On Amelia.

A bullet whizzed past his ear, coming from behind. He had to make sure she was clear of the snipers. He swept her off the ramp, twisting in midair so his body would catch the impact—

Oof. He slammed to the ground. The impact shattered through him, but for once he was grateful they only had a dirt runway rather than asphalt. He rolled her under him, shielding her as the ground shuddered beneath them.

"Amelia?" he shouted, needing to know. "Are you—?"

"Yes..." Her fists gripped his shirt, her teeth chattering. "Yes, yes, I'm okay..."

His arms locked harder as the shouts around them grew so loud he couldn't hear her anymore. But he could feel her, warm, vibrant, and alive. Relief rocked through him so hard he could have sworn another aftershock shook the earth. She was talking and coherent. The rest they could fix later. He tried to put his eyes on Jocelyn to make sure that threat wasn't coming for Amelia and he saw what looked like the woman's unmoving form a few yards away.

He started to roll to the side—

The ground trembled harder. Damn it all. It truly was another aftershock. Even though they'd been through at least twenty already, still the smell of panic, of fear, filled the air. People dropped to the ground, covering their heads, while others scrambled away.

And the shuddering continued, a rougher one this time as the world around him rattled. Lights on poles swayed. Generators hopped as if they were as insubstantial as Matchbox cars.

Shit. Realization mushroomed inside him. This wasn't just a quick tremble. Another earthquake swelled up from below like an underground train exploding upward. Screams mixed with the thunderous cracking.

Pain shot up his leg, but he blocked the sensation, focusing everything inside him on staying curved around Amelia. He could hear her breathing and chanting the Lord's Prayer over and over.

He couldn't even let himself think of how badly she might have been injured. He would deal with that once he was sure the rest of the world wasn't going to crash down on top of them—or crack open beneath them.

The deafening noise around them shifted. The earth quieted.

No more thunder or screams cut the air. Instead the odd stillness was cut with a low keening, crying and shouts, aftermath noises. The earthquake had ended.

So why was his whole body still shaking?

He forced his eyes open and realized the quake hadn't been as bad this time. The world hadn't caved in. Only toppled light riggings, collapsed a tent, and flipped a couple of generators. Already, uniformed rescuers were making tracks to restore order, check for injured, with Cuervo and Brick leading the pack. Hugh pushed with his arms to lever himself off Amelia, to help.

But he couldn't seem to move.

Amelia stared up at him, confusion pinching her eyebrows together as she stroked his face. "Hugh? You're okay." Her arms wrapped around him. "Thank God, you're okay. I can't believe how you pushed me out of the way of Jocelyn like that, but thank you, and I'm so sorry I didn't say this earlier. I lo…"

The sound of her voice faded as the world went fuzzy, narrowing. Damn, he was losing consciousness… He tried to hold on, to focus on Amelia's face and stay right in the moment. But the darkness dragged him under.

Amelia screamed.

She'd made it through everything life had thrown at her this week, but seeing Hugh's eyes close, fearing he had died? Her composure shattered like the fragmented glass from dozens of broken bulbs glinting all over the ground.

Scrambling backward, she worked her way out from under him so she could get help. Her eyes homed in on the tipped light pole pinning one of his legs. Somehow it had missed her—Hugh had taken the hit for her.

But his trapped leg didn't explain why he was unconscious. Fear dropped her to her knees beside him.

"Help!" she screamed. "We need help over here!"

She stroked Hugh's hair, and yes, she knew she was babbling, hoping the sound of her voice would pull him back to her. Her fingers grazed along a lump, where he must have hit his head when he'd landed.

"Ma'am." A guy in uniform knelt beside her, the patch on his uniform just like one she'd seen on Hugh, "That Others May Live."

She choked on a well of hysteria. Why the hell hadn't she gotten on that plane faster so he wouldn't have needed to save her? Again. "He has a bump on his head. You need to—"

"Yes, ma'am. We've got it. My name is Jose. I'm his friend and we'll take care of him. Now you need to be checked—"

"I'm fine. Him. Hugh." Sheesh, she was turning into a hysterical idiot. She'd survived under a collapsed building for two days, and *now* she was losing it?

Because this wasn't about her. This was about Hugh, losing Hugh, a man she loved so much it was tearing her apart inside to see him lying there lifelessly.

Jose grabbed her shoulders. "Listen to me. That plane is going to leave very soon. And we need to get as many out as we can in case another earthquake hits." His voice was calm and clipped with authority made to cut through panic. "We want him and you on it. We have about five minutes. Understand?"

"Got it." She shot to her feet to prove she was unhurt and cleared back.

With an efficiency and smooth training in action that blew her mind, they began to work on Hugh. Backing toward the cargo plane, she kept her eyes glued to Hugh as a half dozen men hefted the lighting gear off him with Herculean grunts. Then Jose went into medic mode, securing his head and transferring him to a stretcher. No wonder Hugh had told her she would be in the way here.

Turning, she raced toward the plane, running up the back ramp and into the crowded cargo hold. The PJ— Jose—barked out a list of medical terms to a man with a stethoscope around his neck, then beat a hasty retreat down the ramp and outside again.

Hands—she didn't see whose—pushed her into a red webbed seat and buckled her in. Before she could breathe, the plane rumbled forward, faster, nose tipping upward…

And they were airborne.

The passengers cheered, their voices echoing through the cavernous metal tunnel filled with packed rows of webbed seats. Amelia gasped in hitchy breaths of air that smelled of hydraulic fluid and mustiness. She searched the rows of people until her eyes finally found her brother sitting with Lisabeth and Joshua. A moment of guilt pinched her that she hadn't thought to check on them sooner.

Her brother mouthed the words *Are you okay?*

She nodded, answering what he wanted to know even though she knew she wouldn't truly be all right until she knew more about Hugh. His stretcher was only two seats away. So close, but not near enough to touch.

His head was still immobilized, his ankle in a splint. She kept her eyes on him as if she could somehow will him awake. To hell with rules. She slid from her seat and knelt beside him.

A hand fell to rest on her shoulder and she jumped, ready to defend her right to stay by Hugh. Except it wasn't anyone official. It was her brother.

"Aiden, how did you win over the seat police?"

"I'm a doctor. I'm here to check you over while the military docs take care of your guy there. Trust me." Aiden worked some kid of magic that maneuvered a quick seat shuffle so she could sit by Hugh's head. Her brother reached into a first-aid kit and pulled out a stack of antiseptic wipes. He tore one open; the scent of alcohol stung her nose.

"I'm not hysterical." Anymore. Although she wondered what he intended to do next with those wipes. "I just want to be near Hugh."

Aiden crouched in front of her, his eyes so serious behind his glasses. "I hear you, but how about we clean you up before you see him." He swept the medicated cloth over her cheeks. "And I do need to make sure you're okay."

She winced at the sting.

"Just a scrape," he said calmingly. "And some cleanup."

He tossed aside the wipe—stained red—and ripped open another. Only then did she realize she had blood on her arms. From Jocelyn. Amelia shivered in disgust and residual fear as her brother cleaned her up. The past hour became all too real. She'd been that close to dying. The whole horrific moment replayed in her mind, frame by frame as if in slow motion, until the logical part of her legal mind snagged on a stray detail.

"What about the military nurse? The one that took the baby from Jocelyn?"

"Security detained her back at the airfield, along with the child," he explained as he tossed away the final wipe. He checked her pupils and took her pulse.

"And Jocelyn Pearson-Stewart, the woman who held me at gunpoint?"

He shook his head. "She's dead."

Nausea welled again. "I only wanted to make the woman surrender. It never crossed my mind that she would turn the gun on herself…"

Her big brother took her hands and squeezed.

"Deep breaths, kiddo, deep breaths," he said, just as he'd done when he taught her to drive and she'd freaked out over stalling at an intersection. "She made the decision to end her life. You did not put the gun in her hand and you were not the one who took someone hostage. Her decisions. Not yours."

She felt some calm ease through her veins. What had happened today wouldn't leave her anytime soon, but her brother had given her enough peace to hang on when she desperately needed to stay in control. "When did you get to be so wise?"

He glanced across the plane at Lisabeth and smiled. "I married a woman who brings out the best in me." He squeezed her hands again. "Thank you for everything you and Hugh did for us. There's no way we can ever repay you, but know we are here for you and for him. Anything either of you needs. The sacrifices you both made to keep Joshua safe…"

Aiden pulled his glasses off and pinched the bridge of his nose.

And her brother didn't even know the half of how difficult the journey had been for Hugh. He was a larger-than-life man for more than just his strength and survival skills. The way he'd bolstered her spirits as much as her steps. He had a core-deep strength of *character* that was rare to find.

And that fast the roots of her hair started tingling. Her eyes slid back to Hugh and she realized… She didn't just think she loved him. She *knew*.

She loved him, so much she wondered if there could be such a thing as too much. She'd almost missed out on it back on the island, her feelings all tangled up in the sex and survival and adrenaline and, yes, also in the heartrending stories of a man who adored his family. Hugh was a man who could stroke magic from a guitar as fluidly as he did from her body. A man who tenderly held a child even when doing so exposed old grief.

He was everything a man should be. Everything she'd wanted when she got married before.

And when he opened his eyes again—she refused to believe he wouldn't—she was going to make sure he knew she never intended to let him go again.

Hugh punched through the layers of consciousness, knowing there was some reason he couldn't sleep in today. He tried to roll over, but he must be tangled in the sheets because somehow his legs were trapped.

"Hugh?" Amelia's voice penetrated the fog. "You need to be still."

His mind traveled some intriguing paths of exactly what she might have in mind for him, except the more awake he became the more he realized he hurt like hell. His leg. His head. Both throbbed like a son of a bitch.

With the pain, the memories came flooding free, of Jocelyn taking Amelia hostage, of the earthquake after. His eyes snapped open. He opened his eyes and instead of a sky, he saw a metal roof with cables, heard the roar of jet engines.

Amelia leaned over him, smiling, tears streaking tracks through the grime on her face. God help him, she was the most beautiful creature he'd ever seen.

"Amelia?"

She touched his face with featherlight strokes. "You hit your head, which is why you passed out, and your ankle's broken. You're on an airplane heading to the States."

He grinned back at her. "Which means *you* are on a plane heading to the States."

"You are correct," she said, shaking her head and laughing through more tears.

Reaching up, he knuckled aside the dampness on her cheeks. "And everyone else? What happened?"

"Your team, my family, they're all fine. Aiden and Lisabeth are across the row with Joshua."

While unable to move his head, he scanned the seated passengers and was able to find the family seated together. Joshua played with his new father's glasses while his mother fed her son a banana. Hugh's throat went tight at the sight of Joshua's six teeth gleaming with his smile. The family tableau was... perfection.

Amelia kissed his forehead. "Thank you for making that possible."

"You held up your end." And then some.

"Well, my brother wants me to let you know he's permanently on call for you if you need him."

"I'm sure having an extra doctor on hand came in handy after I passed out." He tried to put together the sequence of events in his head. "What happened to Jocelyn?"

"She's dead. The baby she had with her is still on the island, with the military nurse in custody for questioning."

All the pieces fell into place, neatly tied up in his mind. The nightmare was past and Amelia was safe. "It's finally over then."

She placed her hand on his chest, on his heart. "Actually, I was hoping that this is actually the beginning for us."

Hoping his knocked-around brain wasn't playing tricks on him, he said, "You'll need to spell that out a little more for me. I'm still kinda thick from the blow to the head and I wouldn't want to misunderstand."

"I believe we shared something very special this past week and I don't want to lose that." She stared back at him with those beautiful cornflower blue eyes that had so captivated him from the start. "We may not have known each other long, but it's long enough for me to be absolutely certain that I love you, Hugh Franco.

What's more, I'm *in* love with you, so much so, you've filled my heart and life in ways I never even imagined was possible."

His hand fell to rest on top of hers and he wished he could hold her. He let the words sink into him and settle, his future coming into focus again for the first time in five years.

"You do have a way with words, madam lawyer." He lifted her hand and kissed her knuckles, lingering before putting her hand back on his chest. He wanted to do more, but aside from being strapped to a litter, they had a cargo hold full of people around them. "I want to see you again after we get back to the States."

"See me?" Her fingers drew small circles on his chest.

"Date you, be your boyfriend, buy you flowers and candy, take you on dates." Give her all the romance there hadn't been time for while they were on the run. Let her know how much he treasured the gift of having her in his life.

"I like the sound of that very much." She leaned forward, her hair draping over him and offering a silken curtain of privacy as her mouth met his.

This kiss wasn't as long or frenzied as others they'd shared, but the ease with which they came together, the way they connected... He was a lucky man.

"I love you, Amelia Bailey," he said against her lips.

And he looked forward to showing her just how much every day, for the rest of his life.

Epilogue

Four months later

THE WORLD HAD OPENED UP FOR AMELIA. LITERALLY.

She stood alongside Hugh as he pushed wide the French doors leading to the balcony of the beach condo. Gasping, she took in the incredible ocean view. The Gulf of Mexico spread out in front of her from the home Hugh was considering buying.

He was relocating.

For her.

"Hugh? Is this place for real?" She stepped to the white railing overlooking a beach with pristine white sand. The place was a corner unit, townhouse style with three bedrooms and even a little dock slip of its own.

"As real as it gets." He tucked an arm around her shoulders. "I take it you're giving the place a thumbs-up?"

"Definitely, two thumbs-up." That he was consulting her on his home purchase spoke of just how much he'd committed to their relationship too.

So much had happened for them in four short months. But then her whole life had changed in those first days with Hugh, so that now she couldn't imagine her life without him.

Once they'd returned from the Bahamas, Hugh had been put on medical leave to recover from his broken ankle. Thank God his injuries hadn't been any worse.

Amelia had taken vacation as well to play nurse at his southern Florida base—and make the most of his time off to be together in his place and then go to hers. She'd been dreading his return to work, so far away, with even longer deployments looming.

But he'd surprised her on that last day of his leave, telling her that Major McCabe had helped pull some strings to get Hugh a transfer to a base in northern Florida. Hugh would be stepping out of the field for at least two or three years to teach newbie incoming pararescuemen at the Air Force Combat Diver School—located in Panama City, Florida. It was closer to Alabama. Closer to her. And with less time away.

She'd started job hunting in Panama City the next day and accepted a position the next week.

Sliding in front of him and leaning back against his chest, she soaked up the late-day Florida sun, the beauty of a seagull dipping along the rolling shore. His arms slipped around her with an ease that both calmed and excited her.

She tipped her face into the sea breeze, watching sailboats and jet skis on the horizon. "What a peaceful place to end the workday, having supper out here on the balcony."

"When I saw the place, the first thing I thought of was sitting out here with you, my guitar, a bottle of beer—"

"—a glass of wine."

"Together." His chin rested on top of her head.

"I still can't believe you came out of the field for me." That he would make such a life change to help them be together touched her. Deeply.

"The decision wasn't as tough as I thought it would be. I realized I'd been working too close to the edge. You helped me see that. And here? I figure that makes me the right kind of instructor to teach students how to make that distinction between laying it all on the line and being so reckless you endanger others."

"You're a good man, Hugh. They're going to learn a lot from you." She folded her hands over his on her stomach. "I would have moved farther for you." As much as it would have hurt to be far from her brother and his family, she knew her future was with Hugh.

"Thanks"—he dropped a tender kiss on her forehead—"but this is where we're supposed to be."

"I agree." So easily they both already spoke of the future together. Things may have started off tough for them, but the love part? They were in total sync on that.

"Besides, I enjoy seeing you spoil Joshua rotten. You've taken well to the role of indulgent aunt."

Hugh took part in quite a bit of that spoiling. There were still times shadows crossed his eyes when he looked at her nephew—or any child, for that matter—and she knew he was thinking about his daughter. But she also saw he wasn't letting that stop him from enjoying Joshua.

News of Lisabeth's pregnancy had caught her by surprise, but Amelia had done her best to ensure any postadoption paperwork proceeded smoothly. Aiden and Lisabeth had been tapping into every support line imaginable to help Joshua bond securely, and they had additional counseling help in place for any contingency after the baby was born.

Everything was being done by the book. Jocelyn

Pearson-Stewart had shown them too well how playing fast and loose with the rules could wreck precious lives.

Authorities in the Bahamas and the States were still threading through the tangled mess by cutting deals with Courtney, Erin, and the military nurse, Lieutenant Gable, in exchange for information. So far, two young children had been rescued from a transaction Oliver had overseen. Amelia shuddered to think what could have happened if they'd been lost forever in the abyss of a child-prostitution ring.

She shivered and Hugh's arms wrapped tighter around her.

"Do you want to go inside?" His deep voice vibrated against her back.

"Let's stay here a while longer, if the real-estate agent isn't in a hurry."

"Actually, I convinced her to have coffee across the street. We're free to hang out a while longer." He ducked around in front of her, leaning against the rail. "I was hoping we could talk."

His green eyes went serious, crinkles at the sides fanning out. Her stomach flipped as hard and fast as a fish flopping in the distance.

"Okay, is there some kind of problem?" She smoothed the collar of his camo—he'd come straight over from work.

"I was thinking, since your stuff is still in storage, you might consider moving it here rather than searching for another place."

Surprise stilled her. She'd been so careful to give Hugh time and space in the their relationship that she hadn't been fully prepared for this moment. She'd told herself she was fine living separately. Taking it slow. But—wow. The thought of being with him full time grabbed hold of her heart.

"You're asking me to move in with you?"

"That's part of why I wanted to make sure the place met with your approval before I bought it."

Nerves—and excitement—kicked up her pulse. "And the other reason?"

Holding on to the rail, he dropped to one knee in front of her. Her stomach dropped right along with him. There was no mistaking his intent.

He pulled his hand from his pocket, holding a small black-velvet jeweler's box. "Amelia, will you marry me?"

Such simple words, but the feeling behind them, the emotion in his eyes and in his voice, was so far from simple, it humbled her. This complex man who had every reason to fear risking love again was giving himself, his heart, his future to her.

She sank to her knees, clasping both of her hands over his. "Of course, I will—move in, marry you, spend the rest of my life loving you."

Hauling her to his chest, he hugged her hard and close, whispering "Thank God" against her hair with so much relief she couldn't help but be moved. Then he kissed her or she kissed him. They moved so fluidly together it didn't matter. The way he turned her inside out with a touch, a stroke, the glide of his mouth along her lips... her skin tingled, the heat radiating inward and rivaling anything that sun could crank out.

He eased her to her feet again, ending the kiss with a final brush across her lips. "I do have a ring here."

He creaked open the velvet box to reveal...

She clapped a hand over her mouth.

A marquise-cut diamond of orangey pink hue, in a platinum setting with white diamonds on either side, refracted rays from the setting sun. "It was my mom's. It's never been worn by anyone but her. She passed away a couple of years ago. I would like you to wear it. I want you to marry me, be the mother of my children..." He paused, a long swallow working down his neck, hinting at just how big a risk he was taking here, offering up his heart again. "And God willing, should we be so fortunate, I'd like you to grow very old with me."

Too choked up to speak, she simply held out her left hand. And it didn't so much as tremble. She was that sure of her love for Hugh, that sure of how well they fit together.

He slipped the ring in place and pulled her hand back to his heart. "I understand that this is all happening fast, and if you need a long engagement, I'm okay with that. But I can't just date and pretend we're testing the waters when I know that you're the only woman I want to be with. I know that's not romantically poetic—"

"Shhh..." She placed her fingers over his mouth, unable to resist staring at the ring on her finger. "I understand what you mean, I understand you. And your proposal is wonderfully romantic and perfect in every way."

"Ooh-rah!" he whooped, scooping her into his arms. "I think it's time to sign the paperwork on this place so we can start celebrating back at the hotel."

"I'm hoping our celebration will be clothing optional?" She looped her arms around his neck.

"Damn straight."

His green eyes glinted with a heated promise as Hugh carried her over the threshold into their first home and into their future together.

Turn the page for more hot military romance
from Catherine Mann

COVER ME

Book 1 in the Elite Force series

Available now from Sourcebooks Casablanca

Chapter 1

It was a cold day in hell for Tech Sergeant Wade Rocha—standard ops for a mission in Alaska.

He slammed the side of the icy crevasse on Mount McKinley. A seemingly bottomless crevasse. That made it all the more pressing to anchor his ax again ASAP. Except both of his spikes clanked against his sides while the underworld waited in an alabaster swirl of nothingness as he pinwheeled on a lone cable.

Wade scratched and clawed with his gloved hands, kicked with his spiked shoes, reaching for anything. The tiniest of toeholds on the slick surface would be good right about now. Sure he was roped to his climbing partner. But they had the added load of an injured woman strapped to a stretcher beneath them. He needed to carry his own weight.

Chunks of ice and snow pelted his helmet. The unstable gorge walls vibrated under his gloved hands.

"Breathe and relax, buddy." His headset buzzed with reassurance from his climbing partner, Hugh "Slow Hand" Franco.

Right.

Hold tight.

Think.

Focus narrowed, Wade tightened his grip on his rope. He'd earned his nickname, Brick, by being the most hardheaded guy in their rescue squadron. Come hell or high water, he never gave up.

Each steady breath crackled with ice shards in his lungs, but his oxygen-starved body welcomed every atom of air. Lightning fast, he grabbed the line tying them together and worked the belay device.

Whirrr, whippp. The rope zinged through. Wade slipped closer, closer still, to Franco, ten feet below.

"Oof." He jerked to a halt.

"I got ya, Brick. I got ya," Franco chanted through the headset. Intense. Edgy. Nothing was out of bounds. Franco would die before he let him fall. "It's just physics that makes this thing work. Don't overthink it."

And it did work. Wade stabilized against the icy wall again. Relief trickled down his spine in frosty beads of sweat.

He keyed up his microphone. "All steady, Slow Hand."

"Good. Now do you wanna stop horsing around, pal?" Franco razzed, sarcastic as ever. "I'd like to get back before sundown. My toes are cold."

Wade let a laugh loosen the tension kinking up his gut. "Sorry I inconvenienced you by almost dying there. I'll try not to do it again. I'll even spring for a pedicure, if you're worried about your delicate feet chafing from frostbite."

"Appreciate that." Franco's labored breath and hoarse chuckle filled the headset.

"Hey, Franco? Thanks for saving my ass."

"Roger that, Brick. You've done the same for me."

And he had. Not that they kept score. Wade recognized the chitchat for what it really was—Franco checking to make sure he wasn't suffering from altitude sickness due to their fifteen thousand foot perch. They worked overtime to acclimate themselves, but the lurking beast could still strike even the most seasoned climber without warning. They'd already lost one of their team members last month to HACE—high altitude cerebral edema.

He shook his head to clear it. Damn it, his mind was wandering. Not good. He eyed the ledge a mere twenty feet up. Felt like a mile. He slammed an ice ax in with his left hand, pulled, hauled, strained, then slapped the right one in a few inches higher. Crampons—ice cleats—gained traction on the sleek side of the narrow ravine as he inched his way upward.

Slow. Steady. Patient. Mountain rescue couldn't be rushed. At least April gave them a few more daylight hours. Not that he could see much anyway, with eighty-mile-per-hour wind creating whiteout conditions. Below, his climbing partner was a barely discernible blur.

Hand over hand. Spike. Haul. Spike. Haul. He clipped his safety rope into a spike they had anchored in the rock on the way down. Scaled one step at a time. Forgot about the biting wind. The ball-numbing cold.

The ever-present risk of avalanche.

His arms bulged, the burden strapped to his harness growing heavier. *Remember the mission. Bring up an unconscious female climber. Strapped to a litter. Compound fracture in her leg.*

His job as a pararescueman in the United States Air Force included medic training. Land, sea, or mountain, military missions or civilian rescue. With his brothers in arms, he walked, talked, and breathed their motto, "That Others May Live."

That people like his mother might live.

Muscles burning, he focused upward into the growl

of the storm and the hovering military helicopter. A few more feet and he could hook the litter to the MH-60. Rotors *chop, chop, chopped* through the sheets of snow like a blender.

The crevasse was too narrow to risk lowering a swaying cable. Just one swipe against the narrow walls of ice could collapse the chasm into itself. On top of the injured climber and Franco.

On top of him.

So it was up to *him*—and his climbing partner—to pull the wounded woman out. Once clear, the helicopter would land if conditions permitted. And if not, they could use the cable then to raise her into the waiting chopper.

Wind slammed him again like a frozen Mack truck. He fought back the cold-induced mental fog. At least when Hermes went subterranean to rescue Persephone from the underworld, he had some flames to toast his toes.

Wade keyed his microphone again to talk to the helicopter orbiting overhead. "Fever"—he called the mission code name—"we're about five minutes from the top."

Five minutes when anything could happen.

"Copy, the wind is really howling. We will hold until you are away from the crevasse."

"Copy, Fever."

The rest of his team waited in the chopper. They'd spent most of the day getting a lock on the locale. The climber's personal locator beacon had malfunctioned off and on. Wade believed in his job, in the motto. He came from five generations of military.

But sometimes on days like this, saving some reckless thrill seeker didn't sit well when thoughts of people like his mother—wounded by a roadside bomb in Iraq, needing his help—hammered him harder than the ice-covered rocks pummeling his shoulder. How damned frustrating that there hadn't been a pararescue team near enough—he hadn't been near enough—to give her medical aid. Now because of her traumatic brain injury, she would live out the rest of her life in a rehab center, staring off into space.

He couldn't change the past, but by God, he would do everything he could to be there to help someone else's mother or father, sister or brother, in combat. That could only happen if he finished up his tour in this frozen corner of the world.

As they neared the top, a moan wafted from the litter suspended below him. Stabilizing the rescue basket was dicey. Even so, the groans still caught him by surprise.

The growling chopper overhead competed with the increasing howls of pain from their patient in the basket. God forbid their passenger should decide to give them a real workout by thrashing around.

"Franco, we better get her to the top soon before the echoes cause an avalanche."

"Picking up the pace."

Wade anchored the last… swing… of his ax… Ice crumbled away. The edge shaved away in larger and larger chunks. *Crap, move faster.* Pulse slugging, he dug deeper.

And cleared the edge.

Franco's exhale echoed in his ears. Or maybe it was his own. Resisting the urge to sprawl out and take five right here on the snow-packed ledge, he went on auto-pilot, working in tandem with Franco.

Climbing ropes whipped through their grip as they

hauled the litter away from the edge. Franco handled his end with the nimble guitarist fingers that had earned him the homage of the Clapton nickname, Slow Hand. The immobilized body writhed under the foil Mylar survival blanket, groaning louder. Franco leaned over to whisper something.

Wade huffed into his mic, "Fever, we are ready for pickup. One survivor in stable condition, but coming to, fast and vocal."

The wind-battered helicopter angled overhead, then righted, lowering, stirring up snow in an increasing storm as the MH-60 landed. Almost home free.

Wade hefted one end, trusting Franco would have the other in sync, and hustled toward the helicopter. His crampons gripped the icy ground with each pounding step. The door of the chopper filled with two familiar faces. From his team. Always there.

With a *whomp*, he slid the metal rescue basket into the waiting hands. He and Franco dove inside just as the MH-60 lifted off with a roar and a cyclone of snow. Rolling to his feet, he clamped hold of a metal hook bolted to the belly of the chopper.

The training exercise was over.

Their "rescue" sat upright fast on the litter, tugging at the restraints. Not in the least female, a hulking male pulled off the splint Wade had strapped on less than a half hour ago.

Wade collapsed against the helicopter wall, exhausted as hell now that he could allow his body to stop. "Major, have you ever considered an acting career? With all that groaning and thrashing about, I thought for sure I was carting around a wounded prima donna."

Major Liam McCabe, the only officer on their team and a former army ranger, swung his feet to the side of the litter and tossed away the Thinsulate blanket. "Just keeping the exercise real, adding a little color to the day."

The major tugged on a helmet and hooked into the radio while the rest of his team gaped at him—or rather, gaped at McCabe's getup. He wore civilian climbing gear—loud, electric yellow, with orange and red flames that contrasted all the more up next to their bland sage green military issue. Laughter rumbled through the helicopter. The garish snow gear had surprised the hell out of him and Franco when they'd reached the bottom of the chasm. They'd expected McCabe, but not an Olympic-worthy ski suit.

McCabe could outpunk Ashton Kutcher. For the most part they welcomed the distraction at the end of a long day. McCabe's humor was also a needed tension buster for the group when Franco went too far, pushing the envelope.

End game, today's exercise hadn't pulled out all the stops for a mountain rescue. Nobody had to parachute in.

Suddenly the major stood upright as he gestured for everyone's attention. "Helmets on so you can hear the radio."

Wade snapped into action, plugging in alongside his other five team members, some in seats, Franco kneeling. The major held an overhead handle, boots planted on the deck.

"Copilot," McCabe's voice piped through the helmet radio, "have the Rescue Coordination Center repeat that last message."

"Romeo Charlie Charlie, please repeat for Fever two zero."

"Fever two zero, this is Romeo Charlie Charlie with a real world tasking." The center radio controller's Boston accent filled the airwaves with broad vowels. "We have a request for rescue of a stranded climbing party on Mount Redoubt. Party is four souls stranded by an avalanche. Can you accept the tasking as primary?"

Mount Redoubt? In the Aleutian Islands. The part of Alaska the Russians once called "the place that God forgot."

The copilot's click echoed as he responded. "Stand by while we assess." He switched to interphone for just those onboard the helicopter. "How are you guys back there? You up for it?"

The major eyed the rest of the team, his gaze holding longest on him and Franco, since they'd just hauled his butt off a mountain. His pulse still slugged against his chest. Franco hadn't stopped panting yet.

But the question didn't even need to be asked.

Wade shot him a thumbs-up. His body was already shifting to auto again, digging for reserves. Each deep, healing breath sucked in the scent of hydraulic fluid and musty military gear, saturated from missions around the world. He drew in the smells, indulging in his own whacked-out aromatherapy, and found his center.

McCabe nodded silently before keying up his radio again. "We are a go back here, if there's enough gas on the refueler."

"Roger, that. We have an HC-130 on radar, orbiting nearby. They say they're game if we are. They have enough gas onboard to refuel us for about three hours of loiter, topping us off twice if needed." The copilot switched to open frequency. "Romeo Charlie Charlie, Fever and Crown will accept the tasking."

"Copy, Fever," answered their radio pal with a serious Boston accent. "Your new call sign is Lifeguard two zero."

"Lifeguard two zero wilco." *Will comply*. The copilot continued, "Romeo Charlie Charlie copies all."

The radio operator responded, "We are zapping the mission info to you via data link and you have priority handling, cleared on navigation direct to location."

"Roger." The helicopter copilot's voice echoed through Wade's headset, like guidance coming through that funky aromatherapy haze. "I have received the coordinates for the stranded climbers popped up on a data screen and am punching the location into the navigation system. Major, do you copy all back there?"

"Copy in full." McCabe was already reaching for his bag of gear to ditch the flame-print suit. "Almost exactly two hundred miles. We'll have an hour to prep and get suited up."

McCabe assumed command of the back of the chopper, spelling out the game plan for each team member. He stopped in front of Wade last. "Good news and bad news... and good news. Since you've worked the longest day, the rest of the team goes in first. Which means you can rest before the bad-news part." He passed a parachute pack. "Speaking of which, chute up. Because if we can't reach someone, you're jumping in to secure the location and help ride out the storm."

Apparently they might well have to pull out all the stops after all. "And that second round of good news, sir?"

McCabe smiled, his humor resurfacing for air. "The volcano on Mount Redoubt hasn't blown in a year, so we've got that going for us."

<div align="center">~~~</div>

A wolflike snarl cut the thickly howling air.

Kneeling in the snow, Sunny Foster stayed statue-still. Five feet away, fangs flashed, white as piercing icicles glinting through the dusky evening sunset.

Nerves prickled her skin, covered with four layers of clothes and snow gear, even though she knew large predators weren't supposed to live at this elevation. But still... She swept her hood back slowly, momentarily sacrificing warmth for better hearing. The wind growled as loudly as the beast crouching in front of her.

She was alone on Mount Redoubt with nothing but her dog and her survival knife for protection. Cut off by the blizzard, she was stuck on a narrow path, trying to take a shortcut after her snow machine died.

Careful not to move too fast, she slid the blade from the sheath strapped to her waist. While she had the survival skills to wait out the storm, she wasn't eager to share her icy digs with a wolf or a bear. And a foot race only a few feet away from a sheer cliff didn't sound all that enticing.

Bitter cold, at least ten below now, seeped into her bones until her limbs felt heavier. Even breathing the thin mountain air was a chore. These kinds of temps left you peeling dead skin from your frostbitten fingers and toes for weeks. Too easily she could listen to those insidious whispers in her brain encouraging her to sleep. But she knew better.

To stay alive, she would have to pull out every ounce of the survival training she taught to others. She couldn't afford to think about how worried her brother and sister would be when she didn't return in time for her shift at work.

Blade tucked against her side, she extended her other hand toward the flashing teeth.

"Easy, Chewie, easy." Sunny coaxed her seven-year-old malamute-husky mutt. The canine's ears twitched at a whistling sound merging with the wind. "What's the matter boy? Do you hear something?"

Like some wolf or a bear?

Chewie was more than a pet or a companion. Chewie was a working partner on her mountain treks. They'd been inseparable since her dad gave her the puppy. And right now, Sunny needed to listen to that partner, who had senses honed for danger.

Two months ago Chewie had body-blocked her two steps away from thin ice. A couple of years before that, he'd tugged her snow pants, whining, urging her to turn around just in time to avoid a small avalanche. If Chewie nudged and tugged and whined for life-threatening accidents, what kind of hell would bring on this uncharacteristic growling?

The whistling noise grew louder overhead. She looked up just as the swirl of snow parted. A bubbling dome appeared overhead, something in the middle slicing through…

Holy crap. She couldn't be seeing what she thought. She ripped off her snow goggles and peered upward. Icy pellets stung her exposed face, but she couldn't make herself look away from the last thing she expected to see.

A parachute.

Someone was, no kidding, parachuting down through the blizzard. Toward her. That didn't even make sense. She patted her face, her body, checking to see if she was even awake. This had to be a dream. Or a cold-induced hallucination. She smacked herself harder.

"Ouch!"

Her nose stung.

Her dog howled.

Okay. She was totally awake now and the parachute was coming closer. Nylon whipped and snapped, louder, nearer. Boots overhead took shape as a hulking body plummeted downward. She leaped out of the way.

Toward the mountain wall—not the cliff's edge.

Chewie's body tensed, ready to spring into action. Coarse black-and-white fur raised along his spine. Icicles dotted his coat.

The person—a man?—landed in a dead run along the slippery ice. The "landing strip" was nothing more than a ledge so narrow her gut clenched at how easily this hulking guy could have plummeted into the nothingness below.

The parachute danced and twisted behind him specterlike, as if Inuit spirits danced in and out of the storm. He planted his boots again. The chute reinflated.

A long jagged knife glinted in his hand. His survival knife was a helluva lot scarier looking than hers right now. Maybe it had something to do with the size of the man.

Instinctively, she pressed her spine closer to the mountain wall, blade tucked out of sight but ready. Chewie's fur rippled with bunching muscles. An image of her dog, her pet, her most loyal companion, impaled on the man's jagged knife exploded in her brain in crimson horror.

"No!" she shouted, lunging for his collar as the silver blade arced downward.

She curved her body around seventy-five pounds of loyal dog. She kept her eyes locked on the threat and braced for pain.

The man sliced the cords on his parachute.

Hysterical laughter bubbled and froze in her throat. Of course. He was saving himself. Nylon curled upward and away, the "spirits" leaving her alone with her own personal yeti who jumped onto mountain ledges in a blizzard.

And people called her reckless.

Her Airborne Abominable Snowman must be part of some kind of rescue team. Military perhaps? The camo gear suggested as much.

What was he doing here? He couldn't be looking for her. No one knew where she was, not even her brother and sister. She'd been taught since her early teens about the importance of protecting her privacy. For fifteen years she and her family had lived in an off-the-power-grid community on this middle-of-nowhere mountain in order to protect volatile secrets. Her world was tightly locked into a town of about a hundred and fifty people. She wrapped her arms tighter around Chewie's neck and shouted into the storm, "Are you crazy?"

"No, ma'am," a gravelly voice boomed back at her, "although I gotta confess I am cold. But don't tell my pal Franco I admitted as much. My buddies can't fly close enough to haul us out of here until the storm passes."

"And who are these buddies of yours?" She looked up fast.

No one else fell from the clouds. She relaxed her arms around her dog. He must be some branch of the military. Except his uniform wasn't enough to earn her automatic stamp of approval, and she couldn't see his face or read his eyes because of his winter gear and goggles.

He sheathed his knife. "Air Force pararescue, ma'am. I'm here to help you hunker down for the night to ride out this blizzard safely."

All right, then. That explained part. It was tough to question the honorable intentions of a guy who would parachute into the middle of a blizzard—on the side of a mountain—to rescue someone.

Still, how had he found her? Old habits were tough to shed.

"Um"—she squinted up at the darkening sky again— "are there more of you about to parachute in here?"

He shifted the mammoth pack on his back. "Do you think we could have this conversation somewhere else? Preferably after we find shelter and build a fire?"

That much she agreed with.

Staying out here to talk could get them killed. For some reason this hulking military guy thought he needed to save her. She didn't understand the whys and where-fores of anyone knowing about her presence in the first place. However, simply walking away from him wasn't an option.

Easing to her feet, she accepted the inevitable, sheathed her knife, but kept her hand close to it. Just in case.

She would not be spending the night in a warm

shelter, curled up asleep with her dog. She would have to stay awake and alert. With too many secrets, she couldn't afford to let down her guard around anyone, and sprinting away wasn't exactly an option.

Her uninvited hero was already taking charge. "We need to find the best location to minimize the force of the wind, then start digging out a snow pit." He had some kind of device in his hand, like a GPS. "I'll keep the instructions simple, and you can just follow my lead."

"Excuse me, but I've already located shelter. A cave only a few yards away." She knew every safe haven on this pass. She had a GPS too, although it hadn't come out of her case since she'd left her small mountain community this morning. "But you're welcome to work on that pit if you prefer."

"Oooo-kay," he said with a long puff of fog. "Cave it is."

"Follow Chewie."

"Chewie?"

"My dog." She pointed to her malamute mutt, now sniffing his way westward along the ledge.

The man hefted his gear more securely on his back — a pack that must have weighed at least fifty pounds. "Looks like a pissed off wolf to me."

"Then perhaps you need to get out those fancy night-vision goggles you guys use." She felt along the rock wall marbleized by the elements. "Sun's falling fast. Don't lollygag."

His steps crunched heavy and steady behind her. "You're not the most grateful rescuee I've ever come across."

"I didn't need saving, but thank you all the same for the effort."

He stopped her with a hand to the arm. "What about your friends? Aren't you worried about them?"

His touch startled her, the contact bold and firm—and foreign. She came from a world where everyone knew each other. There was no such thing as a stranger.

She gathered her scrambled thoughts and focused on his words. "My friends?"

How did he know about what she'd been doing today? She'd been on her own, escorting Ted and Madison to a deputy from the mainland who would take them the rest of the way. He worked for a small county along Bristol Bay and arranged for transportation by boat or plane, even bringing in supplies for them in an emergency.

Had something gone wrong after they'd left her? Ted and Madison were seasoned hikers, physically fit. They'd been frequent patrons of the fitness equipment she kept at the cabin that housed her survival and wilderness trek business. She couldn't imagine there would have been any problem with their trek off Mount Redoubt to rejoin the outside world.

"The rest of your group. In case you were worried— which apparently you're not—they're all toasty warm with dry blankets up in the helicopter on their way back to the resort cabin, probably wishing they'd stayed in California. How is it that you have managed out here so long away from the group?"

Climbing group, from California? He must think she was a part of some other group. Relief burned through her like frostbitten limbs coming to life again. He didn't know about Ted and Madison or the sheriff's deputy, and he had no idea at all why she was really out here today.

She couldn't afford—her relatives back in their community couldn't afford—a single misstep. There were careful procedures for people who left, methods to protect their location. "I've had better survival training than the average person."

And she would need every bit of that training to ditch this hulking big military savior when the time came to escape.

Acknowledgments

People often ask me how I come up with new story ideas. Obviously, as an air force wife, I'm inspired by my husband and our experiences in military life over the years. But my ideas come via other avenues as well. Such as this one. The story started brewing as I watched reports of the tragic devastation of the 2010 Haiti earthquake. I was deeply moved by the breathtaking way dozens of organizations and countries pulled together to help, showing humanity at its best. From that, my imagination took flight and a story came to life.

Little did I know that just after I completed this book, Japan as well would be struck by a horrific earthquake and tsunami. My prayers are with everyone affected by these unimaginably terrible tragedies as they continue the long journey to rebuild their lives.

As I brought this story to fruition, I was blessed with the assistance of many. However, any inaccuracies, poetic license, or overall pushing the boundaries of possibility can be attributed to me. All characters are from my imagination—any perceived similarity to real persons, incidents, or places is coincidental.

Tremendous thanks to my ever-brilliant and witty editor, Deb Werksman. You and the entire Sourcebooks team are a joy to work with. Endless appreciation goes to my agent Barbara Collins Rosenberg—a tireless wonder and a dear friend. As always, gratitude and hugs to my critique partner, Joanne Rock, for the feedback, the encouragement, and her ability to chase away writer's block with one phone conversation. Many kudos to Jeanette Vigliotti for coming through in a pinch with proofreading. I am so grateful for the generosity and support of Sherrilyn Kenyon, Lori Foster, and Dianna Love, authors extraordinaire! And, as always, sending a big shout out to the ever-awesome Suz Brockmann and the amazing friends she has shared with me — Stephanie, Anne, Ann, Michelle, Erika, Beki, Sue, Jeanne, and Laura.

Technical details are always such fun to research — and then stressful, as I worry if I could ever do justice to the heroic professionals who've shared their time and expertise. I took copious notes as former air force pararescueman Dr. Ronald Marshall, DC, relayed details of harrowing PJ rescues in an earthquake-ravaged region. And as always, I would be lost without my own air force aviator husband, Robert, who is always ever ready with brainstorming help and fact-checking reads. Thanks to them both for their brave and selfless service to our country! Much appreciation goes to my longtime author friend, Vickie Taylor, who is also a FEMA canine trainer. I appreciate her patience with my many, many, *many* questions about USAR.

And of course, all my love to my incredible husband Rob and our four eternally patient children — Brice, Haley, Robbie, and Maggie. Thank you for being every bit as proud of me as I am of each of you!

About the Author

USA Today bestseller Catherine Mann has over two million books in print in more than twenty countries. A winner of the prestigious RITA Award, Catherine resides in Florida with her military-hero husband, their four children, and a menagerie of pets. For more information on her upcoming releases, check out her website at www.catherinemann.com or visit her on Facebook at Catherine Mann (author).

SEALed
with a *Kiss*

BY MARY MARGRET DAUGHTRIDGE

THERE'S ONLY ONE THING HE CAN'T HANDLE, AND ONE WOMAN WHO CAN HELP HIM...

Jax Graham is a rough, tough Navy SEAL, but when it comes to taking care of his four-year-old son after his ex-wife dies, he's completely clueless. Family therapist Pickett Sessoms can help, but only if he'll let her.

When Jax and his little boy get trapped by a hurricane, Pickett takes them in against her better judgment. When the situation turns deadly, Pickett discovers what it means to be a SEAL, and Jax discovers that even a hero needs help sometimes.

"A heart-touching story that will keep you smiling and cheering for the characters clear through to the happy ending." —RT Book Reviews

"A well-written romance... simultaneously tender and sensuous." —Booklist

SEALed with a Promise

by Mary Margret Daughtridge

Navy SEAL Caleb Delaude is as deadly as he is charming.

Professor Emmie Caddington's quiet intelligence and quirky personality intrigue him. When he discovers that her personal connections can get him close to the man he's vowed to kill, will their budding relationship be nothing more than a means to revenge…or is she the key to his salvation?

Praise for *SEALed with a Kiss*:

"This story delivers in a huge way." —RT Book Reviews

"A wonderful story that will have readers experiencing a whirlwind of emotions and culminating with an awesome scene that will have your pulse pounding." —Romance Junkies

"What an incredibly powerful book! I laughed and sniffled, was turned on and turned inside out." —Queue My Review

SEALed
with a *Ring*

BY MARY MARGRET DAUGHTRIDGE

SHE'S GOT IT ALL...EXCEPT THE ONE THING SHE NEEDS MOST

Smart, successful businesswoman JJ Caruthers has a year to land a husband or lose the empire she's worked so hard to build. With time running out, romance is not an option, and a military husband who is always on the road begins to look like the perfect solution...

HE'S A WOUNDED HERO WITH AN AGENDA OF HIS OWN

Even with the scars of battle, Navy SEAL medic Davy Graziano is gorgeous enough to land any woman he wants, and he's never wanted to be tied down. Now Davy has ulterior motives for accepting JJ's outrageous proposal of marriage, but he only has so long to figure out what JJ doesn't want him to know...

Praise for *SEALed with a Ring*:

"With a surprising amount of heart, Daughtridge makes a familiar story read like new as the icy JJ melts under Davy's charm during a forced marriage. The supporting cast, including one really unattractive dog, makes Daughtridge's latest one for the keeper shelves." —RT Book Reviews, 4 stars

HEALING LUKE

BY BETH CORNELISON

She can't escape her past...

Occupational therapist Abby Stanford is on vacation alone, her self-confidence shattered by her fiancé's betrayal. Romance is the last thing on Abby's mind—until she meets the brooding and enigmatic Luke...

He won't face his future...

Scarred by a horrific accident, former heartthrob Luke Morgan is certain his best days are behind him. Abby knows how to help him recover, but for Luke his powerful attraction to her only serves as a harsh reminder of the man he used to be. Abby is Luke's first glimmer of hope since the accident, but can she heal his heart before Luke breaks hers?

"Beth Cornelison writes intriguing, emotionally charged stories that will keep you turning the pages straight through to the end. Fabulous entertainment!" —Susan Wiggs

"Healing Luke is a breath of fresh air for romance fans... a stirring novel and a five star read!"
—Crave More Romance